WILD MAGIC

THE IMMORTALS ✦ BOOK I

Books by TAMORA PIERCE

SONG OF THE LIONESS QUARTET

Alanna: The First Adventure (Book I)
In the Hand of the Goddess (Book II)
The Woman Who Rides Like a Man (Book III)
Lioness Rampant (Book IV)

THE IMMORTALS QUARTET

Wild Magic (Book I)
Wolf-speaker (Book II)
Emperor Mage (Book III)
The Realms of the Gods (Book IV)

WILD MAGIC

THE IMMORTALS ✦ BOOK I

TAMORA PIERCE

SIMON PULSE
New York ✦ London ✦ Toronto ✦ Sydney

SIMON PULSE
An imprint of Simon & Schuster Children's Publishing Division
1230 Avenue of the Americas, New York, NY 10020
Text copyright © 1992 by Tamora Pierce
All rights reserved, including the right of reproduction
in whole or in part in any form.
SIMON PULSE and colophon are registered trademarks
of Simon & Schuster, Inc.
Also available in an Atheneum Books for Young Readers
hardcover edition.
Designed by Tom Daly
The text of this book was set in Sabon.
Manufactured in the United States of America
First Simon Pulse edition June 2005
20 19 18 17 16
The Library of Congress has cataloged a
previous edition as follows:
Pierce, Tamora.
Wild magic / Tamora Pierce.—1st ed.
p. cm.
Summary: The mage Numair, the knight Alanna, and Queen Thayet
enlist thirteen-year-old Daine's help to battle the
dreadful immortal creatures that have recently begun
to attack the kingdom of Tortall.
[1. Fantasy. 2. Supernatural—Fiction. 3. Human-animal
communication—Fiction.]
I. Title.
PZ7.P61464 Wi 1992
[Fic]—dc20 91-43909
ISBN 978-0-689-85611-2 (hc)
ISBN 978-1-4169-0343-7 (pbk)

TO RAQUEL WOLF-SISTER
AND
TAS HORSE-HEARTED

Who opened my heart to the songs of all beasts

CONTENTS

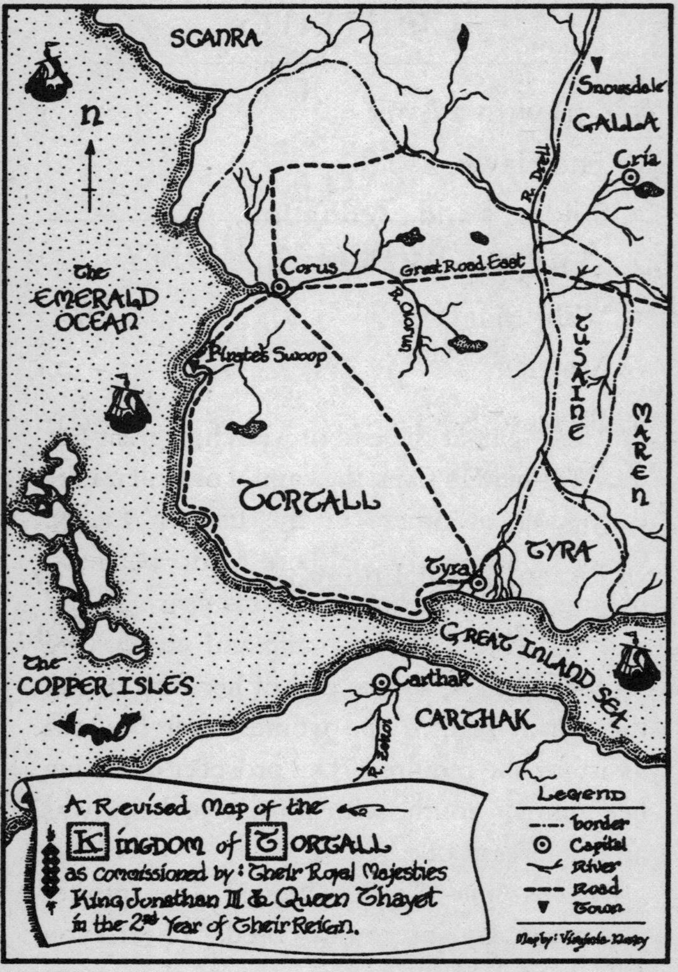

SCANRA
N
Snowsdale
GALLA
Cría
R. Drell
The EMERALD OCEAN
Corus
Great Road East
R. Olorun
Pirate's Swoop
TUSAINE
MAREN
TORTALL
TYRA
Tyra
GREAT INLAND SEA
The COPPER ISLES
Carthak
CARTHAK
R. Zekoi
A Revised Map of the Kingdom of Tortall
as commissioned by: Their Royal Majesties
King Jonathan III & Queen Thayet
in the 2nd Year of Their Reign.
Legend
border
Capital
River
Road
Town
Map by: Virginia Norey

⊙ne

Girl with a Pony

Each year, at the end of March, a great fair was held in Cría, the capital of Galla. Like thousands of others in the Eastern Lands, Onua Chamtong went there to do business: buying ponies, in her case. This year she had another transaction to make and was having no luck with it. By the end of her fifth day at the fair, it seemed she would never find the assistant she required. The prospect of taking her animals south, with no one to help, was an unpleasant one.

"Excuse me—Trader Onua?" The speaker was a girl, shy and country bred. "I heard you was hiring. I'm—" she paused, then went on—"a fair hand with animals, all kinds." She waited as Onua looked her over: a girl in a green wool dress, skirts short enough to show leggings and boots. Brown curls tamed by a head-scarf fell to thin shoulders. A soft, full mouth said she was vulnerable; her chin was entirely stubborn. A quiver filled with long arrows hung on her back, a bow rested in her hand, unstrung.

"Is that yours?" the trader asked, pointing.

Blue-gray eyes flashed. "I'd not have the nerve to carry it otherwise."

"Hmph. String it." The girl hesitated. "Just what I thought," Onua jibed. "Whose is it, really?"

The girl brought a coiled string out of her sash. With ease she fitted it to one end of the bow and set it against her foot. Raising the free end of the string, she brought the other end of the bow down, hooking them together neatly. The bow strung and in her grip, she turned sideways to it, caught the string in two fingers, and drew it back to her ear in a smooth, practiced gesture. Now Onua could see she wore an archer's wrist- and armguards.

"I'd put an arrow up," the girl said, gently

releasing the string, "but I'd hit someone, surely."

Onua grinned. "I'm impressed. I can't draw a bow that big."

The girl took the string off the bow, coiled it, and put it away. "Nor did I, at first. I keep this one limber, or I *still* couldn't draw it."

"Crossbow?" The question was out before Onua remembered, I don't want to hire her— I want to send her home to her mama. She's a runaway for sure.

"Yes'm. We have—" Something flickered in her eyes. She looked down. "We *had* bandits at home. I stood watch with the sheep, so I learned crossbow and longbow. And sling"—a half smile appeared—"not that I'm bragging."

We *had,* Onua thought. Did she change it 'cause she wants me to think she's been gone from home awhile? Or hasn't she *got* a home?

Something looked around the girl, inspecting Onua with a large brown eye. It was a shaggy mountain pony, a steel gray mare. She was plump and well combed, and bore two packs easily.

"Yours?" The girl nodded. "How much would you ask for her?" Onua motioned to a pen filled with ponies at her back. "I'm in the market."

"I can't sell Cloud. She's family—all the family I got." Again Onua saw a flash of sorrow that was pushed aside.

"What's your name?" The K'mir stuck her fingers into a pouch filled with powder known as "eyebright."

"Daine, mum," came the soft reply. "Veralidaine Sarrasri."

The eyebright made her fingers itch when Onua called on her magical Gift. "How old are you, Daine?"

"Fifteen." An aura of red fire, visible only to Onua, flared around the girl's face. The lie was a good one—she must have practiced on the way, the trader thought wryly—but a lie nevertheless. She looked about thirteen.

"Where are you from?"

"Snowsdale, up north. About two weeks' walk."

There was no flare of red—she had told the truth. Onua sighed. "Are you a runaway? From home, or a bad master—"

"No, mum." The soft mouth trembled. "I got no family—just Cloud."

4

No red fire this time. Onua dusted the powder from her hand. "I'm Onua Chamtong, of the K'miri Raadeh."

Daine looked puzzled. "The k-k—the what?"

"The K'mir are a people to the east. Raadeh is the name of one of the K'miri tribes." Daine looked only slightly less baffled. "Never mind. You say you're good with animals. C'mere." She led the girl to her pen. Inside, twenty-seven shaggy ponies in all colors and sizes milled around.

"I buy horses. I had an assistant, but he got offered a better job working for a horse merchant here, and I wasn't about to hold him back. *If* you hire on—and I didn't say I'd hire you—you'll help me take these south. It's three weeks' drive —*if* we don't bog down in mud, *if* we aren't hit by raiders, and *if* we go before all these people take the road to the next fair. It'll be just you and me, and my dog, Tahoi. Why don't you climb in and look 'em over? I want to see how you manage 'em."

Daine glanced back at her mare, Cloud. "Stay put, and *no biting*," she ordered sternly, and clambered over the fence and into the pen.

Poor thing must have been alone a long

time, to be talking to a mare as if she could answer back, Onua thought. She sat on the fence rail to watch.

The ponies watched as Daine passed among them. Ears went back. Those close to her appeared to wonder which would do better: a bite or a kick.

When a yellow stallion, the king of the small herd, minced into place at her back, the girl spun and put both hands under his muzzle, lifting his head to stare into his face. "No, sir," she told him firmly. "I'll not stand for any tricks. I may be human, but I'm not stupid." The stallion tried to rear. She forced him down, then blew gently in his nostrils, to teach him her scent. He shuffled, then fidgeted—then bowed his head in submission.

Horse Lords, Onua thought. She's establishing domination over him and the entire herd!

In years of managing horses, she'd never seen the like. This particular breed was famous for its fiery nature (one of the reasons she purchased them for her employers). She had achieved peace—of a sort—with them using her strength, her wits, and bribes. All horse folk handled their animals that way.

Only this child was different: Daine treated the stallion as if she were a pony herself, a dominant one.

She isn't lying about her folks or running away—just about her age. If I let her go, she might get into trouble. There are too many predators around, looking for a pretty like this one. The road isn't too safe—but what is?

She watched the girl move among the ponies, running her hands over each one. She was giving them bits of apple and sugar from her pockets. Onua was glad to see she *could* deal with the animals in a normal way. One display like that with the stallion was more than enough.

"D'you ride?" she called.

Daine came over to the fence. "Some. Mostly bareback, but I can use a saddle, and I know how to look after tack."

"What about hunting, fishing, tracking?"

The grin lit a face that was too thin and eyes that were too weary. "I do all that—had to, to get this far. I couldn't trust folks on the road. Some looked like—bandits."

As Daine climbed over the rail, the shadow was back in her eyes: grief, Onua decided, but anger too. "Tired of them already?"

The girl shook her head. "I'm getting an oil I have, and a swab. The strawberry has ear mites. They're not too bad—if I get them now, he won't spread them to the herd." She went to the gray mare, who was plainly sulking, and opened one of her packs.

"How do you know you can trust me?"

Daine shrugged. "I don't. How do you know you can trust *me*?"

"Was that a joke?" Onua's voice was stern, but her eyes laughed. Her last two assistants had possessed no sense of humor.

Daine gave her a quick smile and climbed into the pen, a clay bottle and swabs in one hand. Onua watched, amazed, as the strawberry gelding trotted up to the girl. If someone had said that morning she'd see one of her charges willingly submit to an ear cleaning, she would have laughed herself sick.

I shouldn't do it. She's a baby. There're all those rumors—no smoke without fire. Still, my magic will keep us safe at night, and she can handle a bow. "Daine!" she called.

The girl had finished the gelding's ears. She came over. "Yes?"

"I'll tell you right now—I've heard a lot of weird stories lately, about monsters in the wild, attacking travelers. Things out of legend, so folk say. I haven't seen any myself, but that doesn't mean I won't. Are you sure you want to hire on?"

Daine shrugged. "I hear tales. I need work, mum. If I see monsters, I see monsters. My family was killed and my home burned by human ones."

"All right, then—here's the job," said the K'mir. "You, me, and my dog take the herd south, like I said. I have the Gift, and I can shield our camp at night. It's two coppers a day, two silver nobles as a bonus at the end. I pay all expenses, and we share chores. No drinking, no drugs. If you leave me on the trail, you'll wish you died as a child." Daine giggled. "At the end of the road—we'll see. We're bound for the capital of Tortall—"

The girl's face lit up. "Where a lady knight is the King's Champion, right? And they let girls in the army? *That* Tortall?"

"You heard the stories too," the K'mir murmured. "Well, they don't let girls in the regular army, mind—just the Queen's Riders.

Why—have you a fancy to be a soldier?"

Daine shook her head. "Not me. But if they take girls for that, maybe they'll let a girl be a hostler, or work around the camp, or some such." Her eyes were filled with painful hope.

"As it happens, they *do* let girls work as hostlers—or at least, they let me. I'm in charge of the horses for the Riders."

"Oh, glory," the girl whispered. "I'll do whatever you want, if you'll take me on—"

Onua put a hand on Daine's shoulders, touched by her eagerness. "We'll see. If we don't get on, I'll make sure you have some kind of work. I won't leave you stranded. Sound fair?"

Daine nodded vigorously. "Yes, Mistress Onua."

Onua offered a callused hand. "Then shake on it. And stop calling me 'Mistress.' My name's Onua."

Daine returned the woman's firm grip. "Onua Chamtong, of the K'miri Raadeh," she said. "I remember."

Onua smiled. "Very good. Now, will your Cloud mix in with the others?"

"No reason not to." Daine removed packs and saddle from Cloud's back.

"Stow your things with mine." Onua pointed to a canvas-covered mound in one corner. "They'll be safe—these ponies are better than guard dogs."

Daine ushered Cloud into the pen and stored her packs with Onua's. She finished in time to stop Cloud from biting the yellow stallion, and then from kicking a blood bay mare. "You behave," she ordered her pony. "I mean it."

Cloud flicked an ear back, and lifted a hind foot experimentally. Daine leaned down and whispered in her ear. The mare snorted, then stood on all fours, looking as innocent as a summer sky.

"What did you tell her?" Onua asked, letting the girl out of the pen.

"I said I'd sell her to the man that makes dumplings down the way."

Onua chuckled. "That's the threat my mother used on *me*. Look—I want you to meet my dog, Tahoi." She put her fingers to her lips and whistled two short notes. A large form surged over the rear wall of the pen and wound through the ponies, ducking hooves and teeth with the ease of long practice. Coming over the fence in another easy jump, he sat panting at

Onua's feet. He was as tall as his owner's hip, and covered with curling gray fur.

"He's near big enough to be a pony himself." Daine offered her open palm. The dog rumbled in displeasure, and warily sniffed her fingers.

"*Tahoi* means 'ox' in K'mir. Careful—he's a one-woman dog—" Onua shut up. Tahoi's plumed tail had begun to wave. The wary guardian of her stock turned into an eager-to-please pup that licked Daine's hand, then stood to sniff her face. "He's *supposed* to be a guard dog," Onua continued, frowning. "*Not* a pet. *Not* a dog who believes every human's his friend."

"Don't blame him." Daine looked up at Onua apologetically. Her fingers scratched Tahoi in a place he couldn't reach, while his tail thudded in the dust on the ground. "Animals just take to me, is all."

"Hmph. Can you spare her, Majesty?" the woman said to Tahoi. "I'd like to get some grub, saving your presence. And your new friend is coming with me. Guard!" She steered Daine away from the pen.

At one of the cook tents littering the fairgrounds, Onua ordered a rich meal for them both. When it was over, they explored. After a while Daine's eyes hurt from staring so much. Coming from a poor mountain village, she couldn't believe the variety they found at every turn.

"How are you fixed for gear?" her new employer asked. She was eyeing a pair of boots in a leatherworker's stall.

"I'm fine," Daine assured her. Meeting the K'mir's warning look, she insisted, "Really. It was too wet"—she swallowed, trying to speak as if it were someone else's farm that was attacked—"too wet for our place to burn much, so I saved a lot. Clothes, boots, my sleeping gear. I really don't need anything." Seeing the woman's gray green eyes remained suspicious, she raised a hand. "Swear by the Goddess."

"All right, then. Just remember, it's my responsibility to keep you decently clothed and outfitted. I don't want people saying I'm a skinflint."

Daine thought of the huge meal she had consumed. "Just point them out to me, and I'll set them straight."

Onua chuckled. "Good enough."

On their return, the K'mir raised a sleeping

platform outside the pen. "We'd best turn in," she advised. "We leave an hour before dawn."

Daine laid the bedrolls out, wriggled into hers, and took off everything but her shift under the sheltering blankets. "Onua?"

The woman was nearly asleep already. "Yeah?"

"Thanks."

They had a cold breakfast: fruit, cheese, and bread. Onua said little as they ate and packed. She split a pile of lead reins with Daine, indicating she was to connect half of the ponies into a string, while she did the same with the others. They worked quickly as the fair came to life and the air filled with breakfast smells. When the ponies were ready, Onua placed their packs on the first animal in each string.

"Aren't you going to put her on a lead?" Onua pointed to Cloud, who stood free of the others, wearing only a halter and a cross expression. The mare snorted and shook her head.

"She'll be fine," Daine assured the K'mir. "She's as good as a guard dog, that way."

"You know best," Onua said, dubious. "Let's move 'em out."

The K'mir led them away from the fair-grounds and the traffic coming in. They had reached open road when she called for a mid-morning break. Digging apples out of her pocket, she gave Daine one. "*You* eat this," she ordered. "I've more in a basket for the ponies. I should've warned you, by the way—I'm a real bear in the morning. It's no good talking to me—I'll only bite your head off. You didn't take it personally, did you?"

Daine *had* begun to wonder if the K'mir regretted hiring her. She smiled her relief. "It's all right. Ma always says"—her lips tightened—"Ma always said there was no living with me until lunchtime."

"You miss her," Onua said gently.

Daine twisted the stem off her apple. "Her, Grandda, our farm—" Her face was grim. "They took my life, those bandits. I saved *things,* like clothes and food, but all my family was gone except Cloud. They wouldn't even have left her, except she was with me and we weren't there." She got to her feet. "I'm sorry. I didn't mean—"

"To speak of it?" asked the K'mir. Daine nodded. "You have to, just to bleed off the poison from the memory." The girl shrugged. "Well, it doesn't have to be today." She peered at the sun. "We'll be at Coolspring by noon—a village, good-sized. Let's pass that before we stop again."

If Onua and Daine were now well awake, so were their charges. They fussed at every turn. Luckily, many who passed them were traders who knew mountain ponies: they kept a respectful distance. Only Cloud, who seemed to realize she would go into a string the moment she misbehaved, walked meekly beside Daine. The only time she offered violence to a bystander was when he, or she, was too interested in how well the strings were tied together.

Daine worked on the ponies one by one, talking, pleading, cajoling. Repeatedly she explained why she wanted them to follow Onua, *without* making a fuss. One after another the ponies listened as she appealed to their better natures. Some people would have said these creatures had no better nature, but—as Daine told Onua—she had found most animals listened, if things were properly set out for them.

Onua had explained things to ponies and

horses for twenty-eight years without the success this thirteen-year-old was having. How does she do it? the K'mir wondered, fascinated. They're *ponies,* by all the gods. They're wonderfully clever animals, but they don't *think,* not the way people do.

Past the village of Coolspring lay a rest stop, one of the springs that gave the town its name, sheltered by elms. Picketing the animals, the two women sat down to share a meal of bread and cheese.

"Tell me if you get tired," the K'mir ordered. "I can go for hours, once I get moving."

"I'm fine," Daine said. It was the truth. It was good to be in fresh air, headed away from the city. "It's easier than it was coming all the way here. The roads were muddy, you know—with the spring floods."

"Ever been to Cría before?"

Daine shook her head. "Never saw a village bigger than Snowsdale, till yesterday." She sighed. "How can folk live like that, all mashed together?"

Onua shrugged. "City people. They're different, is all. They look down their noses if you didn't grow up penned in." Getting to her feet, she stretched. "Unless something goes wrong, we'll make Wishing Hollow by dark— we'll camp there. We're making wonderful time, thanks to you."

Daine looked at her, baffled. "Me?"

"This is the fastest I've gotten clear of the fair in six years of trade. That's *your* doing. You must have the Gift—though I never heard of it being put to such a use."

Daine laughed. "Oh, please! I've a *knack* with animals, but no Gift. Ma—" She stopped, then made herself go on. "She tried to teach me, but I never learned. I can't even start a fire, and Gifted *babies* manage that. She was so disappointed. Wanted me to follow her path, I s'pose."

Onua touched the girl's hair. "Your mother will be proud no matter what path you take, Daine. I don't know you well, but anyone can see that."

Daine smiled at her. "Thanks."

They sat quietly for a few moments, until Onua remembered something. "I saw you draw that bow of yours, but I don't know what kind of shot you are."

Daine shrugged. "I'm good."

"Mind giving me a demonstration?"

Daine got up and took her longbow from her packs. "Name your target." The wood was warm from the sun and bent willingly for the string. She drew it a couple of times back to her ear, loosening her muscles.

Looking around, Onua spotted a fence that would serve. It lay well within the range of such a powerful bow, but it wasn't so close that Daine would feel insulted. Walking out to it, she fixed her handkerchief to a post with her belt-knife and returned. "How about three arrows?"

"Fair enough." Daine had already fitted one arrow to the string, and her quiver was on her back. Carefully she set her feet, and gently she brought the string back as she focused on her target. The arrow, when she loosed, flew straight and true. Two more followed it.

Onua gasped. All three arrows clustered neatly at the center of her handkerchief. Their heads were buried so deeply she had to cut them loose.

"I take it this is something else you have a 'knack' for," she said when Daine came to help.

"Grandda thought so." The girl shrugged. "It worked out for the best. His bones got to hurting him so bad he couldn't even string a bow, so I brought in all our game."

The yellow stallion screamed a challenge to a passing draft horse and reared, pawing the air. "Odd's bobs!" Daine yelled, exasperated. "Can't a person take her eye off you for a moment without you acting up?" She ran to the stallion's head and dragged him back down to all fours, holding him until the draft horse walked calmly past.

Onua came up to them, smiling. "Time to get back to work."

Well before dark, Onua led them out of sight of the road and into a grassy hollow sheltered by trees. It was plain other travelers stopped here: the fire pit was lined with stones, and a lean-to kept stacks of firewood dry.

"Toss you to give the ponies a going-over," Onua suggested. "For ticks, stones, whatever. Winner gets to dig the latrine trench and catch fish."

Daine considered. "I druther check the ponies."

Onua grinned. "Wonderful—I feel like a bit of fishing just now."

Smiling, Daine went to work. It made no sense to give the ponies a thorough grooming while they were on the road, but she got rid of the worst tangles and checked the animals' hooves. The strawberry's ear mites had to be treated again, and Cloud and Tahoi had picked up ticks in forays off the road.

The girl was finished when Onua returned with two fat trout. "Think this'll feed us?" the K'mir asked, holding them up.

"More than. I'm so tired I couldn't eat but a mouthful." Daine saw that Onua's hair was wet and her face pink from scrubbing. "It's safe to wash?"

"If you make it fast."

"It's too cold to be slow." She hesitated. "Need my help with supper?"

Onua waved her away. "Tahoi'll keep watch for you."

The water was *very* cold. Daine scrubbed quickly and jumped out, feeling deep respect for Onua's courage. Supper—fish and a pot of spiced white cereal grains Onua called "rice"—was hot and filling. They ate without talking, but the silence was a comfortable one.

After the meal, Daine washed up. The fire

was banked; their beds lay on the ground, ready for slumber, when she finished. She got into hers with a sigh. It was warm, and the heavy pad underneath eased the day's aches. As she watched, Onua got several pouches out and tied them to her belt.

"I told you I had the Gift, right? Well, I'm going to place the wards now. Last call for the latrine."

Daine yawned. "I'm set, thanks." She watched as Onua drew a circle around the camp, ponies and all, first in salt, then in water. Soft chanting came from the woman as she walked the circle a third time, calling on magic powers to guard its contents. Red fire spilled from her hand to follow the circle and complete it.

"Ma did that," Daine commented sleepily when Onua finished. "She wasn't very good with it, though." It was easier to speak of her mother when she was so tired. "Maybe she'd be alive now if she'd'a been better."

"Or not," Onua said, sliding between her blankets. "There's always somebody with stronger magic. Lots of raiders have their own witch or mage. That's why every Rider group has at least one member with the Gift."

"Tell me about the Riders. I only know they take girls. Aren't they like the regular soldiers?"

"Not exactly. The fancy name is 'irregulars.' Tortall has a bad time with bandits, and the army's too big and too slow. Bandits hit and run. To fight 'em you need to move the same way. The queen, Thayet, she started the Riders seven years back. The groups run six or eight Riders each, male and female, mounted on ponies. Right now there are six groups, posted all over Tortall. They live off the land, protecting the small villages from raiders."

"Who runs it?"

"Queen Thayet is commander in chief. Her guard, Buri, handles day-to-day affairs, so she has the title 'Commander.' A black man, Sarge, comes just under them. The King's Champion you heard of, Alanna, she helps out." Onua looked over and saw that the girl was fast asleep. Smiling, she pulled up her covers and closed her own eyes.

The badger crawled in with Daine soon after that. Although he was big, he didn't wake her: she was used to nighttime visitors. Without waking, she caressed the animal's head. He sighed gratefully and slept too, his muzzle pressed into her palm.

She did notice him when she woke later and was careful as she sat up.

"I tell ye, I saw 'em. Two strings of ponies— gold on the hoof down in Tortall." The speaker's voice was rough and country bred.

Reaching for the crossbow beside her, Daine saw that Onua and Tahoi were also awake. The dog's hackles were up, his teeth bared in a snarl, but he made no sound. Seeing her, the K'mir put a finger to her lips. Daine nodded, easing the bow onto her lap. Inside her bed her guest shifted nervously, quieting only when she rested a hand on his head.

"If ye saw 'em, then where'd they go?" Leaves rustled as men prowled the hollow around their campsite.

"I'm no witch, to guess such things! It's like they vanished off the face of the world."

"Shut up. They prob'ly found a farm, or kept movin'. Let's get back t' the rest." The new voice held authority; the others grumbled, but obeyed.

They had been gone some minutes before

Daine relaxed enough to put down her weapon. Tahoi licked Onua's face, his tail wagging.

"It's all right," Onua whispered. "Nobody can hear us if we're quiet."

"That's some protection," Daine breathed. "With Ma's circles, you couldn't get in, but you knew it was there."

The K'mir grinned. "Now you know how I can take the road with just my assistant and Tahoi." She curled up in her blankets. "'Night."

The badger grumbled as Daine settled, and walked in her dreams.

"It's about time I found you," he said. "Do you know how long I've been looking? I actually had to come into the Human Realms to get a scent of you!"

"I don't wish to seem rude," she apologized, "but why were you looking for me? I don't believe we've met—have we?"

"Not exactly,"' he admitted with an embarrassed snort. "You see, I promised your father I'd keep an eye on you. So I looked in on you when you were a kit, pink and noisy.

Then when I looked for you again, you were gone. I forgot time passes differently in the Human Realms."

If she had been her waking self, his saying he knew her father would have made her unbearably excited. Now, though, her dream self asked—as if it weren't too important—"Have you met my da, then?"

"Yes, yes, of course. Now, see here—I'm not coming to the Human Realms any more than I have to. If you're going to wander, we must be connected in some way." He looked at a paw and sighed. "I know it barely hurts and it grows back and all, but I still hate it. So messy." He began to chew at the base of one of his claws.

"No, don't—please!" she protested. "I can't think—"

The claw came off. He spat it into her lap. "There. Hang on to it no matter what. This way I won't lose track of time, and I'll be able to find you. Understand?"

She nodded, then gulped. A silvery mist gathered around his paw, and vanished. A new claw had appeared in the bed of the old one.

"Now go back to sleep."

Cold air on her feet woke Daine in the morning. Her guest, working earlier to leave the bedroll, had pulled it apart entirely. She sat up with a yawn and a smile. To think she'd dreamed of a badger who knew her father . . .

Her hand was locked around something—a large animal's claw, or a semblance of one. Complete and perfect, it was made of shiny silver.

"Goddess," she whispered.

"Daine?" Onua was dressed and cooking breakfast. "Let's go."

No time to think about it now, she told herself, and scrambled out of her bedroll. Because if I do, I won't know *what* to think.

Later that day, she wove a thong to grip the base of the claw tightly, and hung it around her neck. Just because she wasn't entirely sure of where it came from was no reason not to keep it close by—just in case.

TWO

THE HAWK

A week later they crossed the River Drell into Tortall on a ferryboat. Watching the Gallan shore pull away, Daine searched her soul. I should tell Onua all the truth, she thought. (By then she had given her new friend the less painful details of her life, and had come to see Onua was right—it felt better to talk.) I should tell the rest—but won't she turn on me, like they did? Maybe it's best to keep shut. The madness, the scandal—it's all back there. Maybe that's where it should stay.

She went forward to look at Tortall as it moved closer. I could start fresh. It can't be worse than home, with folk calling me "bastard" and scorning me. Nobody here knows I've no father, and they don't know about the other thing—the bad thing. They don't need to know.

"You worry too much," Onua ruffled the girl's hair. "It'll work out. You'll see."

Cloud butted Daine's shoulder; Tahoi pawed her leg. Their concern and Onua's gave her comfort. I'll manage, she told herself as the ferry bumped the landing dock on the Tortallan shore. Silence is best.

The country beyond the crossing was a mixture of hills and wide valleys, some of it farmed and grazed, but most left to the woods. Towns here were back from the road, and traffic this early in the spring was thin. There was little to keep them from their usual routine of camp and march, riding the ponies, hunting for game birds or fishing for their supper.

The third day from the river brought rain, slowing them and the animals down before the sky cleared at day's end. Both women were up late, getting mud out of shaggy coats and off their own skin and clothes.

It was the first time on that trip that no animal crawled in with Daine overnight. She slept badly, flipping back and forth, never quite waking or sleeping. Her dreams were thin and worrisome. She remembered only one:

The badger was in his lair, neatening up. "There you are. I'm glad to see the claw works so well."

"Excuse me, sir—" she began.

"No questions. Kits must listen, not ask. Pay attention." He squinted at her to make sure she was listening. "If you look hard and long, you can find us. If you listen hard and long, you can hear any of us, call any of us, that you want." Rolling onto his back, he added, "The madness was to teach you something. You should mind the lesson."

She woke a little before dawn. The sky was gray and damp, the air sour.

"Onua." When the woman only stirred and muttered, she went over and shook her. "I think trouble's coming. Last time I felt this way, a rabid bear came out of the woods and killed the blacksmith."

"A rabid *bear*?" The K'mir yanked on her clothes and Daine followed suit. "Goddess, how many of *those* do you see in a lifetime?"

"One's more than enough." She rolled up her bed and fixed it to her pack. The animals were restless and ill tempered. Tahoi paced the camp, his hackles up. He stopped often to look down the road, only to resume pacing.

"Maybe it's another storm?" Onua suggested over breakfast.

"I don't think so." Daine gave her barely touched porridge to Cloud. "My head aches— not *aches*, exactly. It's—itchy." She sniffed the breeze, but picked up only the scent of water and plants. "The wind's not right, either."

Onua looked at her thoughtfully, then doused the fire. "Let's go." She hitched the ponies to lead reins while Daine secured the packs. "There's a fief on the other side of this next valley, near a marsh. If need be, we'll ask for shelter. I'd prefer not to." She strung her curved bow. "Lord Sinthya doesn't like the queen; he loathes the Riders. Still, we can wait a storm out in his barns, particularly if no one tells him we're there. If we're caught in the marsh, we're in trouble. I don't have any marsh craft."

Daine warmed her longbow and strung it. The quiver's weight on her back made her feel better as they took the road. Past the next ridge she saw a wide, shallow valley filled with reeds and water, with nowhere to hide.

By the time they reached the center of the green expanse, the hair was standing straight out on the back of her neck. Where are the frogs, and the birds? she wondered when they stopped for a breather. I don't even see dragon-flies.

Something made her glance at the wood that bordered the far edge of the marsh. "Onua!" She pointed as a bird shot from the cover of the trees. It was black and hawk-shaped, flying crazily, as if drunk.

Shrieks, metallic and shrill, tore the air. Eight giant things—they looked like birds at first—chased the hawk out of the cover of the trees. Immense wings beat the air that reached the women and ponies, filling their noses with a stink so foul it made Daine retch. The ponies screamed in panic.

Daine tried to soothe them, though she wanted to scream to. These were *monsters*. No animal combined a human head and chest with a bird's legs and wings. Sunlight bounded off talons and feathers that shone like steel.

She counted five males, three females: one female wore a crown of black glass.

Onua gave a two-fingered whistle that could be heard the length of the valley. When the monsters turned to find the source of the noise, their quarry dropped into the cover of the reeds and vanished. The monsters swept the area, over and over, trying to find the black hawk, without success.

"Look at them," Onua whispered. "They use a grid pattern to search by—they're working that part of the marsh in squares. They're *intelligent*."

"And they can't land easy on level ground," Daine pointed out. "Those claws aren't meant to flatten out. They have to fly—they can't walk."

When the creatures gave up, they turned on the women.

Daine watched them come, her bow—like Onua's—ready to fire. The attackers were smeared with filth. When they spoke or smiled, she saw razor-sharp teeth caked with what she knew was old blood. Halting over the road, they fanned their wings to stay aloft. Their smell was suffocating.

"We almost had the motherless spy," one of them snarled.

"But *you* had to interfere," another said. "*Never* interfere with us." It lifted its wings above its head and stooped. The others followed.

"Daine, *fire*!" Onua shot: her arrow struck the first, hitting a wing with a sound of metal on metal, and bounced off. Daine struck a man-thing square in the throat. He dropped with a cry that brought sweat to her face.

Onua and Daine fired steadily, aiming for the flesh of heads and chests. A female almost grabbed Daine by the hair before Onua killed her. Cloud got one by a leg, and Tahoi seized its other foot. Together pony and dog tore the monster apart. Birds—herons, bitterns, plovers, larks—rose from hiding places to fight the creatures, blinding some, pecking others, clogging the air so the enemy couldn't see. Many paid for their help with their lives.

The glass-crowned one was finally the only monster alive. She hovered just out of Onua's range, one of the K'mir's arrows lodged in her shoulder.

"Pink *pigs*!" she snarled. "How dare you defy me, maggots! You *filth*!"

"Look who's talking," Daine shouted, sliding an arrow onto her string. She lowered her bow, wanting the creature to think she was done. "Your ma was a leech with bad teeth," she taunted. Onua laughed in spite of herself. "Your da was a peahen. I know chickens with more brains than you!"

The queen screamed and dropped, claws extended. Daine brought the bow up, loosing as she reached the best point in her swing. Her arrow buried itself in the queen's eye as Onua cheered.

Daine had another arrow on the string and in the air, but the queen pulled away. Blood dripped from her ruined eye. If she felt pain, she ignored it, hovering well out of bow-shot, her good eye furious.

"Ohhh, I'll remember *you*, girlie." The hate in her voice forced Daine back a step. "Your name is on my heart." She looked at Onua. "I'll return for you two ground crawlers. You belong to Zhaneh Bitterclaws now." She launched herself into higher air and was gone.

"I can't believe it." Onua sounded as if she were talking to herself. "The rumors said there were monsters abroad, but *these*? Where did they come from?" She went to examine the body of one of the creatures, the stink so bad she had to cover her nose to get close to it.

Limping, Daine followed. She was unhurt, but she *felt* battered and cut and torn in a thousand places.

A chickadee lay in the road. She picked it up, to find a wing was attached by only a bit of skin. Tears rolled down her cheeks to fall on the dying bird. All around her, birds lay in the rushes, bleeding, dead.

"I'm sorry, little ones," she whispered. "You should've stayed hid." Her temples pounded. Stripes of black-and-yellow fire crossed her vision. Her ears filled with a roaring sound, and she fainted.

Onua saw her fall. The bird that had been in Daine's hand jumped into the air and zipped past, nearly missing the K'mir's nose. In the marsh, she heard a rush of song. Birds took off, clumsily at first, as if they were stiff. An owl that lay in the road moved, then flew away as she stared. She was positive that the bird's head had been cut half off.

Shaking her head, she went to the fallen girl. As far as she could tell, Daine was unhurt.

With a grunt the K'mir levered her onto a shoulder, surprised by how light she was. "You need to eat more," she told her burden as she carried her to the ponies. Cloud trotted over to nuzzle Daine, worry in every line of the pony's body.

"I don't suppose you know a place where we can get off the road," Onua asked, half jesting, never thinking these animals would understand her as they did the girl. Cloud trotted into a nearby stand of reeds. Just beyond her, Onua saw a clearing, floored in solid ground.

This was food for thought. Onua followed Cloud. The remainder of the ponies followed her, Tahoi bringing up the rear.

Coarse hairs tickled Daine's face. Opening her eyes, she saw nothing but Cloud's nose.

"Let me up." Her voice emerged as a croak. "I'm fine." She wasn't really—her whole body ached—but the pain that had knocked her out was over.

"Swallow this." Onua brought over a cup of water. Drinking it, Daine tasted herbs. A tingling filled her veins and left her feeling much improved. The only sign of the pain that had knocked her down was mild stiffness.

"I didn't faint 'cause I'm a baby or anything—" she began, afraid the K'mir would be disgusted by her weakness. She struggled to sit up, and finished the water.

"Don't be silly." Onua gave her a silvery feather. "Don't touch the edges," she warned. "They're razor sharp."

It was metal, etched and shaped like a feather. If it was steel, as it seemed to be, it was paper thin, impossible to bend. Moreover, it *felt* wrong, as the sight of the creatures had felt wrong. If she knew nothing else, she knew nature. Such creations did not belong in the world: seeing them made her feel wobbly and sick. "What *were* those things? Do you know?"

"I've heard tales, but—they aren't supposed to exist, not here. They're called Stormwings." She heard awe and fear in Onua's voice.

"What are Stormwings?"

"The Eaters." Onua wrapped the feather and put it away. "But they're *legends*. No one's seen them for three, four centuries. They lived on battlefields, desecrating bodies—eating them, fouling them, scattering the pieces." She crouched beside Daine again. "Listen—I need to leave you and the ponies for a while—I hope not too long. I can't tell you why."

"Then I'll follow." Daine was comfortable enough with her now to be blunt. "This is a marsh, remember? Quicksand, mud bogs, snakes—you told me you don't know anything about marshes."

"I can't help that. What I must do is important. You stay put—"

A picture of the Stormwings as they'd first seen them flashed into Daine's mind. "It's that hawk, isn't it?" she asked, and Onua looked away. "That black one. You tried to call him, but he couldn't make it, so he hid in the reeds. Now you want to go after him. Why is a *bird* so important?"

Onua's eyes glittered with annoyance. "Never you mind. He is, that's all—he's more important than you could imagine. If something happens to me, take the ponies to the Riders. Tell Buri or Sarge what happened—"

Daine saw how she might repay some of what she owed this woman for taking her in. "I'll go."

"Out of the question."

She retrieved her crossbow and quiver from the packs. "Don't be silly. It's only a few hundred yards out. How much trouble can I get into? Besides, I know about bogs. And I can find lost animals." If she waited, the K'mir would find a good reason to keep her back. She saw a game trail leading into the reeds and took it. "I'll yell for Tahoi if I get stuck," she called.

"Daine!" There was no answer. "When *I* was that age, *I* listened to my elders," Onua muttered, conveniently forgetting she had done no such thing. She grabbed Cloud's rein as the pony tried to follow her mistress. "No, you stay here. And don't try to argue." She tied the mare's rein into a string for the first time since they'd left the fair, and settled down to wait.

The trail took Daine to a pond. She skirted it, always making for the spot where the monsters had left the wood. A grouse darted out of the brush. Following it, she walked a trail that lay on firm ground to reach the trees at the marsh's edge. There she sat on a rock, wondering what to do next. If the bird was alive, it had come down somewhere nearby to hide from the Stormwings.

It was nice, this green wilderness. The scents of growing things filled her nostrils; the sounds of animals and plants waking from their winter sleep filled her ears. What had the badger said, in her dream? *If you listen hard and long, you can hear any of us, call any of us, that you want.*

Surely *listening* wouldn't bring on the madness. She wasn't trying to *be* an animal; she just wanted to *hear* them. Definitely she'd taken advice from worse people than badgers in her time.

Besides, if the hawk was alive and hurt, it might be thrashing or crying its pain. She'd hear it, if she listened.

She'd have to be very quiet, then.

She settled herself and slowed her breathing. Her blouse itched; she eased it. A burn throbbed on a finger; she put it out of her mind.

A breeze fanned the tips of the reeds, making them sigh.

Two plops ahead: a pair of mating frogs. She had no interest in *that*.

A rustle to her left, some feet behind: a pair of nesting ducks. Didn't people think of *anything* else?

A gritty noise at her side was a grass snake, coming up to sun. It was nice on the rock, the warmth just perfect on her face and on the snake.

There—left, closer to the trees. She frowned. It didn't sound like a bird—like the hawks and falcons back home. She felt dizzy and befuddled, almost like the time she had swiped a drink of her mother's home-brewed mead.

That yip was a fox, who had found a black bird. A large one.

Daine headed in his direction. The fox yipped again when she almost made a wrong turn. She found him next to a large, hollow log. The hawk had concealed itself inside.

"Thank you," she said. The fox grinned at her and vanished into the reeds while Daine looked at her new patient. "Clever lad, to think of hiding there," she murmured. (And since when did hawks ever think of concealing themselves?) "Come on out—they're gone." She put her hands into the log's opening, praying she wasn't about to get slashed.

The bird waddled forward, easing himself onto her palms. Moving very slowly, she lifted him out and placed him on top of his hiding place.

He stared at her, beak open as he panted. One outspread wing seemed broken in two places, maybe even three. Her hair prickled at the back of her neck. Anyone less familiar with hawks might have taken this bird for one: she could not. He was too big, and hawks were not solid black. His color was dull, like velvet—there was no gloss to his feathers at all. He wasn't wrong as those Stormwings were wrong, but he was not right, either.

She cut reeds for splints. "I'm from Onua— Onua Chamtong of the K'miri Raadeh," she told him. "You recognize the name?" She didn't expect an answer, but she knew a kind voice was something any hurt creature responded to. "I have to splint that wing. It's broken." She cursed herself for not having bandages of any kind, and cut strips out of a petticoat.

"It'll hurt," she warned. "Try not to peck me, or we'll never get you fixed." Ignoring his gaze, she gently spread the wing. The hawk cried out only once. That was *another* strange thing, she thought; other birds had savaged her for less pain than she was giving this one.

She secured the outspread limb onto its reed framework, feeling him shake under her hands. "You're being a find, brave lad," she crooned, securing the last cotton ties. "You're ma'd be fair proud of you—wherever she is. *What*ever she is."

Repairs made, she slung the crossbow on her back. "I've got to carry you," she explained. "Try to keep still." When she gathered him up, taking care not to bump the wing, he trembled but didn't bite or slash. "You're the oddest bird I've met in my life," she murmured as she followed the trail back to the road. "Heavy too." She was sweating by the time she found Onua. "His wing's busted."

"Horse Lords be praised, you found him!" The relief on the K'mir's face was scary, as if he were a friend or something, Daine thought. Onua lifted the hawk from Daine's arms, examining him with delicate fingers. Somehow Daine wasn't surprised to see that he was as calm with Onua as he'd been with her.

"If we move the packs onto one of the gentler ponies, he can ride on them," Onua suggested. "We have to get well away before we camp." Daine nodded and shifted the packs to a mild-mannered chestnut gelding. On the road, the bird rode quietly, panting without making any other sound.

They left the marshy valley and entered the wood, moving on after dark. Onua lit the way ahead with her magic. They had walked for hours before she took them off the road, onto a small path.

Here she lit a torch and gave it to Daine. "Farther up there's an open shed for drying wood. It's big enough to shelter us and the ponies." She dug out the materials she used to work her magic. "Get a fire going. I'll be there as soon as I can." She went back to the road, a bag of powder in her hand. Tahoi started to follow: she ordered him to go with Daine.

"I think she wants to hide our trail," Daine told the dog. She led the pack pony, and the others followed obediently. "But why? The monster—what's her name? Zhaneh Bitterclaws— can she see in the dark? Apart from revenge, why follow us?" She glanced at the hawk. Meeting his eyes directly still made her head spin. "Not for you, surely."

The bird shuddered.

The shed was big, with three walls to keep

out the wind. Moreover, it had a fire pit inside, and a well outside. With relief she freed the ponies, watered them, and fed them grain from the extra stores.

Tahoi had brought in three rabbits that afternoon. As soon as the fire was going, Daine skinned and gutted them. Two went on the spit for her and Onua; Tahoi got half of the third. Cutting strips from the remaining half, she offered it to her patient. He turned his head away.

Perhaps he hadn't gotten the scent. Daine waved it in front of him. Again he turned his head aside.

She sniffed the meat: it was no different from what Tahoi crunched so happily nearby. She laid it on the pack in front of the bird, having moved his travel arrangements to the floor of the shed. The hawk picked the morsel up in his beak and threw it away.

Getting the rejected meat, she offered it to Tahoi. The dog ate it and returned to his bones. Planting her hands on her hips, Daine scowled at the bird. She'd heard of captive animals refusing to eat, but such a thing had never happened to *her*.

"There's many a hawk would be happy for a nice bit of rabbit," she told him, not even realizing she sounded like her ma. "Now, I'll give you another piece. Don't go throwing that away, for I won't give you any more." She offered a fresh strip to the bird, who sniffed it—and turned his head. She placed it before him, and he threw it to Tahoi.

"He won't eat," she told Onua when the K'mir joined them. "What's the matter with him? I never had an animal that wouldn't eat for me."

The woman crouched near the hawk, her gray green eyes puzzled. "Let me try. Maybe it's 'cause he doesn't know you."

"I've fed plenty of animals that never met me first," Daine snapped, cutting another strip of meat for Onua. The hawk refused it as well.

Onua scratched her head. "Try cooked meat. I have to ward this place. There're armed men all over the road, searching." She walked outside the shed.

"For us?" Daine asked. Onua shook her head and began the now-familiar spell. "Not for you, surely," the girl whispered to the hawk. Cutting meat off the spit, she cooled it

47

with water and offered it to her patient. He sniffed it for a while, but refused it in the end.

"Maybe he's sick," Onua suggested as she ate. "I broke my collarbone once, and I was queasy for a day or two."

"That's shock." Daine rested her chin on her knees. "I s'pose that might be it."

"He's not just any creature." Onua finished her meal. "He may be a little strange to care for, Daine. Just do your best—please?"

The girl awoke in the night to hear a quiet murmur. Peeking with a half-closed eye, she saw that Onua sat with the hawk, talking softly to him. *And Ma said I was fair foolish with animals,* she thought. Rolling over, she went back to sleep.

They moved on in the morning. Searchers passed them on the road, men on horseback and men afoot, but none appeared to see the bird riding in state on ponyback. "I can't throw fire or heal," Onua told Daine, "but when I hide a thing, it stays hidden."

For three days they pushed on. The hawk's eyes still would not focus, and his balance was poor. After some debate with herself, Daine lightly bound his claws to the pack he rested on. He didn't seem to mind, which bothered her still more. Even the mildest sparrow would have fought the ties.

Her patient worsened. He refused any and all meat, raw or cooked. Their third day together she offered him raw egg and then cheese. He ate both, to her joy, but vomited it up later. That night she woke to hear Onua chanting a spell over him, but it didn't seem to help. The K'mir still talked to him about human things—road conditions, the fair in Cría, the doings of the Queen's Riders.

Once, after meeting the bird's eyes, Daine walked into a ditch. Another time she fell over her own feet. After that, she avoided his gaze and resented it. Why *couldn't* she look at this bird? And why did she not feel connected to him, as she felt with other creatures?

His wing did not heal. The fourth night she stayed up with him, coaxing water mixed with honey into his beak. It did no good. The fever she had fought to prevent set in and began to climb.

She woke Onua sometime after midnight. "He's going to die. Not today—tomorrow, maybe. I *hate* losing one I've nursed!" To her shame, she felt tears on her cheeks and wiped them away with an impatient hand. "He's not right! He's not like any bird I ever met, and *I can't fix him!* Can we stop at a village or town, and find a sorcerer who might—"

Onua shook her head. "Out of the question." When Daine opened her mouth to argue, the woman said, "There are *reasons*. Important ones." She tugged at her lip, and came to a decision. Get some rest—I'm calling for help. Horse Lords willing, somebody will be in range."

Daine was too exhausted to protest or ask questions. It was hard even to crawl into her bedroll. The last thing she saw was Onua, kneeling before a fire that now burned scarlet, hands palm up in a summoning.

She slept until dawn, and Onua greeted her cheerfully. "I got lucky—help is closer than I thought. Eat something, and you might want to wash up. There's a bathing pool behind that hill. They'll be here around noon."

"They who?" Daine's voice came from her throat as a croak.

Onua shook her head.

"Wonderful. More secrets. My favorite,"

Daine muttered grumpily as she found towels and soap. Since the day was warm, she washed her hair and took extra time to scrub every inch of her skin. Why hurry? she thought, still feeling grouchy. *They* won't get here till noon—whoever *they* are.

The hawk's eyes were closed when she returned, and he was shivering. She warmed small rocks and wrapped them in cloths— towels, scarves, handkerchiefs. Carefully, talking to him the whole time, she cocooned bird and rocks in a blanket, hoping to sweat the fever out. After an hour of the extra warmth, he took some heated water and honey when she coaxed.

Onua had worn herself out with her magical efforts, and slept all morning. Daine had to content herself with frequent trips to the road, looking for the promised help. Cloud and Tahoi followed her, as worried as she was.

The sun was at its height, covered by thickening clouds, when she saw movement to the east. She raced back to camp. "Onua, there are people coming."

The K'mir grabbed her bow and arrows; Daine got hers. They went to the road to wait.

It wasn't long before Onua said, "It's my friends. The ones in white are in the King's Own. They answer directly to King Jonathan."

Daine gaped at the company that approached. Mail-clad warriors on beautiful horses rode in four rows, their white, hooded capes flapping grandly at their backs. The earth shook with the pounding of their steeds' hooves. Before them came a standard-bearer, his flag a silver blade and crown on a royal blue field.

Beside him was a full knight in gold-washed mail, his gold helm mirror bright. He bore a lance; on his left arm was a red shield with a device like a gold cat rearing on its hind paws. The knight's horse was larger than those of the white-caped warriors, though not as large as the chargers normally used by those who wore full mail or plate armor. It was as gold as the cat on the knight's shield, with a black mane and tail.

Together the company made a picture out of legends. "Oh, glory," whispered Daine.

Reaching Onua, the knight halted the warriors with a raised hand. His horse refused to stop and walked up to butt his head against Daine's chest.

"You beauty," she whispered, running her hand along his mane. "Oh, you pretty, pretty thing."

Laughing, Onua went to the war-horse's head and gently made him back up. The knight peered down at the K'mir through his open visor. "Are you camped here?" Onua nodded, and he turned to his company. "Hakim, this is it."

A brown man in the front rank of the white-caped riders nodded and called out instructions. The result was instant activity: men dismounted, giving their reins over to a few of their number while others removed packs from their mounts and from the spares. Within seconds they were off the road, erecting tents to share the clearing with the ponies and Tahoi.

The knight secured the shield and helm to his saddle. Dismounting, he gave the reins to one of the others, then stripped amethyst-decorated gauntlets from his hands. "I should've changed to leather," he complained. "My back has been one whole itch the last mile." He grinned at Daine. "The outfit looks nice, but it's not very comfortable."

Daine was *very* confused. Out of the saddle, the knight was two whole inches shorter than she was, and built on stocky, not muscular, lines. His cropped, coppery hair was tousled from being inside a helmet. Amethysts winked at his earlobes, stones that matched the color of his eyes.

"My wits have gone begging," Onua said. "Daine, this is Sir Alanna of Pirate's Swoop and Olau—the King's Champion. Alanna, this is Daine. Wait till you see what she can do with animals."

Daine stared at the hand offered her, then into purple eyes. "The *champion*? The knight they call 'the Lioness'?"

"Don't tell me," Alanna said. "You expected someone bigger."

Daine took the offered hand. Remembering her patient, she asked, "Can you help? I can't fix 'im at all."

Onua took the champion's elbow. "Alanna's a healer and a sorceress—if she can't come up with something, no one can."

"Aren't you going to be sorry if I can't?" the knight asked as Onua steered her toward the ailing hawk.

Daine unwound the bird from his wraps. "He won't eat anything but a little honey and water," she explained. "Not meat or fish. And he's dizzy all the time."

The purple eyes looked at her sharply. "How would you know that?"

Daine met that gaze squarely. "I just do. I've—"

"'A knack with animals,'" Onua chorused along with her, and grinned.

Alanna lifted the bird with a care for the splinted wing. The hawk blinked, looked at her—and buried his head against her chest. "He knows me. Good." She carried him to a tent the warriors had set up, and went inside.

"Wait here," Onua told Daine. "Don't let these men bully Tahoi or the ponies." She followed the knight inside.

Daine realized she ought to picket the strings so the smaller horses wouldn't disturb the big ones. Tahoi stuck close to her as she worked, and Cloud was on her best behavior. The warriors smiled at her as they set up more tents and built cook fires. A handful went to the nearby river with fishing lines in their hands. She would have liked to go too, but she couldn't bring herself to ask these businesslike Tortallans.

"Great merciful Goddess!" The shout came from the tent where Alanna and Onua had taken the hawk. "Of all the gods-cursed, simpleminded—"

Daine gaped. The man the knight had called Hakim smiled. "The Lioness has a temper," he told the girl. "Sometimes it gets the better of her."

The knight stamped out of the tent. She had discarded mail for breeches and a white shirt. At her throat a red gem burned like a coal in the fire. "I can't see—" Her purple eyes lit on Daine. "You, girl—come here!"

Tahoi growled, bristling. He didn't like the knight's tone.

Alanna stared at the dog, then smiled. "I'm sorry. Daine, would you come here, please? I think I need your help." Steering the girl into the tent, she said, "Onua says you found him under—unusual conditions." The hawk lay on a man-size cot, his eyes wide and frightened. "How?"

There was something here that pounded on her ears, making her nervous. "Honest, Your Ladyship—"

"Alanna," was the firm interruption.

She thought of calling the champion, the only lady knight in living memory, by her first name, and winced. "I listened for him, is all. I sat down and just—listened."

"Would you do it for me now, please?"

Daine swallowed. "But he's right there, mum. Lioness."

"Turn your back to him, if that helps." Alanna fiddled with the red gem at her throat. "Listen for him *exactly* as you listened back then."

Listening's fine, Daine thought nervously. You only listened before, and had no trouble. And the badger said it was all right. Well, then!

Closing her eyes, she emptied her mind, letting her breath slow until she couldn't hear it. She concentrated on her ears. Outside, Cloud chewed on a clump of grass, thinking she ought to check on Daine, alone with strangers. The gold war-horse shifted; he wanted to run some more.

There! A strange and distant voice, one that sounded like no animal she knew. That had to be the hawk. Was he *muttering* to himself?

"I hear him." That sleepy voice was hers.

"He's a prisoner. He can't get out. But he's just on the bed—"

"Hush." Purple fires played inside her eyelids. "Call him, Daine—with your *mind*. His name is Numair Salmalín."

"Alanna—maybe Arram's better." That was Onua, sounding distant. "He's only been Numair for eight years—he's been Arram all his life."

"True. Call to him as Arram, Daine." The fires evened into a steady purple light, warming her face like the sun.

"Why—"

"Call him." The knight's voice was gentle, but firm.

Daine sighed. "Arram Salmalín? Arram— come on. You're too far off. It's all right, Arram—it's safe—"

Something behind her snapped, breaking her concentration. She opened her eyes as wooden sticks hit the tent wall in front of her: the hawk's splints. "Now look at this," she scolded, picking them up. "His wing won't get any better that way." She turned to show them the evidence.

The hawk was gone. Onua pulled a sheet up to cover a large, naked man.

He smiled drowsily at the three of them. "Can I have something to eat?"

Daine's jaw fell open. "Where did *he* come from?"

Alanna bent over the newcomer, peering into his eyes. Onua grabbed the girl's elbow and steered her out of the tent. "Explanations later," the K'mir said. "There's a lot to be done for him still."

"Onua, where's my hawk? Where'd that man come from?" Her knees shook.

Onua put a hand on Daine's mouth. "Hush. No more questions. I'll explain everything—later." She went back into the tent, pulling the flap tightly shut behind her.

"Later," Daine muttered to herself. "Wonderful. Hawks disappearing, men appearing—why not? Later." She stamped off to look after the ponies, who at least would tell her things and not wait for any "laters."

THREE

SPIDRENS AND MEDITATION

Hedgehogs woke Daine as they wriggled into her bedroll, shaking in terror. It wasn't the controlled fear they felt around hunters, but the wild panic that made them run before a fire. She eased out of the covers. "It's all right," she whispered. "Stay here."

She dragged on her clothes and boots. She felt it now, heaviness in the air and in her mind—not like the Stormwings or the rabid bear, but there was a flavor in it that reminded her of the winged monsters. In the camp around her, the men slept quietly—no snorers like Grandda. Onua was mumbling in her sleep. Tahoi was not with her or the ponies.

"Stay," Daine told Cloud, who wanted to follow. She fitted the string to her bow and checked its draw as she looked around. A light burned in the Lioness's tent. The other one, where the man who'd been a hawk lay, was dark.

The wood outside their camp was thick with fear. Tiny beasts dug as far into burrows as they could. The big ones were gone. An owl sitting overhead was almost mindless with terror. That was bad: owls didn't scare.

Tahoi sat at the edge of the trees, nose to the wind. When Daine rested a hand on his shoulder, the dog flinched. "What is it?"

He knew only that it was bad, and it was coming.

"Stay with the ponies. Guard them." Tahoi whimpered a protest. Waiting for trouble to reach him was hard; better to hunt it out. "Go on." He obeyed, reluctantly.

A sentry nearby raised a hand in greeting. Looking past him, Daine saw another. "Do you hear anything?" she asked. "I think something bad is coming. Something *wrong*."

"I hear nothing." It was Hakim. He didn't take his eyes off the woods beyond. "Go back to your sleep."

There was no sleeping, not now. Checking the ponies, Daine found they were afraid too. Beyond them the horses were alert, watching the trees like sentries. The war-horse pawed the air: he *knew* danger was close. Wanting to fight it, he pulled his tether to see if it could be yanked from the ground.

"Not yet," she said, patting his withers. "Watch. Wait." She walked toward the forest.

"Don't go alone."

Daine wrenched around and lost her balance. A strong hand grabbed her elbow and raised her to her feet. It was the Lioness, wearing a shirt, breeches, and boots. The red gem at her throat glowed steadily; a naked sword lay in her right hand.

"Easy," the knight cautioned. "What brings you out here?" They walked to a small clearing almost thirty feet away.

Daine took a deep breath and made herself calm down. "There's something close by that isn't right. I can't explain better'n that."

The Lioness scanned the trees all around them. "I feel it too." She tapped the gem. "This warns me of trouble, sometimes."

"Look." Her ma had said she had an owl's

nightsight. That was how she saw the rabbit in the clearing, when someone else would miss it. Kneeling to lift the body, she found it was still warm.

White light—Alanna's magic—appeared over her hands. The knight touched the body with a palm and felt its warmth, then touched the red drops at the rabbit's nose. She sniffed her fingers. "*Blood?* Its heart burst—"

"It was scared to death." Daine was sure of it. Gently she lay the dead creature atop a nearby stump. "There's something else, Lioness. The big animals—there isn't a one within a mile of this place right now. Listen."

The knight doused her light and obeyed. "Nothing's moving out—"

A bat darted between them, chittering a warning. Startled, the knight and the girl jumped back—and a rope that glowed a sickly yellow green dropped into the space where Alanna had been standing.

Noise overhead made Daine look up as she put an arrow on the string. A monstrous spider hurtled down at them. She shot it before she even knew what she fired at. A man screamed above; black fluid fell onto her hand, burning like acid. She put two more arrows into the thing and jumped aside when it hit the ground.

Alanna was shouting a warning to the camp. Daine was about to wipe her hand on a leaf when something moved on the edge of her vision. She leaped out of the way and the Lioness moved in, as smoothly as butter. Her sword flashed once—a powerful cut sliced two of the near legs off a new attacker—then twice, beheading the thing. It happened so fast Daine wasn't quite sure it happened, till Alanna dragged her out of the way of the monster's death throes. Knight and girl waited, breathless, for a moment or two, to see if another giant spider would appear.

"I don't think there are more," Daine said at last. "It felt—*wrong*—out here, before. That's almost gone now."

Many-jointed legs moved, and she knew the one she'd shot was alive. Gulping down nausea, she drew her dagger and walked around front to kill the thing—cutting off its head was best.

She had thought they were spiders, almost as big as she was, with bodies dressed in dull black fur. That was bad enough, until she saw this one from the front. Head and neck were human—its teeth as sharp and pointed as a giant cat's. It screamed with a man's voice, enraged at seeing the knife.

Her mouth dropped open; a cry of fright and repulsion came out as a strangled croak. Her knife dropped from numb fingers. No wonder these had felt like Stormwings in the night. They were just as wrong, an eerie mating of animal and human that had no reason to exist.

"Great merciful Goddess." Alanna came up behind her. It made Daine feel better to know the paleness of the knight's face wasn't due entirely to the light she had called so they could see. "Have you ever heard, or—"

"Never." She turned her back on it—let it die slowly—and found a log where she could sit, shuddering in horror. Grandda had told her stories about monsters, human-headed and spider-bodied, named spidrens. A brave man hunted them best at night, he'd said: their webs glowed in the dark.

A hand rested on her shoulder. "Little girl, your ancestors are proud tonight." It was the sentry, the man Hakim. "You are the best archer I have ever seen—better even than the Lioness."

Alanna nodded. She knelt beside the thing, examining it with a stick rather than touching it herself. "We're lucky you sensed them coming, Daine."

The girl swallowed, thinking, You couldn't *pay* me to touch that, even with a stick. "The hedgehogs woke me. They didn't know what was out there. I could feel something wrong was close, but I didn't think it'd look like—like this." Wincing as the knight pulled the thing's head back by the hair—it was dead now—she added, "Grandda told me stories about spidrens, but he said they were killed, ages and ages ago."

"Not killed." Hakim's voice was steady, but his face glowed with sweat. "They were imprisoned in the Divine Realms four hundred years ago, by the greatest of shamans."

"You mean they're *gods?*"

"Immortals and gods aren't the same. They just live in the same place." Alanna dusted her hands. "Like the Stormwings, Daine. They were shut into the Divine Realms at the same time, along with a great many other creatures. Griffins, dragons, and so on."

Daine swallowed: there were *more* of these? What if they were loose too, escaped from the prison where they'd been locked for so long?

"Horse Lords." Onua had found them. "Lioness, what—"

"They're called spidrens." The knight's voice was almost matter-of-fact. "Goddess knows how many of us they would have killed and dragged off to munch on if your Daine hadn't been alert."

"You killed one too," Daine reminded her. She went to the clearing's edge and listened to the woods beyond, just in case. All around she heard creatures stirring, large and small, as they resumed their night's business. I don't know if I'd ever come out of my burrow again, she thought.

Remembering an obligation, she glanced behind her. Hakim and Onua were going over the spidren, using sticks. Most of the camp had come to watch, and to marvel. One of the soldiers was vomiting at the edge of the clearing, which made her feel better. At least *she* hadn't thrown up.

She faced the trees where the bat had fled after warning them. "Thanks, wing-friend," she whispered. "Thank you for both of us." In the darkness ahead, a bat squeaked in reply. Daine smiled and went back to the humans.

"It's over," she told Alanna. "The animals are coming out." She felt suddenly exhausted; the burn on her hand throbbed.

Onua put an arm around her. "We've *both* had enough excitement. Come on." She steered her to their fire. "Are you all right?" She hissed in sympathy when Daine showed her the burn, and got her medicines. Daine barely remembered having the burn cleansed and bandaged, she was so tired. The pain gone, she got into bed.

"You're *certain* you're all right?" The woman was plainly concerned.

Daine smiled at her. "I think so." The hedgehogs snuggled in around her once more. "I'll have nightmares, for sure."

"Me too," Onua sighed. "At least we're alive to have them." She eased into her own bed.

"What of him? The hawk—the man?" Daine pointed at the patient's tent.

Onua smiled. "Master Salmalín slept through

the whole thing. He'll be mad as fire when he hears too. Spidrens are more *his* line than ours."

Daine said shyly, "Why didn't you tell me the truth? About the hawk?"

A sigh came from the other bedroll. "His shape-shifting—it's a secret. Only a few people know, and we're not supposed to tell. It isn't that I don't trust you—I do."

"He's a spy?"

"Only sometimes, when the king's spymaster can't send anyone else."

"He was just supposed to get well and fly off, and I'd never know."

"That was the plan." There was a rueful note in Onua's voice.

"I know now."

"Yes. You planning to tell somebody?"

Daine thought about that. "You just said it's a secret, didn't you? I won't tell."

"Good. Now go to sleep."

No one left the camp by the river the next day. The men of the King's Own burned the dead monsters and searched the woods for more. The Lioness and Onua sat with their patient all morning. In the afternoon they summoned Hakim and another soldier who carried a writing desk.

Daine kept out of the way of the men. She wasn't used to being noticed and greeted by so many people. Her caution did not extend to their mounts, of course. Once she'd cared for her ponies, she looked at the big horses. Her favorite was Alanna's mount, the young stallion who had greeted her so happily the day before. She examined every inch of him, crooning praises into his ear.

"I think the feeling's mutual."

Daine jumped—once again the Lioness had come up unheard. She grinned at the knight. "He's a beauty."

"His name is Darkmoon." The stallion lipped Alanna's breeches pockets. "He's spoiled rotten." Fishing a lump of sugar out, she fed it to him. "His grandam was my first horse—a fine mare, true to the bone." Giving Darkmoon another sugar lump, she added, "You saved my life last night."

Daine blushed. "You saved mine." Purple eyes are very discomforting when they look at you, she thought. Or is it that she's got so much Gift it leaks over to all she does?

"Where did you learn to shoot like that?"

"My grandda taught me. Carved me that bow too."

"You'd think, your size, you'd only be able to manage a smaller one."

Daine shrugged. "I've always been a fair shot."

The woman snorted, but her eyes never left Daine's face. She toyed with the gem around her neck. "Three times you shot overhead and hit a mark that moved, in the dark. That's more than 'fair' shooting."

Daine shrugged again. "I practice a lot."

Alanna grinned. "I'll stop. I didn't mean to interrogate you. I've been so busy getting Arram's story out of him that I forgot I just wanted to say thanks. You saved my life, and the life of one of my best friends. Arram wouldn't be here if you hadn't nursed him. I'll remember it."

Daine swallowed. "It was no trouble—"

Alanna took her hand. "If you need anything, come to me. A place to stay, money, work—I don't care. If I'm not around, go to my husband." Startled, Daine looked at

Alanna's ring finger and saw a wide silver band. "He's the baron of Pirate's Swoop. He'll do anything for you I would."

Daine gulped. A King's Champion in debt to *her*? An offer with no limits, and she to apply to the lady or her baron husband? People like her had no business bothering the great and wealthy! And if Alanna knew the truth about her, about what she'd done once, she'd hate Daine. She'd have to.

The knight must have seen refusal in her face. "Promise me."

Daine wondered if there was any way to get out of it. Alanna had the look of someone who wouldn't let this go, however. "I promise, Lioness."

"Alanna," Onua called from the tent. "We need you for a minute."

"Coming," the knight replied. "By the way— can you wield a sword?"

"*Me?* Gods, no!" she said, shocked. A sword was a weapon for nobles!

The Lioness grinned. "I shouldn't be glad, but I am." Seeing Daine's puzzlement, she explained. "If you were as good with the sword as you are with a bow, I couldn't take the competition." She clapped Daine on the shoulder and returned to her patient.

The next day everyone rose at first light, Onua and Daine from habit, the others from necessity. "You're staying here?" Alanna wanted to know.

Onua spooned porridge into a bowl and gave it to her. "Just for today—give Arram a little more time before we go west. How about you?"

"I'll see the local magistrate, now I have Arram's information," Alanna explained, drizzling honey into her bowl. "Once I get a writ of arrest from him, Sinthya's mine."

"So *that's* why you were so near when I called for help," said Onua. "Springtime you're usually at Pirate's Swoop. You were waiting for Arram?"

Alanna nodded. "He has proof now that Sinthya is dealing with Carthak."

Onua smiled grimly. "I knew it!"

The knight frowned. "I'm sending word to the king, to tell him about our visitors last night, and the Stormwings." She shook her head. "I can't understand why these immortals are reappearing *now*. We've had reports from all over Tortall, and from our neighbors as well. Also, I don't like it that they were on hand to chase our friend when he escaped."

"You don't think it was a coincidence?" Onua asked. "Or does Sinthya have an arrangement with those—things?"

Daine winced. The idea of humans welcoming such creatures was chilling.

Alanna sighed. "I don't know. That's one of the questions I'll ask His Lordship—when I arrest him. In the meantime, I leave you to your travels. Don't let Arram overdo things. And it might be best if he kept from shape-shifting for a while, not that I think he'll have the strength to try." The knight finished her breakfast and got to her feet. "Time to ride."

With the consent of the man who tended Darkmoon, Daine brought the saddled horse to his mistress and held him as the Lioness mounted. This time the knight wore a leather jerkin studded with metal rings, instead of her mail. Seeing Daine look at it, she said, "I drew it from our spares. They always bring one in my size. It doesn't look as nice as the mail, but it's more comfortable." She offered Daine a gloved hand to shake. "I'll see you again—if not at the palace, then later on. Take care of my friends, and take care of yourself."

Daine returned the woman's firm grip. "Safe journey, Lioness. Give that Sinthya man a few lumps for me."

Alanna laughed. "I hope to do just that." She looked back: the men of the King's Own were in the saddle. "Forward!"

Daine, in awe, watched them go. *This* was what she'd dreamed when Onua said they were going to Tortall. Well, *some* things are different, she thought as the riders retreated from view. Pulling the badger's claw out of her shirt, she polished it with a thumb. She's shorter than I expected. And I never thought she'd swear, or make jokes. She's a legend, sure enough, but she's so *human*.

An idea made her jaw drop: if *she's* a legend, and a hero, then *anyone* could be a hero. Tucking the claw back into her shirt, she ran back to camp. If anyone might be a hero—could I? she asked herself, and smiled. No, not me.

Still, she mulled it over as she started on a pile of reins that needed mending. Onua joined her at their fire with leatherwork of her own. They worked quietly until she heard her friend say, "Look who's up."

Their patient stood in front of his tent. Someone—Daine assumed one of the men—had given him a shirt and breeches, as well as a pair of boots.

She stared up at him. He was five inches over six feet in height, with broad shoulders and a well-muscled body. His mass of coal black hair was combed back and tied into a horse tail to show a face that was dark and sensitive. He moved with the ease of a giant cat as he sat on a log beside Onua, but Daine suspected that he hadn't always been so graceful. As a boy he must have resembled a stork, all elbows and knees. In his late twenties now, he had grown into his looks, and he seemed completely at home with himself.

"How'd you find a pair that fits?" Onua pointed at his feet with the awl she'd been using on her tack. "There's tea in the kettle, and a clean mug right there."

His lips parted to reveal white teeth in a shy smile. "Thanks." He poured and blew gently on his tea to cool it. "Alanna witched them so they'd fit." He regarded his boots with a wistful grin. "Nobody else had a pair even near big enough."

"What about your own magic?" Onua asked.

"I'm dry for the moment. Tapped out." His voice was midrange for a man's, warm and a little hesitant—nice to listen to, Daine thought. She kept her eyes away from him as she wrestled with her leatherwork.

A pair of large hands came into her field of vision to hold the strap while she set the final stitches.

"Thanks," she whispered, blushing.

"You look different."

Startled, she looked up into long, shadowy eyes. "What?"

He smiled. "You were a *lot* bigger."

She grinned in spite of her shyness. "Seems to me *you* was a bit smaller, now I think of it."

The strap was fixed. He gave it back and returned to his seat on the log. "I'd be dead if it weren't for you. You're called Daine?"

She nodded.

"I'm glad to meet you, Daine. I'm Numair Salmalín."

"I thought it was Arram."

His eyes flicked to Onua and back to her. "Arram's my boyhood name. I go by Numair now."

Daine took the hint. "The honor's mine, Master Numair." Then, because she *had* to know, she asked, "Why didn't you change back?"

"I was stuck."

"Stuck?"

"When Sinthya caught me, his mage fed me drugs. I panicked, and shape-shifted. I didn't remember I was full of all the drugs it takes to knock out somebody my size."

"You're lucky they didn't kill you," Onua pointed out.

"You're right. By the time you found me, I couldn't tell ground from air anymore. The food you offered? I didn't know it was food. Not that I was able to keep anything down." He sipped the tea. "It'll be a long time before I take hawk shape again."

"*That's* why you had funny eyes," breathed Daine. "And that's why you made me dizzy."

"I wanted to ask you about that. Onua says you got sick, disoriented. I can't understand *how.* She says you don't have the Gift—"

"Odd's bobs!" Daine snapped. Would all her new friends harp on that one thing, like Ma? "I don't see why this *Gift* is so grand. It comes and goes. You can't do too much at once, and you need all kinds of rules. It's more trouble than it's worth." She got up. "But whenever I turn 'round, somebody asks if I have it. I'm good with animals—isn't that enough?" Furious, not knowing there were tears on her cheeks, she stamped off into the woods.

Numair looked at Onua. "What did I say?"

The K'mir sighed and put down her work. "Her mother was a hedgewitch." (She meant someone with basic Gifts, taught by other hedgewitches, never hoping to be more than village healer-midwives.) "She and Daine's grandfather were killed by raiders in January. She wanted Daine to have the Gift, not just whatever she has with animals. Fool woman kept testing her, as if she thought the girl would develop it overnight. I'd better go after her."

"No—when she cools off, I'll go. You and Alanna were right. She has real power. Not the Gift, though." He tapped a pair of twigs together, looking thoughtful. "It's wild magic, pure and simple. She's brimming with it. I've never seen a human with so much."

"You felt it then."

He smiled. "I felt it when I was a bird, half-crazy and dying."

Onua sighed. "Be careful with her, Arram. She's hurting."

"I will." He rose, unfolding his length with a groan. "Use Numair, will you? I know you trust Daine, but there's no telling who else might overhear. I still have enemies in Carthak who'd like to know where I am."

Onua made a face. "You're right—Numair."

He grinned. "Come on—what great sorcerer has a name like Arram Draper? I have to have a name to fit my calling, don't you think?"

"All mages are Players at heart, I swear. Can't do magic unless you have all kinds of robes and props and a big audience to cheer you." She waved him off and returned to her work, smiling.

Numair found Daine greeting a woodchuck, and stayed in the trees to watch. The girl lay on the ground, her eyes on a level with the chuck's. The animal stood on his hind legs, chattering to her. She giggled, then offered a hand: the chuck snuggled against it for a moment. Then he chirped a farewell and trotted off into the bush.

Numair came forward slowly. "He seemed to have a lot to say."

Daine was thinking about the chuck, how *nice* he was after the monsters two nights before. "Oh, it's the usual spring talk. Freshening up the burrow, getting nice-smelling leaves. I told him where to find some wild mint." Her memory returned, and she felt her cheeks get hot. "Master Numair, I—"

He smiled. "No offense taken—if you stop calling me 'Master.' If I'm to help with the ponies the rest of the way, we may as well use first names."

"Is Onua mad at me? For losing my temper?"

He shook his head. The motion popped open the tie that held his black locks, and it fell. "Gods bless it . . ."

Daine came to help him look. By the time they found the tie, she'd forgotten to be nervous with him. "It's easier if you wet it before using it on your hair," she explained as they returned to camp. "When it dries, then it shrinks."

"Good advice. Your hair gives you trouble?"

"Oh, Goddess, my hair's so dratted thick I don't even bother with ties." She giggled suddenly. "This is a very strange talk we're having."

He grinned down at her. "Boys worry just as much about their looks as girls do. We only *hide* it better."

"Seriously?" she asked, delighted. Living with only Grandda and Ma, away from the males of the village, she'd begun to think young men were totally alien.

"Seriously," he assured her. "You should see the lotions I put on my hair to get it to behave." He winked at Onua when they reached the campfire.

Onua and Daine spent the next day exercising the ponies and practicing hand-to-hand combat, something Onua said a woman alone should know. Numair dozed, mended his spare shirt, or did exercises with the arm that had been broken. "Is he up to the road?" Daine asked during one of his naps. She kept her voice low—he was stretched out under a nearby tree. "He maybe should ride, but he's too big for the ponies."

"We'll take it easy," the K'mir replied.

"Alanna laid a slow healing on him, to fix the arm and build his strength. She said in two or three days he'll be fine."

"Did you know him, from before?"

"We're old friends." Seeing the look on Daine's face, Onua said, "Not *that* kind of friend! He goes for shapely blondes, and I like a man that likes horses. No, our hawk took pity on me when I didn't know anyone but the queen and Buri. If he likes you, he's the best of friends. Horse Lords help you if you get on his bad side." Seeing that Daine looked puzzled, she explained, "He *is* the most powerful sorcerer in Tortall."

Daine stared. A boyish man who talked hair-ties? Looking over, she saw a butterfly hovering over Numair's long nose. *"Him?"*

Onua chuckled. "Yes, him. It takes a powerful Gift to shape-change."

Numair opened his eyes. "You're talking about me. I can tell."

"He's vain too," Onua said loudly. "He takes as much time to dress for court functions as any lady. Which is bad enough, but then he ruins his clothes sitting on the grass to watch meteor showers."

83

"But that's my good side," protested Numair. "You really should tell her some of my faults." He paused then added, "Then again—please don't. I forgot you actually *know* my faults."

Daine laughed. She could see the rest of the trip would be fun.

The adults were arguing about protective circles when she began to think of supper. It wasn't fair to let Onua hunt all the time. Like her predator friends, Daine ate meat, taking care to make her kills swift and clean. Now she got hooks and line, and told the adults where she would be. There was a big tree on the riverbank where she could sit and mind her lines in comfort, and Onua had a very good way of preparing trout.

It wasn't long before her lines were baited and set in the deep pool under the tree. With the hard part done, she watched the sky and daydreamed, rousing herself only to greet the animals who came to say hello. Cloud found a nearby patch of clover and grazed, keeping her company.

Tahoi joined them, looking disgusted. He lay down where Daine could easily scratch his ears. Onua and Numair were doing the sitting thing, not talking or working or paying attention to him. It bored him silly.

"What's the sitting thing?" Daine asked.

The dog showed her an image in his mind: Onua, seated with her legs crossed, hands resting on her knees, eyes closed. To that picture he added Numair, doing the same thing. A shimmering, pearly light gleamed around each of them, rippling over their faces.

"What's that?" Daine asked him. "That light, there?"

Tahoi didn't know. It was a thing some humans had and others didn't.

Magic, Cloud said. Your dam had it, and some of the others back home. Not so bright as these two—more like a glitter. But it's magic, all right.

Onua only does the sitting thing with humans that have the light, Tahoi commented, and sighed.

The girl smiled. "Find a stick—I'll play with you. Not here, though—I don't want to scare the fish." Tahoi wagged his tail and hunted for a stick that wouldn't hurt his mouth. "Cloud? Do *I* have the light inside?"

No, the mare replied. *The light's only for humans. You may look like a human, but you aren't. You're of the People: the folk of claw and fur, wing and scale.*

"Impossible," the girl said flatly. "Look at me. I'm pink, my fur's patchy, I walk on two legs. I'm human, human all over."

On the outside, the pony insisted. *Not inside. Inside you're People.*

Tahoi brought a stick, and Daine went to play with him. Cloud was joking, of course. She was human. Ma would have told her, if she weren't.

They left their camp the next day. Onua set an easy pace, stopping twice in the morning to rest. Numair kept up without appearing to tire. Catching Daine's eyes on him once, he thumped himself on the chest and said, "When the Lioness puts a healing on a man, he stays *healed*!"

"Does your ma know you're this silly?" she demanded tartly.

He nodded, comically sad. "The few gray hairs she has on her head are my doing. *But*"— with an exaggerated change of mood—"I send her plenty of money, so she can pay to have them dyed!"

"I hope she beat you as a child," Onua grumbled.

The day passed quickly. Numair and Onua told stories about the people they knew at the palace. The man even juggled for her, a most unmagelike feat. By the time they made camp, she felt she had known him for years.

Building their fire, she ran into trouble. No matter what she did with flint and steel, the wood was too damp to catch. At last she coaxed it into a tiny flame and held her breath.

"How does it go?" he asked over her shoulder, and the flame went out.

"Gods bless it!" she snapped.

"What's the matter?"

"Oh, they must've had rain here yesterday. Everything's damp."

"Sit back."

She did as she was told, and the tinder burst into flame. She had to put large sticks of wood on it fast, before the fire used up the tinder. "But you didn't point, or make circles, or chant anything—"

He shrugged. "Some people need those things. I don't."

She gasped at his arrogance. "Well, excuse me for breathing!"

His laugh was full throated and made her grin. "What—did they have to enact fire-making rituals before anything would burn, where you came from?"

Her spirits dropped. "Things burned easy back home," she said flatly. "*Real* easy." She'd been having a good time while her family lay in the ground. Grabbing the shovel, she went to dig the latrine.

Teeth dug into the mage's elbow, making him yelp. He looked down at his attacker, Cloud. "Stop that, or I'll light a fire under your tail." The mare squeezed a little harder and released his arm.

"It was going so well." Onua was grooming the ponies. "She *laughed*."

Numair rubbed his elbow. He'd gotten off lightly—Cloud had only barely nicked the skin. "She'll laugh again."

Daine kept to herself, and the adults left her alone, talking quietly. When cleanup was done, they did the sitting thing. It was as Tahoi had shown her: with eyes closed and legs crossed they sat, hands on their knees, breathing as if they were asleep. In fact, Daine went to sleep watching them.

That night it came to her that Ma and Grandda probably wouldn't mind if she had fun now and then. They'd been partial to fun, making berry strings or playing catch with the bread dough. In her packs were two of the dancing puppets Grandda had made for her birthdays: the horse and one that looked just like Ma. The others had been ruined, but she had saved these.

She got up in the morning with caution and sent the raccoon and the marten who had spent that night with her on their way. She hated apologies, but if Onua and Numair were angry, she would make some.

Luck was on her side. Their grouchiness seemed to be normal morning grouchiness; all they wanted to do was drink their tea, eat their food, and get moving. Daine let it go at that. If they weren't angry about how she'd behaved, why remind them?

They made good progress that day. Once supper and cleanup were done, Numair stretched. "Let's go, Onua. You won't improve without practice."

Daine knew what came next. "What's the sitting thing?" They looked at her blankly. "You know—what you're going to do now."

"Meditation," Numair said. "It clears the mind, and rests it. If you have the Gift, meditation helps your discipline." His eyes were thoughtful as they rested on her. "Would you like to learn?"

"I don't have the Gift." Was he going to start on that?

He shrugged. "It's not only for the Gifted. I told you, it rests the mind. It helps you get a— a grip on the way you think."

"It helps you decide what you want," Onua added. "And how to get it."

Daine scuffed her foot in the dust. "Is it hard?"

Both of them smiled. "You won't know till you try," Numair pointed out.

Daine shrugged and sat as they did, tailor-style. "Now what?"

"Hands on your knees. Sit straight. Close your eyes. Let the thoughts empty out. For tonight, that's enough. Just let your thoughts go."

Daine heard Tahoi sigh. Now he had no one to play with.

The next morning they weren't far from their camp when riders overtook them on the road: Alanna and the men of the King's Own. Daine was startled to see that the Lioness, so friendly before, was now pale with fury. Darkmoon was as angry as his mistress. He pranced and fidgeted until Daine went to his head. He calmed slowly under her hands.

"He's gone," the knight told them. "From the looks of it, he fled the minute he knew you were safe. Curse him! Those dungeons of his—"

"I know," whispered Numair. He looked suddenly tired.

"I don't understand," Onua protested. "You searched?"

"We did." Alanna rubbed her neck. "His servants claimed Stormwings came, with a box, like a sedan chair. They flew off with him in it."

"Then they can be talked to," Numair said. "They're intelligent."

"Sure they are," Daine said. "They talked to Onua and me in the marsh."

"She's right," the K'mir told them. "And

they searched for Numair in patterns after they lost him."

The Lioness sighed. "Lovely. More fun. All right—we have to see the king. Come along as soon as you can now. Be sure to ward your camp at night!"

"We'll do fine," Numair told her. "See you at the palace."

The knight and Hakim nodded, and within a few moments the company was galloping out of sight.

Four mornings later Onua and her companions topped a rise, and Daine thought her eyes would fall from her head. Before them a river halved a valley that cupped a walled city and more houses than she could count. At the heart of the valley three bridges linked the northern and southern banks, and roads entered the city from every angle. In the west, the city broke through its wall to climb a long slope dotted with estates and temples.

Above everything stood a huge castle shielded by high walls. Its towers, flying bright-colored flags, shone in the early sun. A small dome placed among them glowed silver like a giant pearl. Black dots like ants climbed a broad, white-paved road from the city below, to scatter before the walls and stream in through several gates.

"That's the palace," Numair said. "Home of the most unusual royal couple in all history and their peculiar court."

"I don't think 'unusual' and 'peculiar' are the right words," protested Onua, and Tahoi barked agreement.

"Do you live there?" Daine asked the man.

He shook his head. "I live south, along the coast. They have rooms for me here, though." He looked at Onua. "Press on?" She nodded.

Their road took them around the city until they reached a bridge over a deep moat. Here the palace wall was only ten feet high; the gate was a simple affair of wood and iron. Inside lay a small town, its air scented with molten copper, pine, cows, and baking. All this, Numair said, supported the palace. Daine shook her head in awe.

Guards in maroon and beige waved them across the bridge. Inside the gate, Numair pointed to the palace. "I go that way—I need to report in."

Tears stung Daine's eyes. You knew he'd leave sometime, she scolded herself. This is it. Don't be a baby. He's got important things to do!

A big hand patted her shoulder. "Just for now," the man said quietly. "I'll see you again soon."

Onua grinned when he kissed her cheek. "You just can't wait to lay hands on your books again. *I* know that look in your eye."

"She does too," Numair admitted. "Take care of our Daine." He waved and headed toward the palace, hands in his pockets.

"Come on," Onua told her. "It's this way."

Following her out of the gate's inner yard, Daine saw more wonders. Around them soared the levels of the palace, with wings and turrets in many styles telling of additions over time. She saw more glass in a look than she'd seen in her life. Her nose smelled flowers, both plain and exotic; her ears were filled with creaking wagons, shouting people, and the clang of metal.

Onua led them downhill. Chief among the buildings they passed were large stables, rich with horse smells. Daine would have stopped there, but Onua walked on. Before them lay meadows dotted with grazing animals. Behind the herds were masses of trees—the Royal Forest, said the K'mir.

The road ended at the meadows, where two long, wooden buildings had been built. One was a stable, a neat and quiet one. The other, connected to the stable by a covered walk, was a two-story barracks. Before it was a tall pole, a flag at its tip. As if showing the banner off, the wind lifted it up with a pop. A red horse reared on a gold brown field.

"The Queen's Riders," said Onua. "Home, or at least as much of one as *I* need. Let's put the ponies in the meadow, and then we'll talk."

FOUR

THE QUEEN'S RIDERS

U nloading the packs, they shooed the
ponies into the meadow, and Daine followed Onua into the barracks. Climbing
stairs, Onua led them through a door painted
a bright red. Inside was a big room with two
rows of beds, six in each row.

Taking a key from her belt-purse, the K'mir
unlocked a room near the door to reveal a
single bed, several chests, a desk, and a shelf
of books. With a sigh, she dropped her packs
on the floor and motioned for Daine to do the
same. "I'm not here often, but I'm always glad
to see it." She opened the shutters and flopped
onto the bed. "Pull up a chair."

The woman smiled at her. "As to your future. I'd like you to stay with me—you're the best assistant I've ever had. If you don't want that, you have other opportunities. Alanna would give you work, here or at Pirate's Swoop. Numair could do the same. Both of them say they'll mention you to the king."

Daine shook her head. The road was one thing; people might forget their station in life there. Here they'd go on with their real lives. Exalted persons like Alanna would not bother their heads over a homeless Gallan. Surrounded by wealth and magic, Numair would have better things to think of.

Onua drew a leather bag out of her purse and gave it to Daine. "There's your pay, and the bonus. You can sleep here till you decide what you want."

"Don't be silly," Daine informed her. "I'll work for you."

Onua's face lit, and she grinned. "Don't you want to know the terms?"

Daine had opened the bag and was gaping at the contents: a handful of silver coins and two gold ones. "Did you overpay me?" she accused.

Onua laughed. "You earned every penny, girl-child." She ticked points off on her fingers. "You fought Stormwings and spider-monsters. You found Numair and nursed him. That's *besides* what I said I'd pay you for. No, don't argue. Listen. The job's two coppers a day, plus room and board and bonuses for unusual duty. You help me with the trainees—selecting mounts, handling 'em, grooming 'em, and so on. They get two, so they have a spare ready all the time. But you know these ponies—if *one's* a handful for most people, think what *two* are like!"

Daine giggled. "I feel sorry for your trainees."

"Don't. They learn—or they wash out. You and I take care of the rest of the herd. In a few weeks we all go to the field training camp, and we make sure the recruits don't abuse their ponies. You have lots of free time. Socially, you're as good as a trainee—better, 'cause *you're* trusted to know what to do with a horse, and they aren't. Don't let them order you around. Most of the bad apples will go home crying after a week or so, anyway." Onua grinned. "What d'you think?"

Her head spun. Take today as it is, she thought, making herself calm down. Tomorrow I'll deal with tomorrow. "I'll stay." They shook hands.

"You're back!" Two people came in. One was a short K'mir, her face broader, less friendly, than Onua's, her eyes black instead of gray green. The other was a big man, taller even than Numair and powerfully built. His skin was dark brown; his close-cut hair looked like black wire. Pink, shiny skin like old scars wrapped around his wrists.

Onua hugged the visitors. "Daine, this is Buriram Tourakom—Buri, the commander of the Riders. And this is Sarge." To the adults she said, "Daine is my assistant. She's young, but she's worth her weight in gold."

Blushing, Daine looked at the floor. "Onua!"

"She isn't free with praise," Buri told her. A smile lit her face and made her less forbidding. "If Onua says good things about you, then they're true. Welcome." She offered a hand for Daine to shake, and Sarge did the same. Daine was relieved to find both had the palm calluses of those who worked, and worked hard. "Actually," Buri told Onua, "we just saw Numair. Sounds like you had a rough time coming home."

"It wasn't so bad," Onua replied. "Pretty uneventful, in fact, after Numair reached us. How are things?"

"Same-same." Buri leaned against the wall. "The new class is ready. We'll start after lunch. There's the usual lot of soft-hands merchanters and farmers' babies. A Player—George recommended him. He's pretty solid, though he's tall for ponyback. We may have to give him a horse."

"We lost two from the Third Rider Group, one from the Fifth," Sarge added. Sitting on the floor, he still came up to Daine's waist. "Half of the First Rider Group is on the casualty list, but nothing permanent."

Plainly these people had a lot to catch up on. Daine got up. "Excuse me," she said. "Onua, I'm going to look at the herd."

Her friend smiled. "Don't stray far."

"It's good to meet you, Daine," Sarge told her. "We'll get acquainted later. It's just—"

Daine smiled and waved good-bye. She was a *little* envious of Onua, with her home and friends, but she forced the envy down. For certain she didn't want Onua to be alone in the world as she was.

Leaving the barracks, she climbed the fence into the horse meadow. The animals she and Onua had brought hung back. Strange ponies, who had never met anyone like her, crowded around. Heads were thrust under her hands. Colors passed before her eyes: cream, dun, roan, chestnut, gray, odd-colors. She saw stars, blazes and masks, stockings and the spine-long stripe called a list; mares, geldings, stallions. All were the shaggy-coated mountain breed.

Now the ponies who knew her mixed with the strangers, bragging that she was *their* herdmaster. Daine giggled as they butted her with their heads and flicked her with their tails. There was no need to be envious of Onua, not with friends like these.

Time passed—she wasn't sure how much. When a great bell chimed, she jumped.

"It's the noon bell." Daine hadn't seen the woman on the fence. "Lunchtime." She smiled. "Or will you just graze with the herd?" Her voice was low and clear.

Daine grinned and disentangled herself from her friends. Nearing the stranger, she had a good look at her and stopped. The woman was dressed simply in breeches and a shirt, but she turned them into the richest garments ever worn. Masses of coal black hair had been woven into a braid and coiled around her head. She had green hazel eyes set beneath level brows, ivory skin, and a full, red mouth. Her proudly arched nose was strong for classic beauty, but it fit her. Her only ornaments were a diamond on her gold marriage band and diamonds on her earlobes, but she didn't need any more decoration. She was the most beautiful female Daine had ever seen, lovelier even than Ma.

The woman had said something. Daine wiped her hands nervously on her skirts and went to the fence. "I'm sorry, mum—I didn't hear."

"You look like Chavi West-wind." She mistook Daine's surprise and explained, "Chavi is known for horse magic. She's a goddess, where I come from, one of the four—"

"Horse Lords. Onua told me. Bian North-wind, Shai South-wind, Vau East-wind, and Chavi. But they're K'miri gods. Excuse my saying so, but you don't look K'miri."

The woman fingered the arch of her nose. "There's bad blood in my family. I'm half K'mir, anyway. You're a friend of Onua's?"

"I work for her."

The hazel eyes sharpened. "You're Daine." With a smile she explained, "Word travels fast here. You'll get used to it." She offered a small, delicate hand. Shaking it, Daine found calluses on the soft palm and smiled with relief. For a moment she'd been afraid she was talking to some kind of noble. She had never met a noble, apart from the Lioness, and she wasn't sure she wanted to. What would she say to one?

"Let's go eat," the woman told her. "I'm starving—you must be too."

Daine climbed the fence. "I think the whole city knows my name," she grumbled as they set off toward the barracks. "Did you tell me yours?"

"No. It's Thayet."

"The *queen*?"

"Only when I can't avoid it," said Thayet of Tortall. "Please don't get all formal on me now. We were having such a nice talk."

Daine scowled. "Odd's bobs, this is a strange

place! Knights who say call 'em by their first name and wizards that light tinder and queens that run around dressed like real people—"

Thayet laughed. "No wonder Alanna and Numair like you. You have a very unusual way of looking at things!"

Daine blushed. "I'm sorry. I'm just so—confused, here."

"That's normal," the queen assured her. "I felt the same, once." They entered the barracks. "Some lunch will make you feel better." She steered Daine through a door and into chaos. This room was filled with long wooden tables and benches. A third of them were occupied by men and women in their late teens and early twenties, who created enough noise to fill the place.

Daine copied Thayet as the queen picked up a wooden tray and went to the servers at the back of the room. These people confirmed the woman's identity: each bobbed respectfully and called her "Majesty" as they put bread, cheese, bowls of stew, fruit, and mugs of cider on her tray and Daine's.

"Thayet, there you are!" Buri came up as they left the servers. "We've been looking for you. Onua says she and Daine here met up with Stormwings, and some kind of spiders with human heads—" Talking, she led the queen to a table at the head of the room, where Onua and Sarge waited.

Onua beckoned to Daine, but the girl didn't want to be there, under the eyes of everyone. Shaking her head, she went to the corner of an unoccupied table and sat with her lunch. I'm younger'n anyone here, she thought, buttering a roll. How can I make them mind what I say about the horses?

A girl sat down across from her. "Hello!" She had dark hair cut boyishly short and a pair of dancing green eyes. With a tip-tilted nose, a cleft chin, and a dusting of freckles, she looked like pure mischief. "I'm Miri. Are you a new trainee?"

Daine shook her head. "I work for Onua, the horsemistress. I'll be helping you with the ponies, I guess."

"Good—we need more girls. There are too many boys." Miri stuck her tongue out at the tall, blond youth who settled his tray beside Daine.

He smiled. "Do you mind if I sit here?"

She shook her head. He had a very kind smile and bright blue eyes.

"Evin Larse." He sat and offered his hand.

Daine accepted it. "Daine Sarrasri."

He reached for her ear and seemed to pull a roll out of it. "Didn't wash this morning, did you?" He smeared cheese on the roll and grinned at Daine's openmouthed surprise. "My family's Player folk," he explained. "I have all sorts of useless talents."

"She's going to help us with the ponies," Miri said. "I need all the help I can get," she informed Daine. "Up till two weeks ago I could count on one hand the times I've been on a horse."

"You're doing fine," Evin told her soothingly. He looked at Daine. "She's been grooming and riding up at the palace stables."

"But these ponies are different," Miri protested. "You heard Sarge—they're picked to be fussy and mean, and they bite."

Daine grinned. "They're not that bad. Me'n Onua brought some down from Galla, and I've been with the herd. There's nice ones. You'll see." Looking around, she thought that the last time she'd seen such a mixed herd of humans was at the fair in Cría. There were two other blacks, three very brown youths, and five more as blond, pale skinned, and blue eyed as Scanrans. The rest could have come from any of the realms around the River Drell.

"You look overwhelmed," Evin told her. "They're just trainees, like Miri and me."

"Yes, but what does it take to be a trainee?" she asked. "How did you two join up, if you don't mind my asking?"

"Oh, joining's the easy part," Miri said. "They post the rules in all the schools and at recruiting stations in the towns."

"You have to be fifteen or more," Evin said. "Healthy, with all your body parts still attached—no missing hands or eyes."

"Single," added Miri. "No spouse and children. It helps if you ride, but it's not required—they took me, and the only thing I ever rode in my life was a fishing boat. That's what my people do, fish."

"You need good reflexes," Evin went on. "You have to read and write. For Tortallans that's no problem—schools have been open to everyone for nine years now. For the ones that can't read, the Riders'll give you work in the palace till you learn. I think that's all. Oh, and you have to be here by the March full moon. That's when training starts every year."

"That's *all*?" Daine asked, shocked. "That doesn't seem like much!"

"It isn't," said Evin. The problem isn't getting *into* the Riders—it's *staying*. We've lost ten in the last two weeks—sick, wouldn't take orders, couldn't handle the schedule. We'll lose more by summer's end."

Sarge rose and thundered, "Listen up, darlings! Today is your last day of fun at the king's expense." ("He calls running us around the meadow every day 'fun,'" Miri whispered to Daine.) "Here's Onua, our horsemistress." Onua stood up and nodded to everyone. "Daine—stand up, girl"—she obeyed—"is her assistant." Daine sat when Onua did. "They brought the rest of the ponies we need," Sarge went on, "so we're ready to start the *real* work. You have till the bells chime one stroke to do what needs doing. At the bell, come to the horse meadow." He clapped his hands. "Don't sit there gawping, children—you pick your mounts today. Get those trays to the kitchen and get out of here!"

Onua took Daine aside. "What about sleeping arrangements? I can put a cot for you in my room or a storeroom, or you can sleep with the trainee girls. Your choice."

"Please, Horsemistress—" It was Miri. "If nobody minds, Daine could bunk with me—if you want to, Daine."

Daine thought it over and nodded.

"Fine," Onua said. "After supper you can show Daine the bed. Would you excuse us now, though? I want to ask her something."

The girl nodded and raced upstairs. Onua and Daine followed at a slower pace. "I'm glad you're making friends," the K'mir said. "It's good for you to meet people your own age. Listen—I have to ask"—she pointed to Daine's skirts—"doesn't that outfit get hot?"

She'd hit on the burden of Daine's life. The girl scowled: the litany she'd given Ma and Grandda for years bubbled to her lips. "Hot in summer, cold in winter, always getting tangled and ripped and soaked, clumsy, *heavy*—"

Onua smiled. She knew an old grievance when she heard one. "Then why wear 'em?

Get yourself breeches and a shirt like me."

Daine gaped at her. "*Men's* gear? With folk talking about me all the time as is?"

Onua shook her head. "You're not home now. The rules have changed."

Daine opened her mouth to object—then closed it. She looked at her skirts. To be rid of them, and the petticoats . . . it hit her, *really* hit her, that she was free of Snowsdale. What could they do to her now?

From what Evin and Miri said, Riders came from all walks of life. In Galla she was strange. Here, *everyone* was different. These people wouldn't care if Ma was a hedgewitch. Maybe they wouldn't even care that her father was unknown, someone her ma met one Beltane night and never saw again.

But they'll care if they know you went mad, a tiny voice inside her cautioned. Best keep shut about that!

Onua let her think, and was rewarded when Daine's blue-gray eyes shone like lanterns. "I'd *love* to put on breeches."

"Come on, then." Onua took her out of the girls' dormitory and down the hall. "That's men's country," she said, pointing to a bright yellow door. "Off-limits to females, like we're off-limits to them."

In the supply room, a tall woman with red-bronze hair and great kindness in her face looked up from her desk. "Onua, welcome!" She came over to hug the K'mir. "Your assistant?" she asked.

"Daine, this is Kuri Tailor—she's in charge of the girls. If there's anything you need, Kuri's the woman to ask." Onua hugged Daine around the shoulders. "Kuri, she needs breeches and shirts. Daine, I hate to rush, but I need to talk with Sarge. You'll be all right?" The girl nodded. "When you're done, come out to the meadow and we'll get these two-leggers mounted." She left the room.

"The first day or so is crazy," explained Kuri. "They always start as soon as Onua comes, so she has to move fast. You'll be rushing too, once the Riders see how much work they can get from you—my word on it." She measured Daine quickly and wrote down her findings. "I'll have others tonight, but take these for now." From stacks of homespun garments on one side of the room, she chose a pair of worn breeches and a patched white shirt. "No use wearing good clothes when you're with the horses," she explained. "Step behind that screen and try these on—let's see how they fit."

Behind the screen, Daine drew the shirt and breeches on with trembling hands. Doubtless the trainee girls were used to such things. She had seen they all wore breeches. But she was a little scared. Dressed, she stepped out into the open.

"What's the matter?" Kuri walked over to tug and adjust the garments.

"It's—men's gear," she explained shyly. "At home, the priests and the headman—they'd never approve."

"Forget them." Kuri turned her, checking the clothes. "You're ours, now. I'm not saying there won't be people to carp and pinch at you. That's human nature, alas." Daine nodded. *She* knew. "But here life's what you make it. Who you *used* to be doesn't matter. Look at Sarge—he was a slave, once. Onua was beaten by her husband and left to die. Her Majesty and Commander Buri had to flee Saraine. Do you catch my drift?"

It was a lot to digest. Onua? It was impossible to think of Onua as beaten and abandoned by anyone. And Sarge? "I—I think so."

Palace bells chimed one stroke, making Daine jump. "The bells take getting used to," the woman informed her with a sigh.

"How often do they ring?" the girl asked, pulling on her boots.

"Every hour until late in the evening." Kuri smiled. "All set?"

"Yes'm." Daine grinned at her. "Thank you."

"Welcome to Corus, dear," the woman said as Daine ran out the door.

Onua, Buri, and Sarge waited at the fence with a barrel of apples. Daine arrived just as Onua stuffed fruit into every pocket Miri had. "Bribe them," she said, and shooed the reluctant girl through the gate Sarge held open.

"What do I do?" Daine asked.

"Use your instincts." Onua watched the field as she spoke. "You have to make your own authority with the trainees. Not that I think that will be a problem. Just keep an eye out. Remember they have to pick two."

"One for morning, one for afternoon," Sarge added with a grin.

It was one thing to say "Make your own

authority," another to start doing it. For the moment Daine watched. Most trainees met the ponies cautiously or easily, depending on their natures. A mouse-gray mare twined about Evin as if she were a cat.

Looking for Miri, she saw trouble. Some of the more wicked animals had gone to torment the girl, who was plainly scared. Stopping an arm's reach from her, they frolicked, showing more tooth and hoof than was necessary.

This won't do! Daine thought, jumping into the meadow. She bore down on the mischief-makers with a scowl, Cloud following like a lonely dog. "Stop that!" she ordered. "What would your mas say if they saw you acting bad? Shame on you! Scat—and don't come back till you've learnt manners!" The ponies shook their heads, looking properly ashamed, and fled.

"If she wanted to be a Rider, she *ought* to know how to *ride*," a female voice muttered. Daine looked for the source, but none of the nearby trainees met her eyes.

"At home only lords or couriers ride," Miri explained, shamefaced. "I've *been* practicing. It's just—there's so many, and they're so *frisky*."

Daine put a hand on her shoulder. Her new friend was solid, muscular, with a love of life she could almost feel. "Look—there's some you'll like." She pointed to a cluster of ponies milling around a tree in the open meadow.

"I'd have to go through the herd," the older girl whispered.

Daine stuck her hands in her pockets. "See how you kept to the fence, because you're shy?"

"I didn't think 'shy' was the right word," Miri confessed.

"Hush. Those ponies are nice, but they're shy too. If you want to meet them, *you* have to do the walking. They're just animals. They can't know you've kept to the fence because you're shy."

"It can't be worse than sailing through a storm," Evin said from nearby.

"I only did that *once*." Miri looked at the herd and the shy ponies, swallowed—and walked forward. Daine and Cloud followed her to the tree.

"Here, boy." The pony Daine beckoned forward was a gelding, his body hairs a mixture of black and white, his mane, tail, face, and socks black. "I want you to meet someone."

The pony sidled around until he was behind Daine, peering at her human friend. "This fellow is what we call a blue roan. We came south together." Daine looked over her shoulder. "Come out and meet Miri. If you ask nice, she might give you an apple."

The roan's ears pricked forward at the word *apple*. Carefully he emerged from behind Daine to approach the older girl.

"He's beautiful." Timidly Miri offered him a fruit. Within seconds it was gone and he was inspecting her pockets for more. Daine instructed, "Now blow in his nostrils, gentle like. It's how you get acquainted."

"It seems rude to me." Miri obeyed, and giggled when the blue returned the courtesy. "You know, they aren't as scary as I thought."

"Animals are easy to understand," Daine told her. "You just have to know how to talk to them."

"*You* talk to them like they really *are* people." Miri smiled as the roan leaned into her hands.

"Don't say it's like I have magic," Daine said. "I hear it all the time, and it makes me crazy."

"Depends on what you mean," Miri commented. "The sea's full of magic, but we can't use it like the Gift. It isn't the same. My uncle is a wavespeaker—he swims with dolphins. He talks to them, whole conversations. Have an apple," she told a tan mare who had come near. The pony took one daintily. Soon they were breathing into each other's faces.

"Walk with them a bit," Evin suggested, joining them. The reins he held belonged to the mouse-gray mare and to a tall stallion, a cream-colored beauty with a white mane and tail. "Daine, what do you think?"

She went over both. Evin had chosen well: they were tall for ponies, which meant they would suit his long legs. The stallion was a showy, life-loving fellow, reflecting the Player's extravagance of character. The mare was smitten with him, matching the sweetness that lay close to Evin's bones.

"You got lucky," she said when she was done. "This pair will do anything for you, if you handle them right."

Evin grinned. "I'm glad you approve."

Another trainee called her for help, a red-headed youth named Padrach. She gave it to him, then to another. Before she knew it the afternoon was done, and the trainees were taking their new mounts to the stables for grooming. Daine, Onua, Buri, and Sarge helped then too, though Daine couldn't see how *she* could ever be comfortable telling a twenty-year-old man he was missing spots on the pony he was grooming.

She did try it: "Excuse me, trainee—what did you say your name was?"

Blue gray eyes twinkled at her over his cream-colored mare's back. "I didn't. It's Farant." His blond hair curled thickly over his head, almost matching the pony's in color.

"Thank you. Trainee Farant, you're missing spots."

"Not at all, sweetheart. I'm just combing too fast for you to see."

"*Trainee Farant, you're missing spots!*" Sarge boomed just behind Daine. She thought later she actually might have levitated at that moment—certainly Farant had. "*Next time the assistant horsemistress tells you something, don't flirt—correct it!*"

He moved on, and Daine pressed her hands against her burning cheeks. Farant leaned on his mare and sighed. "Yes, Assistant Horsemistress. Right away." He winked at her and went back to work.

Daine went to Sarge as the trainees were finishing up. "Sarge, I—"

He shook his head. Daine thought if he leaned against the stable wall any harder, it would collapse. How did a human, without bear blood in him, get to be so *large*? "Not your fault. These city boys see you, you're young, sweet-lookin'"—he winked at her—"they're gonna try to take advantage. If they can't keep their minds on the job after I've had them two weeks already in my patty-paws, then I ain't been doing *my* job right." His grin was wolfish. "But that can be fixed." Seeing her openmouthed stare, he asked, "Something the matter, my lamb?"

She closed her jaw. "No, sir. I just never met nobody like you."

"And if you're lucky, you won't again," muttered Buri, passing by.

After the stables there was a bath, a hot one. Bathing with other females in a tub as large as a pond would take getting used to, Daine thought, but at least she had plenty of soap and shampoo.

Dressed in clean clothes, she went to the mess hall, where Evin and Miri waved for her to join them. She noticed there was much less talk than at lunch. Afterward, the trainees cleared and scrubbed the tables, and Kuri went to the head of the room. Buri and Sarge were moving a map of Tortall into place behind her as she laid bundles of plants onto the table before her.

"Tonight it's medicinal herbs," she told them, and the trainees groaned. She smiled. "That's not so bad. Remember, last week I was teaching you how to sew your own cuts—without anything to numb the pain."

Daine saw Onua slip out the back, and followed. "Do I have to stay?"

"No, indeed not. *You* aren't a trainee. You can help me unpack."

That sounded like something she could get her exhausted muscles and brain to do. She followed Onua up the stairs to her room. "Do they have to study *all* the time?"

She sat on the bed while the K'mir opened her packs. "Clothes in a pile by the door. Don't get up—just throw them. Packages on the bed next to you. Hand me scrolls and papers."

Daine hoisted a pack onto her lap and went to work. "Well, they have to get their book learning now, while they're here. They won't have much time, once we head for the summer training site. You'll like the one this year: Pirate's Swoop."

Daine's face lit. "Lady Alanna's home?"

"The very same."

Returning to the subject on her mind, she asked, "What do they study? The trainees?"

Onua numbered the topics on her fingers. "Poisons, medicines, edible plants. Tracking and hunting, all terrains. Reading maps, drawing them—maps here are a lot more accurate, now that Riders help draw them. Battle tactics. Weapons and hand-to-hand combat. Teaching combat and tactics—they show villagers how to protect themselves. The ones with the Gift have to learn all they can do with it. Veterinary medicine. I think that's most of it."

"And they learn *all* this?" the girl asked, shocked.

The K'mir laughed. "They do their best. They have to. At the end of fall they go to groups in the field to start their trial year. If they survive, and most do these days, they're assigned a permanent group. Why? Were you thinking of going for a Rider after all?"

"Not anymore!" Daine said emphatically.

Onua grinned. "I have trouble seeing you play soldier, even so odd a soldier as the Riders turn out."

Later, tucked into a bed next to Miri's, Daine thought Onua was probably right. It must be hard, having to account for every minute of the day as the trainees did. Why, she'd never get to meet any new animals!

Dozing off, she woke abruptly, feeling trapped. At first she didn't even remember where she was. Sitting up, she looked around: the five girl trainees were in their beds, asleep. The barracks were silent.

If she didn't get some air, she'd suffocate.

A window opened over her bed. She pried the shutters apart in time to hear a watchman's distant cry: "The midnight hour, and all is well!"

Her bed was too soft after so much sleeping on the ground. She cursed under her breath and took blankets and pillow to the floor. That at least was firm, and the air was cooler too. She waited for sleep again.

Miri turned over and said clearly, "But I *love* to ride." Daine sat up to peer at her. The girl was fast asleep.

She lay back. The badger's claw weighed heavy on her chest. When she turned onto her side, the thong half-choked her. She eased it and closed her eyes. Sheets and blankets rustled. A blond girl who had snubbed her in the baths snored. Another tossed and turned for what seemed like hours before she settled. Outside, Daine heard a dog's bark.

A headache grew in her temples. She missed having animals close by. At home, she'd had a ground-floor room. Even in winter she left the shutters open a crack, and never slept cold. Her friends always kept her warm.

Disgusted, she grabbed her breeches from the chest in front of her bed. Her traveling gear was there, including her bedroll. It was the work of a second to dress and stuff her feet into boots. With her bedroll under her arm, she slipped downstairs and outside.

The night air was a relief. She inhaled the scents of field and forest happily, feeling sleepy and content as she crossed the open pasture.

The tree that had sheltered the shy ponies that afternoon was there, the ground underneath mercifully free of manure. She spread out her bedroll and, already half-asleep crawled in. Cloud lay down to support her back. Someone—a pony she didn't know—lipped the foot of her covers.

"This is *much* better," Daine said. "Good night, everybody." Falling asleep, she knew the free ponies had come to stand nearby and keep her company.

In her dream, she walked down the road with Onua. Instead of ponies, they led people—the trainees—in chains. The night air was thick and sour, and marsh creatures made an incredible noise.

The noise stopped abruptly, cut off. Onua halted. "What's that?"

A stench fell on them in waves. "Storm-wings!" Daine cried.

She was awake and sitting up. Dawn shone between clouds in the east. The ponies milled nearby, restless and afraid. She drew a deep breath, feeling air pour into her chest like soup. Lurching to her feet, she peered overhead. The sky was empty, but that meant nothing. They were coming.

She dragged her boots on and ran for the building; the ponies ran with her. "Ho, the barracks!" she yelled, knowing she was too far away. "Riders!" On the second floor a window was open—her own. "Miri! Onua, wake up!"

A tousled head appeared. "Daine, what's wrong?" Kuri yelled.

"Get Onua!" Daine screamed. "Tell her Stormwings are coming!" She gasped for breath. At her back she felt wrongness surge.

Kuri vanished from the window. The girl turned, knowing she could never reach the barracks in time. They rose from the trees, the sun's first thin rays striking off metal wings. The familiar stink fell over her.

Zhaneh Bitterclaws led her flock, homing in on Daine. "Kill it!" she screeched. Her left eye was a black and oozing ruin. "Kill this beast!"

More than fifty Stormwings stooped to the attack. Cold with terror, Daine crouched against the ground. Cloud reared, ordering the Stormwing queen to come down and fight like a horse. Steel claws groped for her as the mare struck at the creature with her hooves.

The ponies crowded around Daine, lunging at the Stormwings when they came too close.

Goddess, Horse Lords, get me out of this and I will never, *ever* sleep without a bow again, she promised.

Tahoi raced onto the field with a pack of hounds, all of them as big as he was. More dogs followed, baying. Seeing rocks nearby, three of them as big as her fist, Daine grabbed them. Her first struck Zhaneh Bitterclaws square on the nose.

"There, you monster!" she yelled, shaking her fist at the Stormwings. "Come close, so I can do it again!" A little dog that came with the hounds wove in and out of the ponies' hooves to bring her more ammunition.

Black fire filled with silver lights wrapped around a Stormwing. The creature struggled, trying to throw it off: the fire crept into its mouth and blew it apart. More clouds of black fire chased Stormwings to kill them.

Darkmoon came, saddled and trailing his reins. He leaped to seize a Stormwing by the leg. Shaking his prize like a terrier, he snapped its neck.

Other war-horses followed. Behind them

ran Sarge in only a breechclout, armed with a fistful of javelins. He threw the first with a yell. Daine gaped when a Stormwing dropped, trying to drag the weapon from its chest. The black man fixed on a new target and waited for his best shot, as calm as he'd been at lunch. Each time he threw, a Stormwing went down.

Onua raced onto the field in her nightgown, her small bow and quiver in her hands. She had an arrow on the string: lining up her shot, she dropped the Stormwing that was her target. Zhaneh Bitterclaws saw the K'mir and screeched her triumph as she attacked.

Daine yelled. Half of the animals went to Onua, ringing her as the others ringed Daine. More horses and dogs leaped the fence to cover Sarge.

Purple fire—Alanna's magic—appeared, weaving a net around a pair of attackers. They screamed and beat at it uselessly: it dragged them to earth and the hounds. Thunder that was more than thunder pealed. The dogs howled—Daine clapped her hands over smarting ears. The Stormwings shrieked, trying to do the same thing with their steel feathers.

Blue lightning darted from the top of the field, consuming each Stormwing it struck.

Near the fence a bearded man in shirt and breeches was the source of the blue fire. It shone around him, and pooled in his hands. Beside him was Alanna, dressed as he was, for riding. Numair was there too, in what looked like a nightshirt. Fire lashed from their hands—purple for the Lioness, black for Numair—to cut the enemy in two.

Zhaneh spoke in her odd language and began to climb; those that were able followed. A wall of their own fire wrapped around them, coloring them scarlet with an edge of gold light.

The bearded man threw a fistful of blue. The red shield consumed it, but the man continued to hurl bolts until the monsters were specks in the sky.

Daine's knees buckled from exhaustion and shock. Numair came down the rise, looking as tired as when she had first seen him as a man. "I said I'd see you again," he joked, leaning on the tree.

She grinned at him. "You timed it perfect."

Darkmoon and the other horses, ponies, and hounds sat where they were, trembling with nerves. Many were cut and bleeding, but—miraculously—none were dead.

The bearded man crouched beside a Stormwing corpse. He must have discovered their smell: he sneezed and put a hand over his nose. Alanna and Onua went to him, Onua leaning on Tahoi for support. A liver chestnut and an iron gray horse nuzzled Sarge, making sure he was in one piece. Daine giggled, and found she was getting the same treatment from Cloud.

Numair offered Daine his hand. Cloud supported her on her free side, and a stranger mare let Numair prop himself on her. "The trainees usually wait till they're *away* from the palace before starting any wars," Numair told her. "The nobles will complain you got them out of bed."

Daine looked up at him, worried. "Will I get in trouble?"

Sarge had heard. He laughed. "Let 'em complain. It's good for them to be up in time for breakfast."

When she was calmer, she thanked the dogs, horses, and ponies who had come to her rescue.

Only when the men who worked in the palace stables and kennels arrived to retrieve their charges did she return to the Rider barracks.

"Should I go help them?" she asked Onua as she cleaned up. "Some of the animals were hurt. They'll need stitching and bandaging—"

"Calm down," the woman said. "There's a sorcerer attached to each of the stables and kennels, to do any healing. Your animals will be fine."

Daine followed her to breakfast, envious. Wouldn't that be a wonderful thing, to be able to wave her hands and put an end to a creature's hurts?

Evin and Miri besieged her with questions as she joined them. Why was she in the field? Hadn't she been scared? Why did the animals fight for her and Onua? She answered as well as she could, but when Padrach and Farant came to ask the same things, she felt embarrassed.

After breakfast, Sarge ordered the trainees to report to the horse meadow for cleanup. Daine helped Kuri to clear a ground-floor storeroom, freeing it to serve as her bedroom. Its best feature was a door to the outside she could leave open. Other than that, it was tiny, just big enough to hold a bed, a storage chest, a chair, and a small table.

That afternoon she helped the trainees saddle and ride their new mounts. By the time everyone took their day's-end bath, she was exhausted. She was content, at supper, just to listen to her new friends talk. Afterward, as the trainees got ready for their night's lessons, Onua beckoned.

"What's up?" Daine asked.

The K'mir led her to a room across the hall from the mess. "There's somebody who'd like to meet you." She opened the door. "I brought her," she announced, following Daine inside. "Are we late?"

FIVE

WILD MAGIC

Seated at the table was the bearded man Daine had seen that morning. "I just got here," he said in a deep, gentle voice. "I took the liberty of ordering refreshments from the cooks, by the way."

Close up, he was a sight to wring any female heart. His close-cropped hair and beard were blue black, his eyes sapphire blue, his teeth white against the blackness of his beard. Daine gulped. She felt ten feet tall and clumsy. Her face was probably breaking out in pimples as she looked at him.

He got to his feet and smiled down at her. "You must be Daine. You may not remember me from before—you were busy."

Looking up into those eyes, the girl felt her heart melt like butter in the sun. "No, sir, I remember. You threw blue lightning."

He held a chair out for her. "Sit down, please." She obeyed and was glad when he sat again. Having him behind her was wonderful but terrifying. What if she had forgotten to scrub the back of her neck?

A cook entered with a tray loaded with cakes, fruit, and a pitcher of juice. Placing it on the table, he bowed to the man. "Your Majesty."

"Exactly what we need," the stranger told him. "My thanks." The cook bowed again and made his escape.

Daine gaped at her host. "You're the *king*!" she cried. Belatedly remembering she ought to bow, or kneel, or something, she jumped to her feet.

Jonathan—*King* Jonathan—grinned. "It's all right. Please sit. Otherwise good manners say I have to get up again, and I'm tired."

She sat, trembling. This is a *very* strange country, she told herself, not for the first time. Back home, you couldn't *pay* a noble to speak to a commoner!

The king selected a cake and bit into it. "Wonderful," he said with his mouth full. "The Riders eat better than I do."

"It just *seems* as if we do. We don't have six footmen asking if you're *sure* you don't want a taster," Onua teased. She poured juice for all of them.

King Jonathan snorted. "Don't remind me." He looked at Daine. "Seers can tell, sometimes, if the immortals will attack a place. You, however, are the first I know of to sense them nearby. Are there seers or fortune-tellers in your family?" He smiled at her, *just* at her.

She'd tell him anything for another smile. "Ma was a hedgewitch, Your Honor. She had the Gift for birthing, healing. Protection spells—not as good as Onua's. She was best with plants. She never could see any future things, though."

"Did she have the Gift from her family?" he asked.

She nodded, fiddling with the lacing of her shirt. "All the girls in her family was healers but me." She swallowed a throat-lump, remembering how disappointed Ma had been that Daine couldn't follow in her steps.

"What of your father?" His voice was kind, but the question hurt. The king saw it in her face and said gently, "I'm sorry, but I must know. If your father was a peddler or a vagabond, perhaps he sired other children with your ability. We can use more people like you."

"Why? Sir—Your Majesty, that is?"

"Winged horses were seen in Saraine this winter." The grimness in his eyes caught and held her. "Griffins nest in the cliffs of the Copper Isles. There are spidrens throughout the hill country this spring."

Winged horses? Griffins? "Where do they come from, do you know?"

"The Divine Realms—the home of the gods. Four hundred years ago, powerful mages locked the immortals into them. Only the greatest gods have been able to leave—until now."

An arm crossed Daine's vision to pick up a cake. Numair took an empty seat, and the king went on. "Our neighbors—Galla, Scanra, Tusaine—report unicorns, giant birds, even winged people as small as wrens. *We* are plagued by monstsers, ogres, and trolls." He drummed his fingers on the table.

"It's interesting that a weak mage like Sinthya could send rare creatures like Stormwings after you. Where did he get such power? As far as we know, he had only one secret worth protecting: he was dealing with Carthak."

"Carthak's another country?" Daine asked, blushing for her ignorance.

"Across the Inland Sea," Numair said. "They're desperate. Their crops failed two years in a row—not enough rain, and tornadoes that ripped up the fields. There were food riots in the capital last winter. The emperor needs good farmland, and we're the closest target."

"Carthak has the university, its school for mages, and its library—the same library used by the mages who sealed the Divine Realms." The king looked at Numair. "I think the Carthaki mages found those spells."

Numair was rolling a cake into a ball. "*And* spells to compel immortals to obey humans. How else could Sinthya get Stormwings to chase me?"

"We have nothing like those spells," Jonathan told Daine. "Sinthya's papers vanished. We're searching our own libraries, but it might take months. In the meantime, the warnings foretellers give us aren't enough. If we could send those with your ability to sense immortals to our villages and towns, we could better protect our people. If we can find your father—"

It had come back to that. She shook her head, humiliated.

"Daine?" It was Onua, who had give her trust and work that she loved. She owed this woman, at least, an answer.

She looked down. "I don't know who he is. It's in my name. Sarrasri—Sarra's daughter. Only *bastards* are named for their mothers." She spat out the hated word, but its taste stayed on her tongue.

"Why don't you know?"

She didn't look up to see who had asked. "Ma never told me. She never told anybody. She kept saying 'someday, someday.'"

"Do you know *anything*?" Onua rested a hand on Daine's shoulder.

She fought to get herself under control. "It was Beltane. They light fires, and couples jump over the embers when they burn down." So they'll have babies in the coming year, she thought, but she wasn't going to say *that*.

"We do the same thing," the king remarked.

Daine looked at him, startled. "*You* never jumped over no embers," she accused before she knew what she was saying.

The others laughed. She ducked her head to hide her blush.

"The ruler takes part in all great feasts, to show respect for the gods," Jonathan told her gravely. His eyes danced. "Thayet and I do it every year."

"I didn't mean—I wasn't trying to be— disrespectful—"

He patted her knee. "I didn't think you were. Go on."

"Ma wasn't sweet on anybody, so she went walking in the wood alone. She met someone. I used to think it was a man that was already married, but when I asked last year, she said no. And I don't look like anyone from Snowsdale. Most of 'em are blond and blue eyed, being's we're so near Scanra and all."

The king sat back with a sigh. "Well, it was an idea," he said to no one in particular.

"I'll help if I can," she said, knowing that she had disappointed them. "I just don't know what I could do. And the warnings aren't that, exactly. I know something *wrong's* coming, but I knew that much about the rabid bear."

"A rabid *bear*?" the king asked in horror and awe. "Mithros—that's not something *I'd* ever want to see!"

Daine smiled. "I didn't want to see him, either, sir. I just got to."

"Did you get the identical sensation from the bear as you got with the Stormwings or the spidrens?" asked Numair.

"Oh, no. It was different. Bad, but in a brown kind of way."

"In a *what*?" Onua asked.

"Well, animals—I think of 'em in colors, sometimes." She tapped her head. "To me, bears feel brown, only this one had red and black lights. *Very* sick, he was. I get the monsters as colors too, but they're gold with black and green lights in them. I *never* felt any real creature as gold."

"I *told* you she has magic," the mage told the king triumphantly.

"No!" she retorted, jumping to her feet. "Didn't Ma test me and test me? Don't you think I'd've grabbed at magic, if I had it, just to please Ma?"

"Easy, little one." The king put a hand on her arm, guiding her back into her chair. "Numair believes—and I agree—you have magic. You may have no *Gift*, but there are other magics, 'wild magics.' The Bazhir tribes use one kind to unite their people. The Doi read the future with another. There are creatures we call 'elementals,' whose very nature is composed of wild magic."

Daine frowned. "Miri told me the sea people know about it. Some of them use it to talk to fish and dolphins."

"Exactly. From what your friends say"—the king nodded to Onua and Numair—"your wild magic gives you a bond with animals. Your mother might not have recognized it. Only a few people know it even exists."

Daine frowned. "Can't you see it on someone, like them with the Gift can see it on other folk that have it?"

"I can," Numair said. "And you do." Daine stared at him.

Jonathan said, "He's perhaps the only living expert on wild magic."

Daine scowled at Numair. "You never mentioned this on the road."

He smiled. "If you were trying to get a deer to come to you, would you make any sudden noises?"

Her scowl deepened. "That's different. I'm no deer."

Joanthan took Daine's hands. "Will you let Numair help you study wild magic? It may help expand your awareness of the immortals, for one thing."

"Wouldn't it be easier to *tell* creatures to obey you?" Onua added. "All the way here you coaxed the ponies to mind you. You're dominant—you proved that on the stallion, the day you and I met. Why prove it to each pony in the herd, if you could do it just once and never again?"

"Daine." Something in Numair's voice made her look at him, and only him. At the expression in his dark eyes, she even forgot that the king still held her hands. "I can teach you to heal."

"Animals?" It came out as a squeak. "You mean—like Ma did humans? But how do you know if I can?"

"Because I saw you do it once." That wasn't Numair; it was Onua. "At the marsh, after the fight. You were holding a bird, and you fainted, remember?" Daine nodded. "I was looking right at an owl with its head cut almost off. The wound healed; he flew away. So did a lot of birds that shouldn't have been able to fly. I think it happened because their need just *pulled* the healing out of you." The K'mir nodded to Numair. "He can teach you to heal of your own will, without burning yourself up so you faint."

All her life she had splinted, sewed, bandaged. Most of her patients had mended, but some had not. She felt the badger's claw heavy on her chest. To *fix* her friends, like he'd fixed himself after giving the claw to her . . .

She looked at the king. "I still think it sounds crazy, but I'll try."

He squeezed her hands. "You will?" he asked quietly.

I'm in love, she thought, and nodded. "Oh, wait, I hired on with Onua for the summer."

"That isn't a problem," said Numair. "The trainees will be going to Pirate's Swoop. I live near there. Why don't I just go along?" When the king frowned, he added, "Hag's bones, Jon, there's nothing I can do here right now that you don't have a hundred other mages doing already. If I work with Daine, maybe I can devise a spell to warn people that immortals are coming."

The king made a face. "You just say that so I'll let you go."

"You have too many mages eating their heads off around here as is," Onua pointed out. "It's not as if you can't contact him if something comes up."

"Whose side are you on?" the king asked. The woman grinned. He sighed and looked at Daine once more. Squeezing her hands, he let them go. "Thank you." He got up. "Onua, Numair, keep me posted?" They nodded. "I'd best go then. I have to dance with the Carthaki ambassador's wife."

Numair grinned at him. "Wear iron shoes, Your Majesty."

Daine said, "Excuse me—Your Majesty?"

The king looked back at her. "Yes, my dear?"

No one had *ever* called her that. She blushed, and managed to say, "I'm sorry I can't help more. With the sensing, and my da, and all."

Jonathan of Conté smiled at her. "If I've learned anything as a king, it's been I never know when someone will be able to help me. I have a feeling you'll be most welcome in this realm, Veralidaine Sarrasri."

And he was gone, which was really just as well, because it was suddenly hard for her to breathe.

Onua patted her back. "He has this effect on most of us, if it helps."

Numair rose, nibbling on one last cake. "No time like the present to begin. Daine, will you get Cloud, please? We'll meet you by the stables."

Dazed, she went out and called her mare. With the nights so fine, Cloud had asked to stay with the free ponies instead of being stabled with the trainees' mounts. She came racing over at Daine's summons and leaped the fence rather than wait for the girl to open the gate.

Overwhelmed by the day's events, Daine buried her face in Cloud's mane: it smelled of night air, ferns, and horse. "Things are so *weird* here," she whispered. "You ever hear of 'wild magic'? They say I have it."

You have something, and you know it. Who cares what name it has? Or did you really think the wild creatures visit you because they like humans?

"But *magic*?"

Did you call me to worry about the names of things? If you did, I'm going back. There's a salt lick over by that big rock I want to taste.

"Daine?" Numair and Onua were coming. "Good, you have her," Numair said. "If you can persuade her to come with me, I'd like to check your range with an animal you know well."

"What do you mean, my 'range'?" she asked.

"I've observed that when you say you 'hear' an animal, you actually mean hearing in your mind—not with your ears. I want to see how far I can walk with Cloud before you stop hearing her."

"But how will you know?" the girl asked reasonably. "Should I have her tell you when we lose touch or something?"

"No!" Onua said, and laughed. "Daine, knowing Cloud, she'd do it by kicking him. Numair will do a speech spell with me. You and I will sit here, and you tell me what you hear from Cloud, and when you stop hearing her."

"*If* Cloud will do it," amended Numair.

"Of course she will." Won't you? the girl

asked Cloud silently. The mare switched her tail, thinking it over. Daine didn't rush her. Sometimes, if she was too eager, Cloud would refuse just to keep her in her place.

Very well. The pony trotted off down the fence, away from the palace.

"I think you're to follow her," Daine told the mage with a grin.

Numair sighed and trotted off after the pony. "Only one of us can lead here, and that has to be me," he called.

Onua and Daine hoisted themselves to the top rail of the fence, and Onua held her palm out between them. In it glowed a ball of ruby-colored fire. "Numair will take a moment to set up his end of the spell."

"Onua—if the king's on the bad side of these Carthaks, why does he have to dance with the ambassador's wife?"

"Politics," Onua said. "We don't have to mess with that, thanks be to Father Storm and Mother Rain. It means you sit down to dinner with enemies and ask how their children are."

"Aren't we at war, then?"

"Nah," the woman replied. "We aren't at

war till both sides sign a paper *saying* it's a war. The Carthaki emperor can raid us and send monsters against us, but there's no war. Yet."

"That's crazy," Daine said, and Onua nodded. They waited, enjoying the night. Uphill the palace glittered, its lights blurring the stars overhead. Downhill lay the forest, dark, moist, and quiet. The free ponies had come to graze near the two women, their soft movements a comforting sound.

In the distance the girl heard the callings of a pack of wolves. Did I hear them on the road? she wondered. Not so close, that's for certain. I wonder if they miss me, Brokefang and Rattail and the others.

Listen to these wolves. Is it hunt-song? No, pack-song. They're just singing to be doing it, not to celebrate the kill.

If I could just run . . . dive into the forest. Go to them, be hunt-sister and one with the pack—

"Daine? *Daine!*" Onua was shaking her with one hand.

"Onua? What's wrong?" Numair's voice came from the fire in the K'mir's other hand.

Great Goddess—I almost forgot who I am!

"I'm fine," she told Onua, forcing herself to sound calm. "Can you hear them?"

"The wolves? Of course," Onua replied.

The pack had sensed her—their voices were approaching through the trees. The ponies snorted anxiously, huddling near the women and the fence. "I'll be right back," Daine said, and jumped into the meadow. "Calm down and stay put," she ordered the herd. She walked until she was halfway between trees and fence, knowing the ponies would not come closer to the wolves.

"Go away!" she yelled. "There are hunters here, and dogs! Go!" There was that other way to speak to them, but she didn't dare try it. Not after she had almost forgotten, just listening to them!

Their calling stopped: they'd heard a human and run. It was against their own better judgment to approach human dwellings in the first place.

Daine returned to Onua, glad that the night hid the sparkle of tears on her cheeks. "I'm too tired for this—I'm sorry. It hit me all of a sudden."

Onua spoke into the red fire on her hand,

then closed her fingers on it. The globe vanished. "Go to bed, then. Numair will let Cloud back into the meadow. I'll get someone to come watch the herds, in case the wolves return."

Daine watched her go. "I'm sorry," she whispered though only the ponies could hear. They crowded around, needing reassurance after hearing wolves. She couldn't leave them scared. It took her several minutes to pat and soothe them into calmness once more. It wasn't their fault the wolves thought they'd heard a wolf-sister in the night.

She was climbing the fence out of the meadow when Numair and Cloud arrived. Cloud came right up to her, sniffing Daine all over for wolf smell.

"Are you all right?" the man asked, panting as he rested a hand on Daine's shoulder. "I should have remembered you might be tired after this morning. I get carried away sometimes. I forget that not everyone has my academic enthusiasm."

She stared at him, patting Cloud. He was a sorcerer. He'd cut his eyeteeth on the impossible. He'd understand if anyone did, she thought, and opened her mouth to tell him.

"'Evenin', sir, miss." A burly man climbed over the fence, holding a crossbow out of harm's way. Two big dogs wriggled through the rails and came over, tails wagging, to sniff Daine. "Mistress Onua tells me wolves are near the forest rim tonight. Must be a new pack. Most of 'em know t' stay clear of the palace. Me'n my lads'll keep watch for a bit, to discourage 'em, like."

Daine scratched the ears of both "lads," dogs almost as big as Tahoi. Run, pack-brothers! she called to the wolves, under her breath, hoping they'd somehow hear her. Run and keep running—there are hunters here!

She and Numair said good night to the man, and Numair walked her to her new room in the barracks. She let herself in, waving to him as he climbed the hill to the palace. The chance to tell him the truth was gone.

Just as well, she told herself as she changed into her nightshirt. What he don't know won't hurt him—or me.

As she was crawling under the covers, three palace cats entered through the partly open door and climbed in with her. Daine smiled as they made themselves comfortable. It would have been nice, talking with Miri after lights-out, but this was better. Miri didn't know how to purr.

She didn't realize her new room was beneath the boys' dorm until thunder the next morning crashed through the ceiling overhead: "Trainees, *turn out!*" She sat up, tumbling cats right and left and scaring an owl out the door. That thunder had been Sarge's voice. It must have had an equally powerful effect on the male trainees. They were dressed and stumbling blindly on their way to the stable by the time Daine had pulled on her breeches. Neither Onua nor Buri, who slept in the girls' dorm, could roar, but whatever they did seemed just as effective. The female trainees were just as quick down the stairs.

Once the stabled ponies were groomed and fed, the humans performed the same chores for themselves. "You'll work afoot," Onua told Daine as they ate. "Keep an eye on what's low, hooves to hocks, but if you see a trainee misusing an animal or a problem with the tack, don't be afraid to sing out. The rest of us will be mounted, so you'll see things we miss." She clapped Daine on the shoulder with a grin as she got up. "We'll have some fun."

Going to the meadow while everyone else saddled up, Daine was startled to find the queen already there, patting a savage-looking yellow dun mare. Soon the trainees, Onua, and Buri arrived on ponies, and Sarge joined them on a horse, a strongly built liver chestnut gelding. The mounted officers put the trainees through a morning's hard work, trying the ponies at different gaits—walk, trot, canter, gallop—with and without saddles. After lunch, everyone switched to his spare mount and went through it all again.

Daine soon learned a polite "excuse me" went unheard. She also learned she wasn't shy if she thought a pony had picked up a stone or had strained a muscle. By morning's end she had developed a bellow—not as shattering as Sarge's, perhaps, but loud enough for her purposes.

Numair found her after lunch. "How's it going?" he asked, leaning on the meadow fence next to her.

When she opened her mouth, a croak

emerged. She cleared her throat and tried again. "Fine. It's all fine."

"I was wondering—about that range-finding experiment"—he squinted up at the sky—"you're too busy to try it now, I suppose."

Cloud trotted over to them. *Tell the storkman I will go with him.*

Numair looked oddly at Daine as the girl laughed at the pony's name for him. When she caught her breath, she said, "No, don't ask me. You really don't want to know!" To the pony she said, "But there's no hearing spell for me to talk to him with. I can't ask Onua, not now. I shouldn't even really try it myself, not if I'm to earn my pay with these people."

The pony stamped impatiently. *You act as if you're the only clever one. I will tell the storkman when I can no longer hear you.*

Daine relayed the pony's offer to Numair.

"You mean *she'll* undertake the test situation without dealing through you? Can she do that?" he asked, fascinated.

"She says she can. I know she always finds me if one of us wanders off."

"All right, then." He bowed to the pony.

"Lead on." As they walked off, Daine heard Numair say, "And no biting."

The trainees left the stable with their spare ponies, followed by the queen and the other officers. Soon Daine was busy: she forgot about Cloud and Numair. The afternoon followed the morning's pattern, with one difference: the officers were still fresh, but the pace had begun to tell on the trainees.

"Come on, Evin!" yelled the queen, circling the Player at a gallop. "Raiders won't give you a break for lunch, laddy!"

"I don't want to see air between butt and saddle, trainee!" Sarge roared at Miri's heels. "You ride that gelding like he's a separate creature! He ain't! He's part of you, so connect the parts again!"

Onua swooped down on a brunette, Selda, and scooped the bow out of her hand. Circling back, she told the girl, "An enemy might do that with an ax. Every time you have to concentrate on your mount you give a foe a chance."

"Your stirrup's too long!" Daine yelled at one of the men. "Stop and fix it!" He didn't seem to hear. Within seconds Buri, slung low on her pony's side, came up unwatched to grab the stirrup in question. The trainee's pony wheeled away from the K'mir; her rider, Tarrus, slipped off and down.

Buri righted herself on her pony's back and looked at Tarrus. "Your stirrup was too long, trainee. Fix it." She rode off calmly.

"I'm sorry," Daine said as the young man struggled out of the mud. She gave him a hand. "I tried to warn you—"

He grinned at her, his small, pointed nose quivering like a rabbit's. "I figured I'd fix it the next break. Next time I'll do it right off." He looked at his behind and the backs of his legs, where he sported a coat of mud. "It's an ill wind that blows no good. With a mudpack like this, my skin will be lily soft." He fixed the stirrup and mounted up again.

Daine was tired when it came time to stable the trainees' mounts at day's end, but she knew she couldn't be as tired as the others. They moved stiffly as they groomed and fed their ponies, without joking or arguing as the officers and Daine corrected them. Only when each pony had been tended and the trainees had retreated to the baths did the queen say farewell and trudge up the long slope to the palace. She had groomed her mounts while the trainees groomed theirs, still finishing with enough time to criticize their work.

"She does this every day?" Daine asked Buri as she followed the Rider officers to the barracks.

The stocky K'mir nodded. "In the fall and winter she can't be out in the field. That's the social season. She has to travel around being queen. She works with the trainees to make up for when she can't be with the groups."

"But there's times she'll leave a ball or dinner to go to a Rider group in trouble," Onua remarked. "Remember the pink tissue dress?"

Buri rolled her eyes. "Three hundred gold nobles that thing cost, just for cloth and sewing. That's not counting pearls in the collar and cuffs—gray ones, almost perfectly matched in size."

Daine whistled in awe. She couldn't imagine a garment that cost so much. She couldn't even imagine what such a dress would look like. "What happened?"

"Two years ago," Buri said, "the Fifth Rider Group chased outlaws into a swamp and got bogged down. Thayet was visiting some earl nearby."

Daine winced. "And the dress?"

The two K'mir shook their heads as they led the way into the baths. "What happened to the group and the outlaws?" Daine asked as they undressed.

"The Rider group lost two. The outlaws didn't make it, but Thayet and the Riders saved the village girls they'd kidnapped." Buri plunged into the heated pool, and the girl trainees yelped as a wave almost swamped them. Onua and Daine entered more decorously. Buri surfaced and gasped, "Thayet always said it was worth losing the dress."

"And the king wasn't mad?" Daine wanted to know.

Onua replied, "He just told her next time, try to change clothes."

It wasn't until supper was almost over and the mage had come to the mess hall door that Daine remembered he'd gone off to experiment with Cloud. "Ready for lessons?" he asked, sitting next to her.

"How was it this afternoon?" she asked.

"We determined that your range, with Cloud at least, is a mile and a half. It may be more or less than that with animals who haven't been exposed to you for a prolonged period of time."

"You make her sound like a disease," Evin commented with a laugh. "Are we going to need healers or something?"

Numair smiled. "No. But Daine, have you found that animals you spend a lot of time with are, well, smarter than others? Smarter in a human sense?"

She played with her spoon. A friend of Ma's had said as much, when she had nursed one of his falcons. Some of the local herdsmen had liked her to train their dogs for that reason. "Is it bad?"

"No, how could it be? It doesn't make your animals less able to survive in the wild; quite the opposite." Numair took her food tray and stood. "Come on. We're going for a walk." He took her tray to the servants who cleaned up.

Daine rose with a sigh, tired muscles creaking. Miri winked. "If you don't want lessons, I'll take them," the girl offered. "He's cute!"

Daine followed her teacher, shaking her

head. Numair was well enough, as men went, but he wasn't the king.

The mage steered her out of the barracks and through the horse meadow gate. In silence they crossed the wide swath of green, letting their eyes get accustomed to the night. They had to stop every few feet while Daine greeted the grazing ponies and horses. Each time she patted them and excused herself, saying she would visit with them another time.

The horses stayed back as the man and the girl went into the forest along a trail. There was just enough light to follow it without stumbling into trees. Here, away from the torches of the palace, the dark-clad mage turned into a large shadow, a slightly ominous one.

The trail opened onto a grassy clearing. The animals who normally would have been drinking from the large pond in its center had fled on hearing them, but Daine could feel their eyes. Overhead a bat squeaked.

"Have a seat." Numair motioned to a rock near the pond. She obeyed a little nervously. He came up behind her to rest his hands on her shoulders. "I'm going to use my Gift, but through *you*. You must understand that. If I did this with the king or Alanna, they wouldn't see what you will."

"If you say so." The hair on the back of her neck was standing up, and she was quivering. It wasn't fear, exactly, because she wasn't afraid of him. On the other hand, the dark was filled with strange currents that flowed into and out of the presence at her back.

He put his fingers on her temples. "Now, do just as we do when we're meditating," the soft voice over her head commanded. "Slow, deep breath—inhale." He inhaled with her. "Hold it. Let it go, carefully. Again, in . . . and . . . out." Eyes closed, she breathed at his command.

Her mind filled with vines of sparkling light wrapped in darkness—or was it the other way around? When the space behind her eyes was full, the magic spilled out of her. She felt it ripple through the clearing, soaking grass and trees. It dripped into the pond, following the water into the ground.

"Open your eyes." His whisper seemed to come from inside her head.

She obeyed. The clearing, so dark before, was veined with shimmering fibers. All that was green by day grew from emerald threads now. Awed, she reached down and plucked a blade of grass. The needle of fire that formed its spine flared, and went dark.

She gasped, remorseful. "I didn't mean to—"

"Hush," Numair said quietly. "Look at the earth."

A pale bronze mist lay on the piles of dead matter under the trees. When she let the blade of grass fall, its spine turned the same dim bronze as it touched the ground. "It returns to the Goddess," she whispered.

The stone beneath her and the other rocks she could see were veined with dark silver. An owl on a nearby branch gleamed with a trace of coppery fire. A vole grubbed beneath a bush near the spring, a point of copper light.

Daine looked at her hands. They were laced through with strands of reddish light, almost as if her veins had the power to glow. Intertwined with the red were strands of copper fire. She looked at the owl, at the vole, and at her hands—all the same shade of copper.

Half twisting, she managed to see part of Numair. He too was laced with red fire. In addition a white, pearly glow flickered over his skin like a veil. She recognized the light Tahoi had shown her once.

"Sit straight," the mage ordered her quietly. "I have to remain in contact with you to keep the spell going."

She obeyed. "I wish I could see this by myself."

"You can learn. The vision is in your mind, like the power to heal. Just remember what your magic feels like, and practice reaching for it."

"Reaching for it *how*?"

Something between them shifted, and she knew she looked into herself. At her center, deep inside, welled a spring of copper fire.

She called, and a slender thread rose from it to her. She caught it, opened her eyes, and threw it out to the owl.

"You don't need the hand motion," Numair said. "In magic, the thought is the deed."

"If you *want* it bad enough," she added. "That's what Ma said."

"She was right."

The owl glided down through the air. She held out her arm, and it perched, looking her over with solemn eyes. He was a barn owl a little more than a foot tall, with the white ghost-face of his kind and a powerful grip.

You called to me, night-sister?

His voice was cold and precise. It was also clearer than the voice of any animal she'd ever spoken to, except Cloud's.

"Only to greet you, silent one," she replied with respect.

"You don't need to say it aloud," Numair commented.

Daine shook her head. "Can we do this a little bit at a time?" she asked, not looking away from the owl. "Please?"

She *felt* him smile. "Whatever you say."

The owl ruffled his feathers in disapproval. It is not for the nestling to decide the proper time for lessons, he said, and flew off.

"I heard that," Numair remarked. "He's right. And it's time to stop." The ending of the spell felt to Daine as if she were a waterskin and the water was trickling out. She opened her eyes.

"How do you feel?" he asked.

She didn't reply. She felt a tickling in her mind—a feeling similar to the one caused by Stormwings, only faint and far more pleasant—and looked around for its source. It came from the pond. A tiny figure not much bigger than the owl, glittering with scales, was levering itself out of the water.

Numair saw what she was looking at. He spoke a word Daine couldn't understand, and the clearing filled with bright light. The little female creature in the pond whistled shrilly and vanished into the water again.

"Her hair was blue." Daine said it calmly. She had used up her excitement for the day. "She was all over scales and her hair was blue."

"Undine," Numair whispered. His dark face glowed with awe. "I *think* we just saw an undine—a water sprite." He walked over to the pond and knelt beside it. "I'm sorry, little one. Won't you come up again?"

"Maybe if you doused the light," Daine recommended. She sat back down on her rock. Her knees felt a little weak.

"Oh—of course." He said something, and the clearing was dark once more.

They waited until Daine was half-asleep, but the undine did not return. Finally Numair gave up his vigil and roused the girl. "I'll have to tell the king," he said as she stretched. "Or maybe not. She won't harm anyone. They're said to be incredibly shy of humans."

"I noticed," she said dryly.

He produced a globe of light so they could see the trail: they both were tired and needed the help. "To see a water sprite," he murmured, steering her down the path. "We live in marvelous times, my little magelet."

"What's a magelet?" she asked, and yawned.

"Nothing, really. Well, 'little mage.' Isn't that what you are?"

As they left the clearing, Daine saw movement out of the corner of her eye. Another tiny person, a green female, watched them go from the branch of a tall oak. She decided not to mention tree sprites to Numair just now. She wasn't sure that she liked being called "magelet."

The next day passed in the same manner—driving the trainees morning and afternoon—with one difference. As if her time in the undine's clearing had opened a door in her mind, Daine saw glimpses of copper fire in every furred and feathered creature to come near her. It was very distracting until she got used to it. Most alarming were the flashes at the corner of her eye, the ones that made her turn to look.

"Why do you keep twitching?" the brunette Selda wanted to know. "You look like you have palsy."

Daine glared at Selda but held her tongue. The older girl was like some people back home, never happy unless she had something to complain about. Still, the comment was enough to make her guard herself so she wouldn't jump at the hint of copper light. She came to like seeing it. Her only regret was that copper was the only magical glitter she saw— no blue or green threads, no bronze mists and pearly shimmers.

She had a fresh shock that day: when she saw Onua with the ponies, the same copper color threaded the K'mir's head and hands.

"Why so surprised?" Numair asked that night, when Daine told him. They were on their way to the horse meadow once more. "She's— what's the K'miri term?—horse-hearted. Did you think Thayet would commission just *anyone* to obtain mounts? The Riders depend on horses more than any other military company. Onua ensures they have the best."

"Does she know?" Daine asked.

"Of course." He boosted himself up to sit

on the top rail of the fence. "She doesn't have it enough that she needed training in it, like you. There are a few people here with it: a man and his grandson in the palace mews, two sisters at the kennels, some of the hostlers. Stefan, the chief hostler, has a lot of it. He breeds great-horses—the extra-large mounts many knights need to ride in combat. I trained him."

Shaking her head, Daine sat on the rail beside him, looking at the animals grazing in the meadow. "And I only heard of all this two days ago."

He tweaked her nose. "Being all of thirteen, of course you should be omniscient," he teased. "Now, magelet—to work." He pointed to a pony grazing by itself nearly three hundred yards away. "Call to it."

She opened her mouth, and he clapped his hand over it. "*Without* sound."

She glared at him. "Then how'm I supposed to call her?" she asked, his palm tickling her moving lips.

"With your mind. One thing I've noticed is that you tend to be confused about how you speak to and hear animals. We're going to break you of the habit of assigning concrete manifestation to magical phenomena."

"What?"

"Believing you *actually* hear or speak with your body when all of it is done with your mind. Call that pony."

"'That pony' is a mare. Why can't I just talk to her?"

He sighed. "A time may come when being heard will get you killed. Also, your mind needs discipline. If your thinking is more direct, what you can *do* with your thoughts will happen more directly. Learn to focus your mind: focus creates strength. Meditation helps you reach the same end.

"We're doing spring cleaning up here." He tapped her forehead with a long finger. "Once you put everything into its proper place— once you organize your mind—you'll be able to find what you want quickly. Now call her, please."

Daine clenched her teeth and thought, as loudly as she could, *Come here, please!* The mare continued to graze peacefully.

"Think of the magic," Numair said calmly. "Try again."

An hour or so later they gave it up and went inside. Daine's head ached fiercely, and the pony had not come closer by so much as a step.

"We'll keep practicing," Numair said calmly.

"Lucky me," she muttered, following him into her room. A large book lay on her writing table. "What's this?" She opened it to a colored page and gasped in awe: it was a precise drawing of the bones of a wild pig.

"It's a book on mammalian anatomy," he said, sitting down on her bed.

"A book on what?"

He sighed. "I keep forgetting you're not a scholar—sorry. Anatomy is what's inside a body: muscles, veins, organs, and so on. 'Mammalian' refers to mammals. You know what they are; you just don't know the fancy term. Warm-blooded animals with hair-covered bodies that suckle their young are mammals."

"That's most of my friends." She said it quietly, turning page after page of drawings with fingers she had scrubbed on her shirt.

"Exactly. If you're to learn healing, you need to understand how animals are put together."

"I already know some." Here was a bear's skeleton; here the veins and organs of a cat.

Every drawing was done with an eye to the finest detail.

"This book will help you to *organize* what you know and add to your present knowledge."

She made a face. "Why? My friends don't organize their minds. Everything they think about is all tumbled together, willy-nilly."

"For them that's enough," he said patiently. "As animals they remember the past only vaguely. They are unable to visualize a future, apart from the change of seasons. They have no comprehension of mortality—of their deaths. They don't learn from books or teachers, so they have no need to structure their minds in order to find what they learn. You, however, are human and different. If you do *not* find a way to organize your mind, at worst you might go mad. At best, you'll be stupid."

She made a face—she didn't like the sound of either fate. With a sigh she looked at the page before her. The artist had drawn a bat, its frame spread so she saw how bones fitted together. "You'd best take this when you go. My friends come in every night. I wouldn't want it soiled."

"The book is spelled against dirt and tearing.

It's yours. I want you to use it, not admire it."

It took a moment for her to realize what he'd said. "Mine!" she gasped. "No! It's—it's too valuable. The likes of me don't keep such things!" Her fingers shook, she wanted it so much, but peasant girls didn't own books.

He caught her hand, his eyes earnest. "Daine, listen to me." He pulled her down to sit beside him. "You're a student mage. You need books like this to do your work. I am your master. It's my duty—in this case it's my pleasure—to give you whatever books and scrolls I believe you require to learn. Unless you don't want to learn?"

"Odd's bobs, of course I do!"

"Good. Then get your book. We'll start at page one."

They ended some time later, when Onua knocked and stuck her head in. "We're about to meditate. Come one, if you're coming."

"Do we have to?" Daine asked, closing the wonderful book.

"Spring cleaning," he replied, getting to his feet.

She followed him to the Rider mess. She'd been surprised to learn that meditation was required of all trainees, not just Gifted ones. They worked at it every night before they went to bed, along with all their officers, Daine, and Numair, "whether we need it or not," Evin commented once, in a whisper.

That day set the pattern for the next three weeks. It took Daine six days to learn how to deliberately call the nearest pony without using words. Numair then had her summon a pony farther away but still within sight, until she could do that. Next she had to call an animal from inside the barracks or stables, where she couldn't see it: often that was Tahoi or one of the cats that slept in her room. She worked hard. Each task took less time to master.

Anatomy lessons she swallowed in gulps. Every spare moment she had went into studying her beloved book and memorizing its contents.

Meditation was the hardest. She did her best, wanting to control the copper fire that was her kind of wild magic, but clearing her mind was *hard*. Stray thoughts popped into her head; something would itch; a muscle would cramp, and she would have to start over. Often she fell asleep. The best thing about meditating with the trainees was the knowledge that she wasn't the only one who was easily distracted or who dozed off.

Slowly they all grew used to their work. She saw it in the trainees before noticing it in herself, as their bodies hardened and the hard routine became habit. After two weeks she was taken off watching them on foot and put to teaching archery, something even the officers had to work to beat her at. It wasn't until she saw that few trainees were falling asleep in meditation that she realized she no longer fell asleep, either. With practice it got easier to learn to think of nothing at all. The deep breaths emptied her thoughts and quieted her body rhythms. Her mind learned to drift. She began to feel as she had in the marsh, when she had listened for the hawk.

Is *that* what it is? she thought one night, lying awake in bed. She grasped the badger's claw. "I wish you'd come and tell me," she whispered, earning a curious look from the pine marten who had arranged herself and her kits on the girl's blanket-covered legs.

If the badger heard, he did not answer the summons. "Typical," Daine told the martens, and went to sleep.

SIX

MAGELET

The next day, a month after her arrival, she was waiting for the trainees to finish their morning workout when she heard a low persistent rumble. For a week the hill above the barracks had swarmed with men loading empty wagons. Now draft horses had been hitched to the wagons; one by one, they towed the laden vehicles up the hill.

Sarge clapped Daine on the shoulder. "This is it," he said cheerfully. "The king is on his way, so *we* can be on ours. I'm ready!"

"I'm confused," she said, craning to see his face. "He's on *what* way?"

"See, my lamb, in summer the king goes on

progress, to see how fares the kingdom. Soon as he goes, the queen takes the trainees to our summer camp—"

"Pirate's Swoop this year," Alanna put in. She'd been training with the Riders for the last week. "We set out tomorrow."

"That isn't much notice," remarked Farant, who had overheard.

"How much notice do you *need*, trainee?" Sarge asked. "You *have* half a day to prepare. One day you'll have to roll out of *bed* ready for a long ride. Then you'll appreciate this leisurely pace."

Technically, Daine thought that night, the trainees didn't have even half a day to get ready. They'd put in their usual afternoon's work with their spare mounts. The only change in their routine was that they were excused from their lessons before meditation to pack. She hadn't been excused from her lessons, but she had little packing to do.

Meditation was held, as always, in the mess hall, and everyone attended. When Numair gave the word to begin, she decided to try her idea from the night before. Instead of thinking of nothing, she closed her eyes and *listened*.

How could breathing be so *loud*? She concentrated, putting the sound of her lungs aside. As the noise lessened, her nerves calmed. Her neck itched, but it was a distant feeling, not a distracting one. She scratched, lazily, and let her hand settle into her lap. A drumlike thud in her ears was her own heart. Easy, she told it in her mind, and the sound retreated.

Something bumped steadily at the front of the mess: Tahoi, lying near Onua, was wagging his tail. Daine peeked and saw the dog shining with copper fire. She looked at Onua—the K'mir was veined with fine copper threads.

Taking a deep breath, she looked inside. The wellspring of her own power was there, just as it had been the night by the undine's pool.

Remembering Numair's lectures, she trapped how it had felt just now, to listen and to find her power, and memorized it. When she placed the feeling in her mind, she knew exactly where it was and how to find it again, quickly. It's *organized*, she thought with an inner smile.

She let the excitement fade and listened again. In the closed and dark kitchen at her back, mice hunted for scraps. She directed them to a rind of cheese she'd hidden for them beneath the long table, then sent her hearing out of the mess hall, into the night. Sounds crashed into her skull: bats seeking insects, cats on the hunt, kenneled dogs settling for sleep, horses relaxing, the hawks in the palace mews. It was too much to hear all at once: she almost lost her inner silence in panic. Stopping, she pushed the animal sounds back with her mind until they didn't overpower her. Only when she was sure they were under control did she send her hearing out to the horse meadow once more.

A herd of ponies, including Cloud, grazed there. All of them knew her by now, from the silent-calling lessons. She joined with them, entering the herd. A breeze filled the air, bringing lush scents: ripe grass, leaves, the heady, rich smell of the earth. Around her were the others, her brothers and sisters. A king stallion watched over their family, ready to lead them to safety at the smallest hint of danger.

Spring made them all coltish. With a snort, the king horse broke into a run, just to be running. The herd and Daine followed, racing, black earth thudding under their hooves, the night air in their nostrils. With the herd she was safe; with the herd she had all she could need of comrades and family . . .

Cloud knew the instant Daine came into the herd. She'd seen this coming, as the stork-man had encouraged the girl to venture farther and farther from herself. Tonight the feel of Daine's presence was stronger than it had been since they came to this giant human stable, making Cloud edgy. When Daine's spirit began to change, to take on the scent of the herd, the mare knew they were in trouble again.

She ran for the fence and jumped it. From the meadow she felt the herd call her to go with them. She wavered, wanting to follow. Then, with an angry neigh at the part of her that made her think unhorselike things, she broke free of the call and ran to the stable where Daine's body was.

The gate was barred. She flung herself at it, flailing with her hooves. Putting her hindquarters to it she kicked the gate once, and again, until the large human, the wood brown man, yanked it open. She shoved past him—no time to be polite—and looked around this room that smelled of human food.

Sure enough, there Daine sat on the ground, front hooves limp in her lap, eyes closed. Cloud went to the girl and knocked her over.

A warm force slammed into Daine's body. Suddenly she was free of the herd, safe inside her own mind. Opening her eyes, she saw Cloud standing over her. People around them were talking.

"I did it again, didn't I?" she whispered.

Numair knelt beside her, dark eyes worried. "What happened? She nearly kicked down the door to get at you—"

Daine was shaking. They didn't know. They didn't know what Cloud had prevented. *Thank you,* she told the mare.

Don't run with the People again until you remember to hold on to yourself, the mare ordered. *I won't always be here to wake you up!*

Daine fumbled in her pocket and produced two lumps of sugar. "You'd best go outside now," she whispered, and Cloud obeyed.

Numair helped the girl to her feet. "It's all right," he told everyone. "We were just trying an experiment. I didn't realize it would work so well." Shielding her from the stares of the trainees, he guided Daine out of the mess and into her own room. "What happened?" he asked, closing the door.

"I felt sick," she lied. "Just a headache, that's all."

"Cloud wouldn't come here for that," he retorted. "She was in a panic. What went wrong? And what's this?" The badger's token had fallen outside her shirt. He picked it up, squinting at it. "From its appearance, it's a claw."

"It's mine," she retorted, yanking it away from him. "It's *private*. Can't I have anything *private* anymore?"

"Daine—"

Her voice rose. She knew she was about to cry. "Would you *please* go away? I'm tired and my head hurts! Can't you leave me alone for once?"

"Very well." His face was grave and sad. "But I wish you would trust me." He left, quietly shutting the door.

Daine sat on her bed, tears on her cheeks. What could she do? If she went too deep in meditation, she risked madness. If she *didn't* go deep—He said I might learn to heal, she thought desperately, squeezing the claw tight.

But I have to master this first—or I'll *never* be able to heal.

Caught between fear of losing control and wanting the power Numair said she could have, the girl tossed and turned all night. She would doze off, only to dream of running down a forest trail on all fours. Behind her would be the trainees, or the King's Own, or Stormwings, tracking her so they could tear her to pieces.

Habit woke her at dawn, the hour Sarge usually bellowed for everyone to turn out. That morning the trainees had been given an extra hour to sleep, which meant if she hurried, she'd have the stable to herself. Soundlessly she called Cloud in for a thorough grooming and breakfast: there'd be no time for it later on. Onua had asked her to handle the supply wagon, and Daine expected her time before they left would be spent looking over the cart horse and making sure any last-minute additions to her load were safely stowed away.

A stranger was in the stable, a potbellied man the ponies greeted with enthusiasm from their stalls. Copper fire shone inside his red face. When he saw her, his head flew up as if he were a surprised horse.

Suddenly shy, Daine halted just inside the door. "Excuse me—might you be Stefan? The chief hostler?"

"Maybe. Who're you?"

He can't see it in me, she realized. I can see his magic, but he can't see mine. "Daine, sir. Master Numair said you have wild magic. So do I."

The man relaxed—slightly. "You're the one, then. I brung ye a cart horse." He led her to a newcomer, a sturdy bay cob. "This be Mangle."

Daine offered the gelding her hands to sniff. "*Mangle?*" she asked with a grin. The cob felt like a calm well-behaved sort of horse to her.

Stefan smiled and ducked his head. "Oh, well," he muttered by way of explanation. "Anyways, he's good for whatever ye need in th' way of work." Daine leaned down to blow in Mangle's nostrils. "He likes ye. Onua said I needn't worry if *you* was in charge of 'im." Cloud butted him from behind. "Who's this fine lady?" He bent to the task of greeting the mare, while Daine finished getting acquainted with the cob. When she finished, Stefan was looking at her oddly. "You know this little beauty's changed, 'cause of you."

She couldn't tell what the emotion in his pale blue eyes was. "Me'n Cloud have been through a lot together."

He gave the mare a last pat. "It shows." With a wave to Daine, he walked to the stable door.

"Master Stefan?" He turned to look at her. "D'you ever want to run with the herd? To just—be a horse? Do what the herd does?" She sweated, waiting for an answer. It had cost a lot to ask.

"'Course I do," was the mild reply. "Don't everybody?"

She gripped the badger's claw hidden under her shirt. "What keeps you from doing it?"

He rubbed his strawlike hair. "I'm a man. I can't be runnin' with the herd, now can I?" He left, closing the door behind him.

He makes it sound easy, but it's not. There's something wrong with me, she decided. *It's the madness, just waiting for me to drop my guard so it can take me again. That's how he can protect himself—he never forgets what he really is. And I can't remember.*

Taking Cloud into an empty stall, the girl

swore she would never let her guard down again. Better to disappoint Numair in her studies than to run wild and lose the friendships and respect she had found in this new country.

She was almost done with Cloud when Onua came into the stable. "There you are. Did Stefan bring our cart horse?"

Daine jerked a thumb at him. "His name's Mangle."

Onua grinned as the bay sniffed her pockets. "Is that so?" Looking at Daine as she fed the cob an apple, she asked, "Did you meet Stefan?"

The girl nodded. "Onua—about last night—I'm sorry."

"For what?" The K'mir gave Mangle a last pat and went to see to her own two ponies. "Daine, your magic is taking you down a different road from most folk. Your friends understand that, if you don't. Stop worrying so much."

"Thank you," she whispered.

"Don't thank me—get moving. We want to be assembled and ready to go when the first morning bell rings."

Once she'd eaten a quick breakfast, Daine

finished stowing the officers' packs in the wagon, harnessed Mangle to it, and drove it to the flat area in front of the horse meadow gate where the Riders would assemble. The queen, Buri, Onua, and Sarge turned their spare mounts over to her to lead, so they would be free to range along the trainee column during the ride. The girl considered roping the three ponies and Sarge's horse together for appearances' sake and decided not to: all four mounts knew her well and promised to walk in their own column on one side of the wagon.

Alanna waved as she rode past on Darkmoon, going to wait with the queen. Daine grinned, knowing the Lioness would be more talkative after lunch.

She had started to wonder about Numair when several packs thudded into the back of the wagon. The mage rode up on a black-and-white gelding, looking tired. As if to prove it, once he stopped, he lay along his horse's neck. "Wake me up when we stop for lunch," he said, and—to all appearances—went to sleep.

Daine looked at him, smiling. Dressed in a brown tunic, white shirt, and green breeches, he looked like the man she had known on the road to Corus, not the silk-clad friend of kings who'd been giving her lessons. The jeweled pins and rings he'd worn since his return to court were nowhere to be seen. The only hint of his apparent wealth was a large amber drop dangling from one earlobe.

Slowly twenty-three trainees assembled ahead of Daine in two columns, leading their spares on the outside. Each was inspected by the queen, Buri, Sarge, or Onua; some, including Farant and Selda, were sent to the barracks to lighten their packs. Four trainees, again including Selda, were sent back twice, this time with Sarge to harry them. Daine could hear his bellowed "Riders travel *light*!" when he was inside the barracks with his victims.

At last everyone was ready. Alanna and Buri took places on the left, Sarge and Onua on the right, outside the columns. Thayet rode to the head of the company, and Daine nudged Numair. He opened a bloodshot eye. "I think this is it," she whispered. He nodded and straightened in the saddle.

It was. Thayet unsheathed her slightly curved blade and held it aloft. "Riders, move *out*!" she cried, her clear voice rippling through the columns, and started forward. The trainees followed, keeping the prescribed distance between their mounts as they took a well-marked road into the Royal Forest.

Daine's skin quivered with goose bumps. "That's fair beautiful," she said to no one in particular. "Gi' up, Mangle!" His ears pointing forward with eagerness, the cob obeyed.

The company stopped at noon for lunch. After cleanup, the trainees and officers switched mounts. Daine, her shame about the previous night put aside, tried not to smile when Numair asked if she minded if he rode with her. She agreed instantly. It was hard to be aloof from a man whose seat on a horse was so bad that he had to feel every bump in the road. Making friends with his patient gelding, Spots, she told the horse he deserved a carrot for bearing such an ungraceful rider, and gave it to him.

Things went better during the afternoon: they picked up speed, covering some distance before camping for the night. Supper came from kettles that had been stowed in her wagon, their contents gently reheated over that night's fires.

"Tomorrow you *hunt* for your meal," Sarge

warned as they filled their bowls with stew. "You'd best make less noise, my lambs, or you won't eat." Daine, settling between Miri and Evin, fought to hide a smile.

Returning to the fires after she had cleaned and put away her things, she was intercepted by Numair and led away from the trainees to an isolated clearing. "Lessons," he said firmly. "As long as you and I are within riding distance of each other, my magelet, we will have lessons."

She couldn't protest, really. She knew the trainees were having lessons and, unlike them, she didn't have the excuse of having fought two spirited ponies all day. With a sigh she took a seat on a nearby rock.

Numair put her book on another rock, where Cloud—who'd joined them—couldn't nibble on it, and took a tailor's seat next to Daine. He rubbed his large hands together. "Tonight we'll try something a bit different. While you were washing up, I untethered Mangle and Spots. I want you to call them *both* to us, at the same time."

"Why can't I call them one at a time?"

"You're being difficult," was the forbidding reply.

"It don't make sense."

"Remember the Stormwing attack in the horse meadow? You called quite a few animals to you, all at once. You might need to do something like that again one day. Wouldn't it be nice if—instead of calling entire herds—you only called enough horses to keep you safe?"

He had her there.

She found the copper thread in her mind, the one she wrapped around a call to an animal, and held it.

Mangle—Spots, she called. *Would you come here, please?*

They crashed through the brush, coming up to nuzzle her and Numair.

"See? That wasn't so bad," he told her. "Send them back, please."

With an apology and a short explanation to the horses, Daine obeyed.

Numair held up thumb and forefinger: between them sparkled a tiny ball of his magic. "Onua, now, if you please," he said calmly. Putting thumb and forefinger together, he snuffed the ball out. "Our friend is releasing some of the other mounts," he told Daine. "How many has she loosed?"

Daine listened—*not* with my ears, she reminded herself. "Spots and Mangle are still free. Onua's loosed—let's see, Ox and General, Sarge's two horses, and her pair, Whisper and Silk, and also Darkmoon."

"Call them," Numair said.

She struggled with the calling magic. It only worked for one creature, or two at best, because all she did was focus the magic on an easy-to-hear mind. To call several minds, she had to open her mind to her surroundings. She tried it, and lost her concentration when an owl screeched overhead.

"Relax," Numair said, his voice pitched low. "It gets easier with practice. Find them, and call them—softly. You don't need too much."

She nodded, wiped her face on her sleeve, and tried again. Closing her eyes, she listened for the ones who were free of their ropes. That was easy—a tethered horse was always aware of the thing that kept him from getting that extra-juicy clump of grass just out of reach. There—she had them. She opened the cupboard in her mind where she'd put all her calling skill . . .

A scent of deer on the breeze; a frog croaking in the distance; the soft patter of bats hunting overhead. The herd was around her, contentedly browsing on lush, fat grasses that had been amazingly overlooked by the deer. Ox and General were with her, then Whisper, Silk, Spots, Mangle. Darkmoon, young and blood-proud, fought her command. She'd teach him to obey with teeth and hooves if need be, to give way to *her* domination—

She gasped and threw herself out of the magic. The herd had caught her up so much *easier* than last night! "I can't," she told Numair, her voice shaking. "My head aches."

"You *must* learn this." For the first time since he started her lessons, his voice was stern. "You didn't have a headache before. Try again."

I can't, she thought, but there was no sense in telling him that—not unless she wanted to tell him everything. Desperate, she cheated, and hated herself for cheating. She wrinkled her face, clenched her teeth, shut her eyes, all so he'd think she was trying—but she kept her mind blank. She did this over and over, until he sighed.

"Perhaps I push too hard. You've done well— too well, perhaps. Most apprentice mages take over a year to make the progress you have in a month."

She stared at him. "But I thought I wasn't— How can you tell?" Scared, she added, "Can you see in my mind?"

"No. I wouldn't if I could. We all have secrets." Sadness moved over his face, making her wonder what his secrets were. Then he smiled. "I'm a mage, a well-educated one. When I wish, I can see things hidden from normal vision—like a person's magical aura. See mine?" He lifted his hands. White fire laced with shadows outlined his fingers. "The first day I was strong enough to do it, I examined your aura." He let the brilliance fade. "Your magic was like a tangle of vines around you, going in a hundred directions. You've been getting that tangle under control, pulling it inside your skin, and you're doing it faster than anyone I've ever known. Well, perhaps you've earned a night of rest. Come on—let's go back to the others. We'll meditate and stop there for the night."

She started to protest the meditation, and kept her silence. I'll just pretend, like with the calling, she told herself.

When they stepped into the clearing where the Riders were camped, Padrach was saying in his mountain burr, "Why won't he declare war, then?"

"It's true Carthak has the largest standing army in the world," the Lioness replied. Sarge was rolling up a large map that had been spread out on the ground. "But to attack us they have to cross water at every turn—the Inland Sea, or come up our coast on the Emerald Ocean. We have the advantage, being firmly on land when they have to come ashore to engage us."

"The navy's grown since my lord came to the throne," Thayet put in. The queen was dressed like the others in homespun breeches and tunic and a plain white shirt. Her glorious hair was severely pinned down, but nothing could dim the beauty of her face and clear, level eyes. "The emperor's policy of coastal raiding and paying bandits to attack in the mountains and hills has made the people in those areas determined to fight. Also, since His Majesty built his university outside Corus, we've brought a lot of mages to Tortall—enough even to make Emperor Ozorne's trained sorcerers think twice about taking us on."

"And only a fool would want to attack King Jonathan without some kind of real advantage," Numair said. "Not on Tortallan soil."

"Why's that, Master Numair?" asked Miri.

"Jonathan's magic, and the magic of the crown, are tied into every grain of soil in this land," explained the mage. "Unless an enemy has some kind of advantage that will hurt the king, or keep him from calling on his magic, it's possible that every tree, stream, and rock would form death traps for an enemy." Daine could see it in the trainees' faces, the fear a warrior would live with when the land itself fought him. The thought gave *her* goose bumps.

"Very well, my doves, it's that time again," Sarge barked after giving the trainees a moment to reflect on such warfare. "Seat yourselves comfortably, but not *too* comfortably."

Daine settled near the edge of trees around the clearing. Within a few moments the only sound to be heard was the breathing of the others. She watched them, envious. In the month she'd been with the Riders, she'd come to see that meditation supplied them with something they got nowhere else: a time to be calm, a time to find quiet inside themselves. It would be useful when they were living in the wilderness, hunting raiders and being hunted, she realized. Tonight especially she envied them that serenity. She wished *she* could find some measure of quiet in herself.

Carefully, gingerly, she closed her eyes and drew a breath. It was all right; she was safe. She released the breath, took another. Peace wrapped her like her mother's arms. She opened her ears to the night.

In the distance, a wolf howled, and got no answer.

Poor wind-brother, she thought sadly. No one to sing with, no brothers and sisters to hunt with . . . like me. It's so lonely, outside the pack.

As she breathed, her body fell into the habit she'd been making for it. Her mind cleared, her heartbeat slowed. Forgetting her danger, she opened herself to the music of the forest:

The swish of tails, the shifting of feet, the crunch of grass under broad teeth. A sense of peace and solidity flowed out from the humans to infect their mounts. The herd was content . . .

Once again she forced herself awake, to

find she'd sweated her clothes through. What am I going to do? she asked Cloud as the mare nuzzled her. I can't even close my eyes without it happening!

It doesn't happen when you sleep, Cloud reminded her. It's only when you use that fire-stuff—the thing that makes you People—or when you do the sitting thing. Leave the fire-stuff and the sitting thing alone, and you'll be fine.

Daine shook her head. It seems like I can't win for losing, she told Cloud silently. Sometimes I think I never should have left home.

The next day the Riders picked up the pace. There were fewer stops as they headed through the coastal hills; those that were made were shorter.

Daine faked her lessons that night, as she faked her meditation. She thought she'd handled it well too, until Numair stopped her just before she climbed into her bedroll.

"Are you all right?" he asked, feeling her forehead. "Is something wrong?"

Looking up at him, she swallowed hard.

"What's wrong, except for me being worked to death?" she asked, trying to put him off by being rude. "Honestly, can't you stop fussing at me for one *day*?"

Tahoi whined from his spot near Onua's bed, worried by Daine's tone. Glancing over at him, Daine saw that Onua, Evin, Miri, and the Lioness had heard her as well and were staring at her as if she'd just grown horns. "I'm tired of being watched all the time too!" She struggled into her blankets and wrapped herself in them, not wanting to see how they reacted to that.

She heard Numair sigh. He patted her shoulder. "Sleep well, magelet." He walked away as Tahoi came to lie down next to her.

Tears rolled down her cheeks as she hid her face in her covers. I'm afraid, she wanted to tell her human friends. I'm afraid if I go deeper in my magic, I'll forget who I am.

She woke in the morning to a campsite draped in fog. Without speaking to anyone, she groomed and fed Mangle and Cloud, and hitched Mangle to the wagon. She drove in silence all day, ignoring the worry she saw on Onua's and Numair's faces. The fog burned off by midmorning, leaving the air crisp. By afternoon the breeze coming out of the west bore a new scent to it, tangy and strange. She sniffed it often, wondering what it was.

"That's the sea," Miri told her when she saw Daine lift her nose to the air. Her cheeks were flushed; her green eyes sparkled. "It's close. That's brine you smell, and seaweed. I can't believe how much I missed it!"

"If she starts to talk nautical, plug your ears," Evin advised. "She's just showing off." Miri stuck her tongue out at him.

Their road topped a rise, and a new world spread itself before them. Daine dropped her reins. "Goddess and glory," she breathed.

Miri beamed with pride. "I told you."

Nothing had prepared her for this. Endless blue-gray water stretched north to south, and waves pounded the rocky coast. Salt winds nearly plucked off her head-scarf before she retied it. In the distance a toy with a dab of sail bobbed along—a boat, she realized, but far off.

Soon they reached the coast road, crossing it to pitch camp in a sandy cove. Automatically she cared for Mangle and Cloud, barely able to take her eyes off the water that smashed against the sand. Every time she blinked, something new appeared. Even Cloud's accusation that she looked like a cow, standing about with her jaw open, had no impact. She was entranced.

As soon as archery practice was done, Miri and Alanna took the trainees to find supper in the rock pools of the northern curve of the beach, leaving the officers and Daine to entertain themselves. Thayet removed her boots and stockings, rolling up the legs of her breeches. "Come on," she told Daine. "We'll go for a walk."

She ran to join the queen, trying to shed her boots at the same time. The woman laughed and steadied her as Daine wrestled her footgear off. "It won't go away," she said. "Slow down. Onua says you never saw it before?"

"No, mum." She made sure her breeches, rolled above the knee like the queen's, were tucked in securely.

"Then look. See how steep the beach is? It means waves pound it hard. They create a force called 'undertow' that grabs you and drags you out if you aren't careful. The easier a beach slopes into the water, the less undertow you'll find. Never forget it's there, Daine." Thayet's low voice was stern. "Plenty of good swimmers drown because they can't fight that drag."

Daine nodded soberly. This place had dangers, like any other part of the world—that made sense.

"Then, let's go." The queen stepped down as a wave hit the shore, and let the foaming water surround her ankles.

Daine took a breath and followed. The water was icy. When it met her skin, she heard singing. Gasping, she jumped back.

Thayet stood ankle deep in the retreating waves, fighting to keep her balance as they ate the sand under her feet. "Too cold?" she asked, grinning.

She doesn't hear it, Daine thought.

"Come on," the queen urged. "You'll be numb before long." She walked forward, stopping when the water swirled around her knees. Lifting her face to the sun, she gave a loud, bloodcurdling war cry.

"Thayet, stop that," Numair called. His breeches rolled up, he had gone to explore a

lumpy and pitted block of stone on the northern edge of the beach. He held up something.
"Come look at this."

Thayet went to him. Daine walked forward, immersing her feet to the ankles as a
wave overtook her. A few steps more: she was
far enough in the water that a wave's back-
ward crawl didn't leave her dry.

"Singing" was not right, but she had no idea
of what the proper term might be. Part of it
was a croon, the speech of a wolf mother to
her cubs, but held past a wolf's ability to hang
on to a note. A moaning whistle followed,
then a series of short, high notes. The quality
of the eerie calls was something like sound carried inside a cave—almost, but not entirely.

Hello? she cried silently (all she needed was
for Numair to ask why she was talking to the
ocean). Who are you?

There was no answer, not even the shift of
attention she felt in most animals. Were these
monsters? No—there was no gold fire in her
mind. She gripped a thread of her magic, as
much as she dared use, and tried again. Is
anyone there? It's me—it's Daine! Can you
hear me?

The songs—there were many, all beautiful and different—faltered.

—*Call?*— The voice was faint and alien, unlike any animal voice she'd heard in her life.

She strained to hear without using her power to help her listen. Yes! I'm calling! Me, here by the rocks—

—*No call*—

I called! *I* did! Where are you? *Who* are you?

—*Calf-call?*—

—*No call*—

I'm not loud enough, she realized. If I used my magic, maybe they could hear me, but I don't dare.

Thayet yelled, trying to get Daine's attention. Daine turned, but before she could answer a heavy form slammed into her. Down she went, mouth filling with brine. Trying to rise, she was slammed again and thrust deeper in the water by the animal's impact.

She opened her mouth to scream, and breathed seawater.

Miri and Evin said later she popped into the air to hang upside down from an unseen hand, pouring water as she fought. She only knew she was free to cough and vomit out the liquid that had nearly killed her. Looking down, she shrieked, clawing at the invisible grip on her ankles. Then the hands that weren't there whisked her to the beach, where Onua waited with a blanket. Daine was put gently on her feet, but her knees gave. Onua caught her before she fell.

Numair strode down the beach toward them, his face like a thundercloud. Black fire shot with white light gathered around his outstretched hand. Sarge grabbed up a quiver of javelins, Buri her double-curved bow. Both raced to attack the brown creature lumbering up onto shore.

Daine saw them just in time. "No, don't!" She threw herself in front of the animal. "Don't!" she screeched when fire left Numair's fingers, flying at them. He twisted his hand, and it vanished.

Clutching the blanket around her, she faced the one who had tried to kill her. He returned her look with huge, liquid brown eyes set in a pointed face capped by a small crest. His body was wide in the center and pointed at both ends. Covered with slick, blond brown fur that went light and shaggy around his head, he waddled toward her on fins that ended in claws. Curiously she touched his chin and lifted his head, the better to see his slitlike nostrils and small, curled-leaf ears.

Like most of the big predators she had met, he chose to speak in sounds. He chattered away in sharp, varied barks. He was confused: he'd thought she was a rival male, coming to take his harem. She looked where he did: twelve furry lumps, all a fourth to a third smaller than the male, watched her from the most southern arm of the cove.

"Why did you think I was another male?" she asked, curious.

She *felt* like one, a king bull. He'd been terrified. He was young, and the power of her mind had convinced him she could easily take his females.

"Well, I'm no king bull," Daine assured him, tickling his curving whiskers until he calmed down. "I'm just me—whatever that is."

He was relieved. His harem was safe.

"May I visit after supper?" she asked.

Food? Pictures of fat, juicy fish were in his mind, and the knowledge he couldn't leave the females to hunt.

She promised to bring something. It seemed the least she could do, after giving him such a scare. He barked his thanks and slipped into the water, anxious to return to his mates before another male sneaked up on them.

"I forgot to ask what he was," Daine muttered to herself.

"Sea lion." Miri had come to stand beside her. "They're touchy in the breeding season. The way he went for you, it looked like he thought you were another male, coming to steal his wives."

"Do they eat in the breeding season?" Daine asked, curious.

"Not the beachmasters. If they hunt, another male will take their harems. They can go two months without food—Wave-walker defend us—look!"

A huge shape, far bigger than the sea lions, shot out of the water at the mouth of the cove: a great, lumpy gray thing that cleared the water and plunged back in with a tremendous splash.

"I can't believe they came so close to the land," Miri whispered.

"They who?" Daine's heart was thudding. "Is that a fish?"

Miri shook her head. "They suckle their young, like furred animals."

"Mammals," Daine supplied, from what Numair had taught her.

"Oh. That was a humpback whale—whales are the biggest things in the sea. They sing, you know."

Daine grabbed her friend's arm. "What d'you mean, *sing*?"

"Well, not singing, not like us. They talk in sounds—whistles, some of them, and moans—eerie noises. You should hear them from a boat in the middle of the ocean. It comes right through the wood, and fills the air."

Supper was ready by the time Daine had washed in a freshwater creek and put on dry clothes. She ate little, pondering the whale songs and her failure to reach the singers. After chores, she gathered up extra food and her bedroll.

"No lessons?" Numair asked quietly.

"I promised I'd bring him something to eat. And I do need a holiday." She looked away, rather than meet his eyes and see the disappointment in them.

"If that's what you want. Good night, then."

But he watched her all the way as she walked down to the sea lions.

The beachmaster greeted her—and her food—with enthusiasm, and let one of his wives show the girl the first of that spring's new pups. When she slept, it was with her cheek pillowed on a yearling's flank, and with heavy, fishy-smelling bodies ranged all around her.

The badger came. His fur was puffed out; he was very, very angry.

"I have lost patience with you," he snarled. "If you were my kit, I'd knock you tail over snout. When will you stop being stubborn? I didn't guide you all this way so you could fail to learn what you must! Tell these people what happened at that town of yours. Tell them what you're afraid of! Did you think I would send you to more hunters?"

"Predators," she told him.

With a smack of one heavy paw he knocked her onto her behind and jumped onto her chest. "Don't talk back, youngster. Have you no sense? Your time is running out! Soon the storm will be here. Lives depend on learning your lessons. I realize you are only a kit, but even you must see more is at stake than your fear of the hunt. Now, promise me you will tell them." She hesitated, and the badger snarled, "Promise me!"

He bore down on her with his will, thrusting his face into hers. She wondered later if it was the force of his mind, or the overpowering reek of his supper (decayed rabbit and a few worms), that made her surrender. "I promise."

"Tomorrow, and not one day later." He climbed off her chest, and she could breathe. She sat up, pulling air into her squashed lungs.

"Well, you're a good enough girl," he grumbled. It was as much of an apology from him as she would get. "I just worry about you, and things are moving so fast." He lifted his nose and sniffed. "Phew—these friends of yours stink of fish!"

She woke to fog, dense and wet, beading in the sea lions' fur. Sitting up, she winced. She felt like one large bruise. Luck had been with her the day before. If she hadn't been in shallow water, she would have died, smashed by four hundred and fifty pounds of fast-moving sea lion. On top of the bruised ache were new, sharp pains. Peering inside her shirt, she found deep gouges, four on each shoulder—as if a badger had rested his weight there.

The morning fog turned into rain, and Thayet announced they would remain in their present camp. Steeling herself, Daine approached Onua and Numair as breakfast was being served. "Can I talk to you later?" she asked. "Alone?" She swallowed. "There's something about me you ought to know."

A few words to Thayet and Buri were all that was needed. Numair and Onua followed her to the south end of the cove, where a rock over-hang kept a strip of sand dry. Numair built a fire. Tahoi sprawled between him and Onua, head on Onua's lap, his belly to the warmth of the flames. Cloud lay down so Daine could lean against her, encouraging the girl silently.

"Is it so hard to begin?" Onua asked.

Daine looked at the high waves, feeling her chin quiver. She gripped the badger's claw for reassurance. "Oh, yes. Don't interrupt me. If I'm stopped, I don't know if I'd have the courage to go on." Drawing a breath through a chest that had gone all tight, she began,

"When the thaw came, end of January, nothing would do for Ma but I go to the next valley over, and visit her friend that married a shepherd there. She heard that Lory—her friend—was coughing a lot, and Ma had a syrup to give her. She made me promise not to come home in the dark, but stay over till morning. Sometimes I wonder if she just knew . . . but prob'ly not. As a foreteller, Ma always made a good cook.

"So, I saddled Cloud and went. Lory was glad to see me. Her 'n' Rand, her husband, always treat me nice. There was a new baby she let me play with. They're sweet when they're that little. And Rand wanted me to take a look at his best ewe. Good thing I did. She was getting set to give him twin lambs, only breech birth, which might've killed them and their ma. So I was up late, and Lory let me sleep till noon.

"Coming out of their place, I couldn't see anything anywhere but fog, couldn't smell, couldn't hear. I was clear to our village before I knew.

"They hit around dawn. The mill was burned, the miller dead. They took the wheelwright's oldest girl and the headman's wife.

Really, they mighta passed my house by, Ma having the Gift, but they remembered she was pretty too, see.

"They fought—all of them. Ma, Grandda, dogs, ponies, horses—even the stupid chickens. Even Ma's geese. Not the rabbits. They left. Well, they never fight, and you can't ask them to go against their nature. But the rest fought. They killed some of the bandits.

"The bandits went crazy. They killed everything on the farm and didn't carry any of it away, Mammoth told me. Mammoth was my boss dog. He said they was too scared of animals who fought like that.

"Mammoth told me what happened, and died.

"So we buried them, me and Cloud, every last one of our family. Cloud's dam and sire, her brothers are in those graves.

"I straightened up the house, what was left. The raiders had tried to burn it, but only the upper story and roof were gone. Ma had a bunch of charms against fire in the kitchen, so most of the downstairs was saved.

"It was two days before anyone came to see. After Ma helped them birth their children, and nursed them when they was sick. *Two days!* She could've been alive and hurt all that time! If the bandits had passed us by, Ma would have been at the village with medicines and bandages, making me and Grandda help.

"When I saw them, I just—popped. I said get out. I threw rocks, and they ran. You got to understand, there was all this mad inside me, all this hate and wildness. I couldn't hold it. My animal friends, they're the only ones who came right off to see if *I* was alive. I was going to them when I found the blood trail the bandits left.

"I knew where the pack of wolves was. The boss male and female thought I was smart, for a two-legger. It took explaining—they don't hunt their own kind. It's one thing to run another pack off your territory, but to hunt each *other* like they're prey, that makes them sick. When I showed them our farm, well, it made them crazy. We picked up the bandit trail and found them, in some caves.

"It was hard, keeping the pack from taking the bandits all at once, but I didn't want the wolves to get killed. We picked off three shifts of sentries, 'cause nobody was awake or sober enough to remember if the old sentries came back. When the other bandits came out in the morning, we took them. I remembered enough to let the women taken from the village loose, and kept my pack-brothers from killing them too.

"By then I was gone wild entirely. I went to all fours, and me and the pack denned in the bandit caves. I was safe with the pack. Cloud couldn't even talk to me. It scared her silly, being around the wolves, but I remembered she was family and I wouldn't let them get her. There was plenty of meat, anyway, from all the bandits stole.

"We heard the humans coming. I told the pack to go to the old den. I waited to see what was what. Maybe I was getting human again, a little.

"I hid in the brush. They sent Hakkon Falconer ahead to talk to me. He used to visit Ma and stay over, before he married again. He'd've wed Ma, but I heard her tell him my da wouldn't like it. She always spoke of my da that way, as if he was just around the corner. Anyway, Hakkon treated me all right, even after he married, because I helped with the birds.

"He said the women we set loose made it home and told what we did. He said I'd best come in now, before I took sick. He said he'd put me up, and I could earn my keep with him. He trained falcons for our lord.

"I came out onto the road. They'd've had me, but Cloud snuck up on one of the archers and kicked him. He shot too soon, and I ran.

"Hakkon said I was crazy, it was for my own good. He said I was like the rabid bear. I had to be put down merciful. If I'd come out, it'd be over in a minute—wouldn't hurt at all. The rest of them were calling me a monster.

"Then they tried to set the dogs on me, but the dogs wouldn't go. When them with ponies tried to come after me, the ponies threw them and lit out for home. The men should've known they couldn't get their animals to come after me.

"Me and Cloud headed up into the rocks. Trouble was, they were mountain men, fair trackers even without dogs. I wasn't thinking like a human, so I didn't remember to hide my trail. The weather didn't help, either.

"I don't know how long they hunted me. I think it was most of a week. I got pretty tired and cold and hungry. Cloud saved me. She started to nip and bite my arms. See—this one left a scar, above my elbow. She only left me alone when I got on my hind feet. When I got used to walking like that, I remembered I was human, and I knew I had to get out of Snowsdale. I snuck back home, got the things I had left, and came south.

"That's why I've been scared with the lessons. It never happened before my folks got killed, but now when I go deep in my magic or the meditating, when I'm by myself, I start thinking like the closest group of animals— like a herd of horses, or a pack. I forget I'm human. I forget I'm *me*.

"I was afraid to tell the truth. You don't know what it's like, having them you knew all your life hunt you like you was a deer. Hearing them on your trail and knowing if you don't start running, your hide'll get stretched on a frame and the rest of you goes into someone's stewpot. And I *was* crazy, running on all fours, hunting with a pack. I wanted to forget all that, if I could. I wanted to be all new here, all normal, just like everyone else.

"Only I guess I can't. The badger says I have to learn."

SEVEN

BUZZARD ROCKS

She hadn't watched them as she talked, and she was afraid to look now. Suddenly Onua hugged her tight. The tears that had stopped coming when she buried her family came again, in a hot and silent flood.

"What about the badger?" asked Numair, when she was calm again.

Daine shrugged. "He comes in my dreams, sort of." She described the badger's visits, showing the silver claw and the marks on her shoulders as evidence. Onua shook her head over the wounds and fetched her medicines.

As she tended Daine's scratches, Numair thought. Finally he said, "'Time is running out'—

'the storm will be here.' What time? What storm?" He sighed. "I hate omens. They depend on translation, and I was never good at it. If he tells you anything more solid, let me know." Daine nodded. "As for the rest . . . I never heard of a human with wild magic losing contact with his essence—the part that tells us we *are* human.

"On the other hand, I've never met anyone with wild magic as powerful as yours. It *is* conceivable that your bond to animals over-whelms your humanity." He rubbed his hands together. "Well, *that's* easy enough to fix."

She gaped at him. "It *is*? All this time I've been afraid of joining a herd or a pack or a flock or whatever, and I could've *fixed* it?"

"With help from your humble servant." He stretched his arms. "Are you up to meditating now? I won't let you swim off with the sea lions." He smiled warmly at the girl, and she smiled back.

Onua patted her knee. "I leave you mages to it. I'm going to camp and torture some trainees." Quietly she added, "Thanks for trusting me, Daine."

"I wish I'd told before," Daine replied guiltily. "Only I was scared—"

The K'mir stood and dusted sand off her bottom. "After your village hunting you, I'm surprised you made yourself talk to another human again. Don't worry about it. And don't let him work you too hard." With a wave, she set off down the beach. Tahoi watched her go: he refused to leave the warmth of the fire to be drenched by the rain.

"She's quite a woman," said Numair. "You have a good friend in her."

"I know," Daine admitted.

"Now—just like meditation." She nodded and closed her eyes, feeling his fingers come to rest on her temples. His hands were warm. Carefully she breathed, pushing the sounds of her heart and lungs out of her mind until she barely heard them. Her muscles relaxed one by one.

Now she heard a thundering—Numair's heart. She pushed the sound back and let her hearing spread. Tahoi slept, dreaming of rabbits. A sea lion cow had started labor nearby, bringing a new pup into the world. Another pup, already born, suckled at his mother's teat. She heard doubled heartbeats in some of the other cows, signs of pups to come.

Inside, Numair said. Obediently she looked for her wellspring of copper fire. She dropped in and they fell through it, until she saw a white core to the fire. It bled into the copper as the wild magic bled tendrils into it. Suddenly she was inside the white column, looking out.

A shadow glittering with bits of light came between her and the magic. In its tracks flowed a glass wall, its surface etched with odd runes. When the shadow had circled her, the beginning and end of the glass connected.

Her head was clear: for the first time in weeks she felt sure of herself. Examining the white fire around her, she found it untainted by her magic, just as the magic was entirely apart now from her inner self. She also knew that she was alone—Numair had gone. She followed him to the real world and opened her eyes.

"How do you feel?" asked the mage.

She tried to stand and nearly fell over. She was stiff! "A bit rusty, but aside from that, wonderful. Am I fixed? Am I all right?"

"You tell me," he said. "Try the listening again. Sea lions live in groups like wolves and horses. If you're going to lose yourself, you should be able to with them. If not, the Rider ponies are just down the beach."

Daine closed her eyes, took a breath—and she was among the females of the harem, hearing their sleepy talk of fish and weather. The cow in labor had given birth: her new pup suckled contentedly. The mother barked at him, teaching him the sound of her voice so he'd always know which female she was.

Daine opened her eyes and grinned at Numair.

The mage smiled back. "Did you forget who Daine is?"

"Nope," she said gleefully.

"Sure you don't want to plunge into salty water and eat live octopi? That's what they eat, among other things."

She looked at him suspiciously. "What's an octopi?"

"One octopus is an octopus. Two octopuses or more are octopi."

"So what's an octopus?"

"I take it what all this means is you were able to stay Daine."

"It does. What's an octopus?"

He laughed. "All right, magelet. Let's go to sea."

She worked the day through, learning about ocean animals (no whales were within range, she was disappointed to learn) and about calling groups of sea animals to her. Afterward, it was a pleasure just to eat, clean, and mend tack with the others, and listen to Sarge talk about daily life in Carthak. Onua had to wake her up to get her into her bedroll.

The sea otter found her in the night, hobbling on three paws. The fourth dangled uselessly. She told Daine she'd been hunting in a tidal pool when a wave slammed into her, jamming her into a rock crevice. A second wave had yanked her free, but the paw got caught and broke. Cradling her patient and whispering reassurances, the girl eased out of the tent where she'd been sleeping. Sticking her head into the small tent the trainees had pitched for the mage, she said, "Numair?"

He sat up in his bedroll. "Daine? Is something the matter?"

"I've an otter with a broken leg here. I hate to disturb you, but—now I'm doing better with the magic, I thought there might be a chance I could—"

"Of course. Come in." Light filled the inside

of the tent, making Daine and the otter blink. "Sit." She obeyed, cradling the otter in her lap with a care to the broken leg. "You'll go deep, but into your patient instead of yourself. You need to see her bones from the inside—do you understand?"

"I understand right enough. I'm just not sure I can do it."

"I can help with that part. What you must do on your own is apply your magic to the break and *will* it to heal. You need to burn out any infection. Make sure the muscles, veins, and nerves knit together, not just the bone.

"The strength of your desire is what will complete the task. You must *want* this to work more than anything, and keep on wanting it, no matter how weary you become. *That's* the hard part—maintaining the concentration to finish. As it tires, your mind will want to attend to something else, just as it does in meditation. You'll get a muscle spasm or an itch, and you'll want to see to it. You can't—not unless you plan to resume splinting your friends and hoping you can keep them quiet long enough for an injury to mend."

Daine looked at her patient. The otter gazed

up at her calmly. She had sensed that Daine could help her, and she was content.

"I'll do it," the girl said grimly. "Let's go."

The magic came swiftly into her hold. Numair guided her into the copper-laced animal in her lap and to the broken limb. Gently he shaped the grip of her mind around the injury and showed her an extra-bright strand of copper fire from the deepest part of her magic. She grabbed it and brought it to bear on the shattered bone.

It *was* hard work. She was tired; her head began to ache. It required patience. For a while it seemed nothing was happening. Once she almost gave up, but she remembered the otter's wholehearted trust and the promise to heal her. Ma had always said, Never break a promise to an animal. They're like babies—they won't understand. Daine hung on.

At last she saw movement. Tiny bone spurs grew across the break, slowly at first, then quicker. Marrow formed, building itself inside the protection of the spurs. Bruising in the muscles around the break began to vanish.

She got sleepy. Her back cramped almost unbearably. Nuh-uh, she thought fiercely.

No quitting—not ever. If I'd known this, I could've saved Mammoth. If I learn it, I can save others.

She did not allow herself to think of anything else until marrow, bone, nerve, vein, and muscles were whole and healthy.

When she opened her eyes, she was cocooned in blankets and fiercely hungry. The otter was gone; so was Numair. She crawled out of the tent to see the trainees practicing hand-to-hand combat in the rain. Day had come.

"How do you feel?" Numair was sitting under a canvas awning, writing in a fat notebook. He capped his ink bottle and put his quill aside.

"How is she?" Daine asked.

"She's fine. I saw her swim off a while ago. We had lunch. I kept some for you." He passed a small bag to her.

She fell on the contents—chunks of smoked ham, bread, cheese, dried figs, an orange— and polished them off in record time. "I can't believe how *hungry* I was," she said when she finished at last.

"You worked hard. Of course you're hungry."

"How long did it take?" she asked, running her fingers through her hair.

"Some hours—that's to be expected. Healing in wild magic is more difficult that it is with the Gift. Wild magic depends on the body's own power to mend what's damaged. The Gift simply restores health that was lost."

"One thing I don't understand. Onua said I must've healed the birds in the marsh—remember? But I didn't know how to heal then, and it took me hours to do it now." She bit back a yawn. "I'm also worn out. Maybe I fainted in the marsh, but I never felt like this."

"Hmm." Numair fingered the bridge of his nose. "Several possible theories exist, but only one fits both of the limitations you just described. I'd have to say the birds' *need* to be healed pulled the magic out of you in raw form. You didn't force it to work within the limits of *your* strength then—you served only as a channel. The magnitude of the power transfer made you lose consciousness, but your overall health and reserves of strength were unaffected. That *is* the problem with wild magic—it has been known to act without the cooperation of the bearer."

"You mean it could happen again, and I couldn't stop it?"

"I'm afraid so. If it's any help, I imagine the need in those connected to you by wild magic would have to be overwhelming. It's only happened once that you know of? No fainting spells as a child?" She shook her head. "Once in thirteen years, then. I wouldn't worry, if I were you." He smiled when she yawned outright. "Go back to sleep. I'll wake you for supper."

He was as good as his word. She was still tired, but forced herself to bathe in the stream and visit with the ponies. By the time the trainees had begun their meditation, she was in her bedroll, asleep.

The otter's return awoke her late that night. She had brought Daine a sea urchin shell, one that was cleaned of its original inhabitant and dried.

"Thank you," Daine whispered, touched. "I'll treasure it." The otter chirped her own thanks, and squirmed out through the gap in the tent wall. Daine smiled and snuggled into her covers, feeling the bumps of the shell with her fingers. I can *heal*, she thought. Ma, I wish you were here to see!

* * *

They moved out in the morning under a clear sky. Daine's studies went on. Slowly, she honed her ability to speak with groups of animals so no other creatures might hear. She learned to put her will on four, then five, then six animals, to make them obey. She used whoever was closest: a flock of gulls, dogs in a village where the company stopped for eggs, harbor seals. Her greatest success came when a herd of mule deer came down to graze near their camp one morning. When Daine rose, she saw them. She watched, keeping Tahoi with her, simply enjoying the sight of deer so close to humans.

At Sarge's *"Turn out!"* the flock prepared to flee.

"Stop!" Daine called, throwing up her arm.

The deer stopped and did not move until she said, "What'm I doing? Go on, scat!" She took her will off them, and they ran. Feeling pleased with herself, she turned around, to find the trainees out of their beds and staring at her oddly.

"It's a good idea not to say anything out loud," Numair murmured, coming up beside her. She looked up at him and was rewarded with a smile. "It keeps the uninitiated from noticing. Just a little professional advice."

The Lioness walked over to them. "Congratulations, Numair. Your student learns fast."

"I have a good teacher," Daine said, and the mage tousled her hair.

"Come on, children, you aren't paid to gawp like a bunch of yokels!" Sarge's training voice could cut through stone, Daine was sure.

Evin was so close that she heard his soft: "We aren't paid at *all*, yet."

Sarge's eyes flicked his way, and a corner of his mouth twitched. "Let's move it or lose it, people!"

They pushed hard that day, stopping only once, to change mounts. By noon Daine felt as if her teeth would never stop rattling from the wagon, even though she'd switched to riding Cloud twice. About then she found a brush rabbit by the road: he'd been slashed by a goshawk and was dying. Daine took him into her lap, giving Mangle control of the wagon, and went to work.

The healing was harder than before, partly because concentration in a wagon traveling over a rutted road was more difficult than it had been in Numair's tent, late at night. Several times Daine was banged out of her meditation. Finally she switched places with Numair, asking Spots to give her as easy a ride as possible. On a large and placid horse, her luck was better than it would have been on a pony, or than it had been in the wagon. Still, by the time she finished, she had drenched her clothes in sweat, and she had been working throughout the early afternoon.

Weary to the bone, she freed the rabbit. He thanked her and fled, promising to keep a better eye out for predator birds in the future. She watched him go, elated in spite of her exhaustion.

They camped on a wide, open space that ended in a bluff over a tumble of rocks. "Daine, look!" Miri said as they were caring for the horses. She pointed out to sea. Three long, sleek, gray shapes broke from the waves and plunged in again, then four shapes, then two. "Dolphins!"

Once her chores were over, she went to the edge of the bluff. This was her first sighting of dolphins, and she wanted to talk to them.

Sitting on the grass, she reached for her magic—and felt it slip from her grip. Working on the rabbit had tired her to the point of being unable to bear down with her mind. She closed her eyes and tried again. Tahoi barked. One of the trainees loosed an ear-piercing whistle. *"Concentrate,"* she ordered herself through gritted teeth. "You can do this!"

Slowly she discarded every sound nearby, until the only one left was her own heartbeat. Bearing down, she pushed it away, and farther. Perversely, it hammered in her hears louder than ever. She forced it back one more time.

Numair saw her collapse.

"Alanna!" he roared. "Come quick!"

A wide, smooth path sloped ahead, bordered in wildflowers. At the top of the hill two people waited in the shade of an old and gnarled oak.

"Ma?" she whispered, her eyes filling, and the woman held out open arms. Daine floated up the path toward her. The man was unfamiliar: he stood by Ma lazily, wearing only a loincloth. He was very brown, heavily muscled, and carried an unstrung bow like a man born with it in his hand. With so much of his skin bare, she could see that there were streaks of green in his tan, a deep green that gleamed in his eyes. Strangest of all, she could see what looked like antlers planted firmly in his curling brown hair.

"New friend, Ma?" she asked dryly.

The woman laughed. "Still mothering me, Daine?"

A bolt of lightning shot through her chest once, twice.

Her mother's face saddened. "No!" she cried. Daine fought, but a force was pulling her away.

"Ma!" she yelled.

"Sarra!" The man's voice was commanding. "It isn't time. Let her go."

Suddenly she felt reality shatter. Now she hung in open air, high over a rocky bluff where ants gathered around a purple fire. She looked back toward the hill, and a Stormwing dropped between her and her mother.

He looked her over, a nasty grin showing filthy teeth. "Well, well—what a surprise. What brings you here, little pigeon? Aren't you the darling Queen Zhaneh has offered so much to have brought to her *alive*?"

"Your queen can eat my arrows!" she screamed. "I want my ma!"

"Kiss my claws and say 'pretty please,'" he taunted, and vanished. Daine fell to earth and back into her body.

Numair shook Daine as he held her. "You fiend!" he yelled. "What on earth *possessed* you? You were *dead*! I ought to kill you myself!"

"Numair, calm down." The Lioness bent over Daine, looking white and drawn. "How are you, youngling? You gave us a scare."

Daine grabbed her hand. "You're the purple fire. You brought me back?"

"I gave you a direct jolt to the heart. We thought we'd lost you."

"My heart?" She frowned, remembering. "It made too much noise. I wanted it to quiet down so I could talk with the dolphins."

"Do you *hear* her?" Numair asked the clouds. "She wanted to talk to dolphins, so she stopped her own blessed *heart*! Mithros, Mynoss, and Shakith!"

Daine sat up. "I never."

Numair opened his mouth and Onua, behind

him, covered it. "Not until you can talk without screaming," she said firmly.

"Daine, meditation is done for control over body responses, and thus over mind." Alanna's purple eyes were amused, but serious as well. "In cutting back the sound of your heart, you were cutting the heartbeat itself."

"Well, I won't do *that* again," Daine promised, sitting up. "I feel like a mule kicked me in the ribs."

The knight chuckled. "In a way, one did. I gave you quite a shot, youngster." She reached a hand to Evin, who helped her get to her feet.

"Will you behave now?" Onua asked Numair. He nodded, and sighed as she took her hands from his mouth. "And men say *we're* emotional," the K'mir told Daine. "Don't do that again. I'd hate to find another assistant at this time of year." Wiping her hands on her breeches, she went back to the trainees.

"May I ask why you couldn't hear dolphins in the *usual* way?" Numair's voice was dangerously pleasant.

Daine rubbed her eyes with her fists. "I was tired."

"You were tired—ah. That makes it much clearer. Listen, magelet. The *next* time you're tired, try *resting* for a while. If you simply *can't* rest, go where you'll get nice and chilled, or step into salt water." He indicated the ocean below. "As you can see, there is quite a bit of it down there."

"I don't get it."

He sighed. "Reductions in temperature or contact with salt water can act as amplifiers for magic."

"So that's why the whale songs are so loud in the water!"

"Yes, that's why they're loud. Daine, you must realize—these things you're doing when you meditate are *real*. When you reduce the inner sound of your breathing, you are reducing your *breath*. When you quiet your heart, you're slowing it *down*. Your body will react—understand?"

"Yes, sir." She got to her feet with a groan. "Do people have visions when they think they're dead?"

His control vanished. "I don't *know*! I've never *tried* it!"

"Oh, well, I can see there's no talking to

you the rest of the night," she said wisely. "Not till you're out of this pet you're in."

"The pet *I'm* in?" he bellowed.

Definitely time to go groom the horses, she thought.

She fell asleep during supper, and slept through the night. She felt rested when she woke, an hour before dawn, with something already on her mind.

It was the Stormwing. He had been nastily real, in a way Ma and her friend had not been. Even now she could smell the thing's reek, fouling the salt air—

Salt air.

There had been no scent to the hill in her vision. She had a good nose, and she would have remembered. There had been flowers. Ma always wore wood's lily or sweet pea sachets, and Daine had smelled nothing at all. But the Stormwing had come when she was in the air over *this* place. She had smelled him.

Standing outside the tent, in a cold wind, she reached out.

She was too tired to go far—less than a mile, only part of her usual range. She brushed the mind of an albatross that wheeled just over the rocks, but that was as far as her senses went. At that distance, she could trust her eyes as much as her magic, and they told her there were no Stormwings about.

Cloud followed her to the ocean, as cross as Numair had been. *Haven't you had enough fun?* she asked, gracefully picking her way down the bluff while her mistress slid and scrambled.

"Not near," Daine replied. She sighed in relief when she reached the strip of sand between cliff and water. "Don't distract me, either."

I wouldn't dream of it, the mare retorted.

If I think about it, I'll only chicken out, Daine told herself firmly. *Like as not it isn't near as cold as it looks, either.* Yanking off boots and stockings, she plunged into the waves up to her knees. Once her feet were numb she tried again, gripping a rock to keep from being knocked off balance.

There—far overhead, hovering behind a long cloud, a tiny dot of wrongness. The hackles went up on the back of her neck.

Why so far up? she wondered. *He just hangs there, waiting. Watching?*

She sat down. "Cloud, keep me from being sucked under!"

I will do no such thing, the mare replied. Come out this instant.

Daine turned and fixed her eyes on Cloud. "Now, please." She used her will—just a touch of it. "It's important."

Grumbling, the pony waded in and gripped the back of Daine's shirt in her teeth. I hope it rips, she grumbled.

Daine reached behind herself to grab the pony's mane. If I go, you go, she retorted. Numb to the waist, she closed her eyes and sent her magic out.

There was her nasty friend, a jarring note in the sky. He was far from a single note, however. He was part of a thin, jangling chord that reached north and south where the waves boomed, as far as her hearing could go.

She dragged herself out of the water. "Get me to the others? Please?" she gasped, crawling onto Cloud's back. "Not the trainees. Umm—"

To Numair's tent? The mare sounded worried in spite of herself.

"Good. Yes. Have Tahoi bring Onua. It's important."

Just hang on and be quiet.

Daine collapsed over her friend's neck. "Of course." Cloud's mane was delightfully warm on her face.

"I'm sure," she repeated. All the adults were gathered around Numair's small fire. "They're up and down the coast as far as I can hear."

"How can they stay in one place like that?" Buri asked.

"They have their own magic," Numair replied, drying his feet from his own seawater dip, taken once he'd heard what Daine had to say.

"Can they see everything?" Alanna wanted to know. "Can they look through walls or stone?"

"I think they see like hawks," Daine guessed. "I don't know what they can do with their magic."

"They can use only a little without being noticed." Numair was still shivering. "If a sorcerer knows where to look, he can see the aura of their magic for miles. All they dare risk is the bit that holds them aloft." He made a face. "Once I thought to *look* that far, of course."

"Don't blame yourself," Alanna said tartly. "I see magic too, and *I* never spotted them." She patted Daine's shoulder. "Good work." She got to her feet. "I have to let Jonathan know. He won't be pleased." She walked away, far from the noise made by the trainees getting up. Within minutes a small fire blazed where she had gone, burning first orange, then purple.

Buri fed their fire more wood. "What now?" she asked the queen.

Thayet sighed. "I *wanted* to stay a few days at Buzzard Rocks, but maybe that's not a good idea. We'll move them along today, camp early at the Rocks, and go before dawn. Onua can ward the camp. There's not much else *we* can do, once my lord gets Alanna's message."

"We've seen fishing boats and villages," Onua said thoughtfully. "They aren't raiding. They aren't raiding, and they aren't killing."

"You sound almost sorry," Buri commented.

"In a way I am. That would make sense." Onua got to her feet. "They're watching our coast like cats at mouseholes, but who's the mouse?"

The Riders moved out briskly, and kept up the pace of the day before. Numair, apparently over his bad temper of the previous night, taught and questioned Daine on the habits of dolphins and whales.

Later in the day, when they took a side road to the village of Buzzard Rocks, Daine picked up a growing hum. With it came a feeling of *other*ness, though not that of monsters, or even of the water and tree sprites of the Royal Forest. She intended to tell Numair once they had pitched camp.

Their talk was postponed. When they reached the cluster of huts and sheds that marked the town, they found it was deserted. Thayet broke the trainees up into groups, and they fanned out to search the cluster of buildings. Daine and Cloud followed Numair, who did a search of his own.

"It happened fast, whatever it was," he said, almost to himself, as he peered into barns, wells, and chicken coops. "Yet they did have a chance to pack and gather livestock." Then turning he asked, "What's the matter with your ears?"

She blushed and stopped rubbing them. "I keep hearing this—*sound*."

"Oh?" His look was skeptical. "Hearing with your ears, or your mind?"

She listened for a moment. "With my mind. Sorry."

"Is it like the Stormwings?"

"No—more like the undine, but not *like* her exactly. And I have this feeling, as if—I don't know—when I see a juggler or something marvelous." She looked up at him miserably. "I'm sorry—I can't tell you anything else."

"Don't worry. Come on—maybe the others have learned something. Tell me right away if anything changes."

They joined the Riders in the village square. No one had found any clues. "They had time to pack," Alanna said. "It wasn't a raid or disease—"

The hum turned into a roaring chime in Daine's head. Selda shrieked.

They came in low over the beach where the fishing boats lay, giant things too large for birds. The mounts went crazy with fear, needing all their riders' attention. Spots, Cloud, and Tahoi shrank close to Daine and Numair, who were frozen with awe. Selda's ponies broke from her hold and ran into the rocks—five other ponies and Sarge's General did the same.

Daine realized poor Mangle was having hysterics, and went to grip his bridle. "Shush," she told him absently. "Calm down." Trembling, he obeyed.

"Weapons!" barked Thayet. Those who could do so grabbed their bows.

The birds—if they were birds—banked and came for another pass, giant wings shining like dim gold in the sun. This time they gave voice to shuddering, screaming roars. One of them raked the cart's roof with its claws, slicing the canvas as neatly as butter.

Daine saw what was about to happen. "Stop!" she called, to attackers and defenders.

Buri got in the first shot, Thayet the second. The great creatures were out of range, but already they were curving around again. "*No!*" Daine yelled now to the humans. "Leave them be!"

"We're under *attack*!" Buri yelled.

"Don't shoot! They don't understand. If you'll *give* me a second—" But she could see fifteen arrows were fitted to strings. She screamed her fury.

Ponies and horses grabbed for the arrows, breaking them in their teeth. Sarge's Ox actually knocked him over. Daine wasted no time watching something she knew she could catch trouble for later. She ran toward the sea and the incoming creatures, waving her arms. "No! *Stop!* It's not what you think! It's not what *they* think!" Closing her eyes, she grabbed her power and threw it out like a net, pleading, *Listen to me!*

They broke off their attack two wingbeats in front of her, curving to each side. Rising above the lapping waves, the female flew out to a rock at the foot of a nearby cliff and perched. The male stalled with his wings and came down, scant yards away from Daine. He cocked his head, predator's eyes glittering down at her, and waited. Sitting on his haunches, he was as tall at the shoulder as Numair; each of his claws as large as a small sword. His body was that of a giant, feathered cat, blending harmoniously into the head, beak, and wings of an eagle. His eyes spoke of a nature that was alien to hers, but intelligent.

His voice in her mind was deafening.

"It's all right to put down the weapons?" Numair asked.

The griffin—it had to be a griffin—nodded regally.

The mage's eyes lit with wonder. "You can understand me?"

The great haunches rippled.

"A little, he says," Daine translated. "It's ideas he gets, like 'weapons' and 'safety.'"

"Thank you," Numair told the griffin. He went to the Riders as Daine examined the two creatures. The female was gray silver in color, her mate brown threaded in gold. Both gleamed and shimmered in the dying light of the sun. In her magical vision, they blazed copper.

"I don't suppose you could tone down your voice? No," she said when the griffin looked at her arrogantly.

Footsteps crunched in the sand. Alanna came up on Darkmoon, shield on her arm, bared sword in hand. The great horse stopped a few feet away, his sides streaked with sweat. Daine knew the knight had brought him so close to a creature that scared him witless because she would need the advantage of

Darkmoon's height if the griffin attacked; but she wished Alanna had tried for less advantage and the horse's peace of mind. She went to the stallion and stroked his muzzle, assuring him he was safe. He believed her—barely.

"Ask him where the village is," Alanna told Daine, her voice hard.

The great head cocked, and the griffin examined the knight. Daine swallowed as the chiming in her head broke into a handful of notes. "What?" she whispered. "Please, sir, I'm very new at this. You have to—" He chimed again, impatient. From the fire that was his presence in her mind, she picked out an image: Alanna's shield. She shook her head, and the griffin repeated the question/image. "Lioness, I—I *think* he wants you to explain the device on your shield. He won't talk about anything else till you do."

The woman's eyes were hard jewels in the light. "It's a lioness, my own sign. A female lion."

The male stretched his wings, and settled. Could you speak more gently? Daine asked him. Your voice hurts—I feel your answers in my bones. It makes translation difficult.

Pressure—a broad hand—settled at the

nape of her neck. Suddenly she was inside a circle of light, shielded from the worst noise of the griffin's speech. "Calm down," Numair said gently. "Relax. I'm shielding you. Take a deep breath—good girl. You can manage this—just go easily."

She ordered her mind, sorting out what was griffin and what came from other animals. Focusing on the griffin, she reached more directly into his mind until each ringing note became a symbol or an idea. Once she could manage what her mind heard, Numair carefully freed her from his shield. Now she had control of the translation.

The griffin spoke again.

"He says there're too many griffins held captive on human shields," Daine told Alanna. "That's why they attacked the village—no, 'attack' isn't right. They flew over, like they did with us, to warn the people not to raid the nest and steal the little ones for shields. They're nesting atop that large spire of rock." She pointed to where the female sat at its base.

"How many villagers did they kill in this 'warning'?" Alanna wanted to know. "And

Daine, you'd best not lie to protect them."

She listened to something the griffin was telling her. "I couldn't lie if I wanted to, Lioness. He won't let us." His correction boomed in her mind, and she sighed. "That's not right. Lies can't be *told* near a griffin. He's surprised we didn't know. That's why they were captured for shields."

"There haven't been griffins here in centuries," Numair put in. "We've forgotten the lore. Does he know how long it's been since they were seen in human lands?"

Daine struggled with the answer. "He— sorry, Numair—he doesn't know what you mean. I *think* he doesn't understand time as we use it. He *does* say they killed no one. The villagers screamed a lot, then they ran. They're at a great stone house about a day's ride down the coast."

"Pirate's Swoop," Alanna said, relaxing. "That's easy enough to check. Is it true, about lying around them, Numair?"

"I'd heard it. You could try."

Alanna opened her mouth—and no sound came out. Her throat worked, but nothing happened. At last she smiled. "I can't."

"How do they live?" Thayet came to stand with them. "What do they eat?"

That at least was easy to understand. "Fish," Daine said. "Dolphins if they can get them, seals, sea lions—but mostly fish. He says there're big ones in the open ocean."

"No cattle? No sheep or pigs?" the queen wanted to know.

Another easy one. "No, mum. They think grass-eaters taste nasty."

The queen hooked her hands in her sword belt, thinking. "Will he agree to let the villagers come back and not harass them?"

The griffin's reply was emphatic.

"Ouch! As long as they keep away from their nest, he doesn't care what people do." Daine smiled weakly at the queen. "Their voices—*our* voices—discomfort their ears. They don't want to come any closer to us than they must, to protect the little ones."

Alanna sighed, leaning on the pommel of her saddle. "It'd be a shame to destroy such magnificence," she said, admiring the great creatures.

The griffin preened his chest feathers and stood a little straighter.

Thayet laughed. "All right. I'll talk to the locals when we see them. Tell your friend we *will* fight them if they harm a human or any livestock."

The griffin's reply was so loud that Daine's temples throbbed. "He says don't insult him by calling me his friend. His kind has better things to do than associate with humans." She knew she was blushing. "He says at least my voice doesn't hurt his ears."

Alanna saluted the griffin with her sword. "Your point is taken, sir. Return to your nest, and we won't inflict our voices on you again."

Opening his beak, the male loosed a great, ringing cry. Before the echoes had faded he and his mate were in the air, spiraling up to their nest.

The humans made camp in the village square. Once the trainees were busy, the officers and Numair took Daine aside. "You shouldn't have turned our mounts against us." Thayet's green hazel eyes were serious.

She gulped. "I didn't—honest. They did it without me asking. If you don't believe me, maybe we could bring the griffins back—"

"No," Alanna said firmly. "We just got the ponies calmed down."

The queen pursed her lips. "You had best study control, mistress," she warned Daine. "If we can't trust our mounts, we're in trouble."

"There's only so much she can do," Numair put in. "This is wild magic, Your Majesty—not the Gift. She can't help animals knowing her feelings any more than she can help breathing. I've tested her control. It's as good as she can make it. Wild magic is unpredictable—thus the name."

Onua slung an arm around Daine's shoulders. "It's got to be harder on her than on us, Majesty. She's a good girl."

Daine bit her lip, glad she had friends—human ones, not just animals.

Thayet rubbed her neck. "I'll be so glad when we reach Pirate's Swoop," she said. "A hot bath and a night's sleep in a bed, and I'll be a new woman." She smiled at Daine. "I'm not going to bite you, youngster. I'm not even angry, not really. I will say this—riding with you has been an eye-opener!"

"Welcome to the club," muttered Numair.

"You know," Alanna remarked, "I have a feeling, if the people come back, this is going to be a *very* honest village from now on."

Onua said, "If so, a lot of husbands will be sleeping in the barn."

In the morning the road swung away from the coast. Daine watched with disappointment as trees blocked her view of the sea. Her sadness grew when Numair left them after noon. He lived in a tower visible to the west; it would take him an extra three hours to reach it if he followed the Riders. He promised that he'd see her soon. She had to be content with that.

By midafternoon the trees thinned and vanished. The main road sloped downhill from there to pass a large, prosperous-looking village on the shore. The road they followed left the main one to approach a strong-looking fortress built around three towers, one much thicker than the others.

"Pirate's Swoop," Evin said. He had fallen back to keep Daine company. "You'll like this place. I think you'll like the baron too. He and my father have been friends for years. He's—different."

The gates ahead opened to reveal the baron's—and Alanna's—domain.

EIGHT

PIRATE'S SWOOP

They climbed a tall mound to enter the castle. Daine was impressed by the thickness of the walls around the outer court and by the alert and well-armed guardsmen. The baron of Pirate's Swoop kept his home in fighting order.

A man in gold-trimmed brown ran up to Thayet, bowing repeatedly as he talked to her. The queen signaled Buri, and the second-in-command turned in her saddle. "Riders, this way!" She and Sarge led the trainees to long, low buildings along the wall: stables, by the look of one, and the guard barracks.

Onua came up beside Daine. "Wait here. I

want them to stable their mounts so they can unload the cart." She grinned. "A bit of advice, for what it's worth. Never do anything you can order a recruit to do for you."

Daine grinned. "I'll remember that." Movement caught her eye: a flag was being run up on one of the three towers. When the breeze caught it, she grinned: it was a gold lioness rampant on a red field, the same as Alanna's shield. On the tower next to it was a brown flag decorated with a gold key.

"The baron's flag," Onua said, noticing the direction of her gaze. "Those flags mean the baron and the lady knight are both in residence."

"No flag for the queen?" she asked.

Onua shuddered. "Gods, no! It's bad enough the whole palace knows where the summer training camp is, without crying it from the towers. George has made this place strong, but why ask for trouble if you don't need it?"

Grooms took Thayet's and Alanna's mounts as the women stretched. Suddenly shrieks filled the air. It took Daine a moment to real-ize the sound was not birds but children screaming, "Mama, Mama!" A pack of them dashed through the inner court's gate and separated: three to Alanna, two to the queen. Thayet's pair—both dark haired, a boy and a girl—bowed when they were a foot away from their mother, then threw themselves at her.

"The prince is nine, the princess eight," Onua explained. "They asked to watch the training this year instead of staying with the younger children in the summer palace."

Alanna's three—the tallest a true redhead, the younger two blondes with a touch of red in their locks—didn't even stop to bow. She laughed and knelt to return their hugs, disappearing for a moment under their bodies.

"You'd think they'd been brought up in a barn, wouldn't you?" a lilting voice asked nearby. "Climbin' on their ma like she was a hobbyhorse." Daine looked down from her seat on the wagon. The speaker was a tall, broad-shouldered man with brown hair lightened by the sun. His nose was too big for good looks, but there was a wicked twinkle in his large, green hazel eyes, and his grin was catching. He wore a shirt and breeches, and had come from watching the sea, to judge from his tousled hair and the spyglass in his hand.

She had to return his smile. "They must love her very much."

"She's easy to love," he replied.

"For you, maybe," Onua said, dismounting. "I know threescore offenders against the king's law who don't find her at all lovable. Hello, Baron."

"Onua, every time I see you, gods be my witness, you make me wish I wasn't married." They hugged vigorously, slapping each other on the back.

"You'd never pull in my harness, George. Daine, this gentleman—"

"Don't call me 'gentleman.' I *work* for a livin'," he interrupted. Daine grinned. Sarge often said the same thing.

"This *noble*man is Baron George of Pirate's Swoop. George, this is Daine, my assistant."

A large hand was offered. Daine shook it. Like all the nobles she'd met in this strange country, his palm was callused. "Welcome to Pirate's Swoop, Mistress Daine. How did you fall into such bad company?"

She blushed, not knowing how to take this charming man.

"Stop flirting with her, George—you'll only break her heart." Onua winked at Daine, who winked back, thankful for the rescue. "How long have the prince and the princess been here?"

"A week only," the baron replied, taking his sharp eyes off Daine.

In a quieter tone, Onua asked, "Any trouble?"

George's eyes flicked to Daine. "You can trust her," the K'mir assured him. "We all do."

Daine blushed again when George raised his eyebrows. "That's quite a recommendation, young lady. I didn't think Onua even *liked* two-leggers." Looking around, he said, "Bless me—so you did take on Evin Larse."

Seeing them, Evin waved and loped over, his long legs taking him across the outer ward court in seconds. "George, I made it," he said, panting as he offered his hand. "I told you I would. Wait till you hear about the trip we've had! Did you know you have *griffins* nesting up the coast?"

"I've got the whole village quartered here," George said, making a face. "Eatin' our food and beggin' me to send soldiers after them.

Tell me true—is it really griffins, or just a pair of mean albatrosses?"

"It's griffins, and you don't have to send a company," Evin assured him. "Daine here got them to make peace."

"I didn't 'get' them to do anything," Daine retorted. With the charming baron she might be tongue-tied, but never with Evin. "They don't do anything they don't want to. But they promised the queen not to attack people or livestock," she told George. "And they can't lie, so I believe them."

"Wait," he ordered. "You've had speech with them, *and* made a treaty—"

"This is a fine welcome you've given me, laddy-buck," Alanna said, trying to imitate her husband's speech as she approached. She bore a gold-haired child on each hip. "Here I am, home from the wars, and you let me be swarmed over by barbarians whilst *you* flirt with my friends."

"Excuse me," George said gravely to the adults, and to the children he plucked from his wife's hold. Gripping the Lioness firmly, he bent her back in a prolonged kiss that looked like a romantic scene in a play. Everyone, even the men-at-arms posted along the walls, clapped, whistled, and cheered.

"Does anyone in this land act like they're supposed to?" muttered Daine.

Onua heard her question. "They do in lots of places," she said, eyes twinkling. "But this isn't 'lots of places,' it's Pirate's Swoop. And if you think *this* is strange, just wait till you've been here a couple of days."

Exploring after the evening meal in the castle's great hall, Daine got directions to the observation deck on top of the third, largest tower. Here the wall rose out of stone cliffs. Looking down, she saw rocks, a thread of beach, and heavy waves. Relaxed, she watched the sun dip itself into the ocean as a cool breeze blew across her face. She liked the Swoop, she decided. If she had to live within stone walls all her days, this would be the kind of place she'd want.

"Beautiful, isn't it?" The Lioness relaxed against the stone wall at Daine's side. "I'm so glad to be home."

You have a home to go to, the girl thought, and was immediately ashamed of herself. How could she begrudge the knight a place of her own? "I don't see how you could ever leave this," she admitted.

"I don't, either, except I took an oath as a knight, then as champion, long before I came here. And I keep my oaths."

They fell silent again. It's odd to see her in a dress, Daine thought. Wearing perfume—it's pretty, whatever it is—and pearl earbobs and silk. And yet she fits here. She sighed. I wish this were *my* place, she thought wistfully. I bet I could fit here too.

A distant cry fell upon her ears. She and Alanna looked north and saw a bird shape wheeling over the ocean. "Griffins," the Lioness remarked. "It's like a story, or a bard's tale."

So are lady knights, thought Daine, but she kept that to herself. "If only the griffins were all of it."

They looked up. Only a handful of clouds were in the sky, but they knew there was a Stormwing behind one, and that more waited up and down the coast.

"My father is a scholar." The woman's voice was soft. "The king asked him to report on what he could learn about Stormwings. He says they live for destruction and the fear that destruction provides. They eat only the products of war, famine, and disease—the bodies of the dead. They drink only the energy of human suffering and fury. They've had a long fast—four hundred years' worth, in the Divine Realms. I have the feeling they won't be as easy to send back as they were to set free."

"Send back?" Daine had a thought, and she didn't like it. "If they *had* to be locked in the Divine Realms, maybe they were never supposed to be there. Maybe they're *our* predators."

"*Our* predators?"

"Surely." She tugged one of her curls. "You speak of locking them up again as if it can be done. What if the gods don't allow it, because the Stormwings are supposed to be here, not there?"

Alanna winced. "That's not a very cheerful thought. I wish you hadn't come up with it. If you're right, we have a lot of battles ahead."

Daine slept in the stable loft, cushioned by the bodies of the castle's many dogs and cats. At breakfast, she listened as the trainees were given a day off (except from caring for their mounts). That meant a day off for her as well, and she could use one. All her shirts needed mending, and a wash wouldn't hurt any of her clothes.

Getting directions to the castle laundry, she returned to her loft and gathered her clothes. On the way back from the laundry, she found Selda checking the saddlebags that had been issued to each trainee for the trip south.

"Smile," the brunette said, shoving her belongings into a pack. "I'm quitting. I've had enough fun in the wilderness."

Daine glanced away. She wouldn't miss the girl at all.

"Don't look so pleased." Selda folded the bags and hung them next to her tack. "One of these days you'll be packing yourself."

"Me? Whatever for?"

The older girl's smile was bitter as she looked Daine over. "Are you blind? How long can they afford to keep you on, do you suppose? After that thing with the griffins, I figured it was all over for you."

Daine felt cold. "I've no notion what you mean."

"What happens if they're in battle and you

get hurt? You think they can risk their mounts coming to *your* rescue? I don't." The girl shouldered her pack as Onua came in. "Don't say I didn't warn you."

Onua looked at her suspiciously. "You'd best get to the wharf. That boat won't wait."

Selda gave both of them an ironic salute, and was gone.

Onua rolled up her sleeves. "This is a surprise inspection. Let's see how the trainees' mounts look while they're off relaxing. You start on that side; I'll start here," she ordered. "We can talk while we work. Look at everything, mind—nose to tail. What poison was she dripping in your ear?"

Daine stroked the muzzle of the first pony with a hand that shook. "She said the Riders can't afford to keep me. She's right, isn't she? If animals know I'm in trouble, they *will* come to me. Numair himself said I couldn't shield all my wild magic."

"Maybe that's so." Onua ran a brush over Padrach's Minchi to see if extra hair fell out after a morning grooming. "But it wasn't the Riders that hired you. It was *me*. As long as I say so, you work for me, not them."

"How can you do that?" she whispered. "You're a Rider."

"No, I'm a civilian expert. I deal with whatever concerns horses, and that's *all*. I'm no soldier." Onua pointed at her with a brush. "You saved my life in the marsh and at the palace, when the Stormwings hit. You saved Numair—he was the first person here I knew liked me for myself. I won't let you down." She reached over and dabbed at a tear rolling down Daine's cheek. "Those of us that's horse-hearted have to stick together, right?"

Daine nodded. "But you'd tell me if I wasn't giving satisfaction?"

Onua grinned. "If we spend more than the morning checking these mounts, I will be *most* unhappy. I was planning to take the afternoon off!"

Daine went to work, smiling. They had just finished when hoofbeats rang outside and a voice yelled, "Daine? They said you were in here."

She ran outside as Numair climbed off his sweat stained gelding. "Come with me," he ordered. "We have to find the Stormwings."

She shaded her eyes to look up at him.

"What d'you mean? Aren't they behind their little clouds, being sneaky?"

He shook his head. "They're gone. Vanished."

She spent the afternoon on the observation deck with Numair and Alanna, searching as far out as she could drive her magic for any sign of the immortals. The Gifted ones applied themselves to scrying, or looking. Numair used a round crystal he carried in a pouch, Alanna used a mirror with (Daine was tickled to see) roses painted on the back.

"It's not *my* taste," the knight said dryly. "This is from Thom—my oldest. A birthday gift. It's the thought that matters." She glanced at the back of the mirror, winced, and turned it to the reflecting side. "That's what I keep telling myself, anyway. And it makes a very good scrying tool."

For herself, Daine sank deep into meditation, listening up and down the coast. She heard the griffin female return to the nest with food: griffin males, it seemed, helped to brood eggs. Her friends among the sea lions were prospering, as were other seals and sea lions.

A number of whales had come to swim in the waters around the Swoop, but she didn't have time to attempt to speak with them. Crossing her fingers, she hoped they'd stay close long enough for her to get a chance. Other sounds she identified as two groups—Miri called them "pods"—of dolphins.

At last she drew her senses back to the castle. "Nothing."

Alanna grimaced. "No luck for us, either."

"So our friends have given us the bag." The baron had joined them at some point. Seeing Daine's puzzled look, he said, "They've escaped us. It's thieves' cant, meanin' a delightful trick whereby you wait for your pursuer and slip a large bag over his head to blind him."

Daine scowled. "Well, I'm not blinded, and they aren't there."

George smiled at her. "I believe you." He looked at Numair. "Is there a way to nab one of these beasties for questionin'?"

Numair frowned. "I'm not really sure. If we can kill them, I assume we can capture them . . . You know, it's moments like this that I really miss the university library."

"We're working on ours," Alanna pointed out. "Maybe the king has the proper books already. And wait—what about the Golden Net?"

Numair's face lit. "You know, with a few adjustments—"

"My lords and ladies." A proper man in the livery of a castle servant had come up to the deck. "We dine in half an hour."

"I think I have the basic spell in a book I've been reading," Alanna told Numair. "If you want to come take a look—" They followed the servant down into the tower, talking about spells and their variations.

Daine looked at the sun; it was low. "No wonder I'm hungry."

"If you hear one of those nasties again, let's catch it," George said.

"I don't think we'll get anywhere talking to one," she pointed out.

The baron's grin was neither warm nor friendly. "You leave that to me." They studied the ocean together. "It's strange how folk look at a thing. Numair sees what's comin' to us— he thinks of the return of old magic, magic that's controlled by none and understood only by a few. My wife sees a threat to her kingdom. Me, I'm a commoner born and bred, title or no. You know what I think of? Omens and portents—like the red star that blazed over us when the emperor Ozorne was crowned, seven years back."

"Then maybe we're lucky the Stormwings are giving us so much time to think about them before they do something really nasty," Daine said.

George laughed. "Now *there's* a practical way to look at it, and I thank you. It does no good to brood about what might come." He offered his arm with a bow. "Let's go to supper and drink to the confusion of our enemies."

Numair kept her at her lessons until the midnight hour was called. She trudged back to the stable the Riders used, yawning heartily as she climbed to her loft bed. Her mind spinning with new animal groups, she kept her eyes open barely long enough to pull on her nightshirt.

She awoke to a stable cat giving birth near her ear and three children—a girl and two boys—watching her solemnly.

"I s'pose you're fair proud of yourself,"

Daine told the cat. "My wondrous book says you're a feline, and a carnivore, and a vertebrate, and a mammal. I wish them that wrote it could smell around here right now and maybe they wouldn't call you all those pretty names." The girl wriggled out from between her blankets and grabbed her clothes. The feline was busy cleaning the last of the new kittens and refused to reply. "It's too early to be paying social calls," she told the children.

"Our mamas said you're a mage." That was Thayet's daughter, Kalasin. She took after her handsome father, sharing his blue eyes and coal black hair.

Daine sat on her bed. "I'm no mage." She grinned. "Numair calls me a magelet, but that's just for fun. It's too early to be answering questions."

"Ma says you help animals." Thom's hair was redder than Alanna's, and he had George's green hazel eyes. "We brung you him. He was on the wall."

The two older children lifted a basket and offered it to Daine. Inside lay an osprey, a fishing hawk, glaring at her over a broken leg. If the cat hadn't been giving birth close by, she would have known about him already.

She sighed and took the basket. "It's all right, then. You can go now." Turning her attention to the bird, she carefully took him from the basket. "How'd you manage this, sir?"

He shrieked and slashed at her when she joggled his leg. "I'm sorry," she murmured, gentling him with her mind. "I'll make it better—I hope."

She went to work, unaware that the children watched her, fascinated. Bird bone was easier than otter bone to mend: it was thinner and hollow. Better still, it wasn't a clean break, but one of the greenstick kind, which meant the bone simply had to be fused together again.

Opening her eyes, she saw that the break was healed, the bird's pain gone. She was dripping sweat onto him. "Sorry," she murmured as he shook himself.

He cocked his head, looking at the mended leg. He was impressed, and intrigued by what she had done. At this moment, however, what he was most interested in was a nap.

She smiled. "Just, when you wake up, obey the rules—no hunting or teasing any other creatures in this castle. They're all my friends too."

The osprey understood. She settled him on a wooden rail and brought water from the stables below. Promising she'd see him later, she gathered her things again and left.

Her early visitors waited for her by the stable door. "You missed breakfast," Prince Roald said. "We brought you some." He handed over a napkin wrapped around sweet rolls.

"Thank you," Daine said. "That was very kind." She wolfed two of the rolls, knowing her manners were terrible and not caring.

"Papa gets hungry when he's been using his Gift," remarked the princess.

Daine wiped her mouth. "It was good of you to bring the osprey, and the food. I thank you. Now, I think you should go back to the nursery, please. Won't the servants be missing you?"

"We're too old for the nursery," replied Thom, with all the dignity of his six years. "Only the twins have to stay there. They're four."

"Poor things. Listen—I have to bathe, and then I work for the Riders, which means I've no time to chat. Good-bye."

They looked at her hopefully.

What was she supposed to say? At home she'd never spoken with a child. Parents had always kept them from her. If I ignore them, they'll go away, she decided, and went to the baths.

When she came out, they were waiting. They trailed her to the stable, admiring the new kittens while she stowed her gear. They followed her back down to the ponies and helped as she looked after Selda's old pair as well as Mangle and Cloud, holding brushes, pails, and rakes for her. They were still with Daine as the trainees, subdued after a morning conference with their officers, came to look after their mounts.

Thayet broke out laughing when she saw what was going on. "I'm sorry, Daine," she said, giggling, "but it's like ducklings. No offense, children."

"You said we ought to learn more about the stables, Mama." Kalasin was more outspoken than her brother. "You said if we wanted to come with you and the Riders when we're older, we'd have to take care of our gear and all."

"Daine has to decide if you can stay, however," the queen said.

The girl wished the children wouldn't look at her piteously. Thayet was right—it *was* like ducklings. She could have shot them easier than resist those eyes. "Onua? Sarge?" she said, hoping. They shook their heads.

"Look at it this way," Buri said. "You'll need help with the new extras—Jacy and Kenelm handed in resignations a little while ago. Starting tomorrow we're taking groups outside the castle walls for days at a stretch. You won't even have Onua then."

Selda had been right, Daine thought, looking at Buri and the queen. They know I won't be helpful in the field, not if the ponies obey me first.

A gentle hand rested on her shoulder—Onua's. "Somebody *does* have to care for the washouts' horses," the K'mir whispered. "It's real work, not just something to do because we haven't the heart to throw you out. And you need to stay close and study with Numair, remember?"

"Once you start, no quitting," Thayet told her children. "If you agree to help Daine, that's what you do. It's a responsibility. You can't stop just because you're tired of it." The two coal black heads nodded seriously.

"Thom?" the Lioness asked.

I don't think he's old enough to bind him, Daine thought, but Thom was already promising. She recognized the expression on his face. He might be only six, but he would keep up with Roald and Kalasin or die trying.

Which means I'll have to watch him, she thought with a sigh. Ducklings.

A week passed. It was easier to manage them than she expected. Being able to meet wild animals was a powerful attraction, one the "ducklings" did not tire of and would not risk losing. Though she incurred the wrath of all the nursery helpers but the chief one, Maude, by introducing their charges to savage beasts, she presented her friends to weasels, crows, bats, and deer. She let them watch as she worked to heal one of the dogs, who'd had a paw smashed by a passing wagon.

She was surprised to find Roald and Kalasin *did* help in the stable, and that only Thom's size kept him from doing as much.

She knew from her meetings with the twins that his maturity came from the possession of two appallingly lively younger siblings. Roald and Kalasin also had younger sibs, but their maturity seemed to result from what people expected Tortallan royalty to do. She was surprised, and a bit shocked, to learn that they fed and groomed their ponies at home. She had never heard of princes and princesses who had chores.

"I'll be a page in a year," Roald pointed out one day as they helped with the constant chore of mending tack. They had settled on the flat area in front of Daine's stable (as she had come to think of it) as a place for such chores. "I'd have to learn then, anyway. It's best to know as much as I can ahead of time. Papa says later the other lessons will keep me busy."

"I'll be a page too." Kalasin had insisted Daine call her "Kally" as the children did. "Papa said girls can be knights, so that's what I'll do."

Daine was about to ask Thom if he wanted his shield when a messenger came through the gate at full gallop. Covered with dust, the man slid from his horse as hostlers came to take it.

"Lioness," he gasped. "Message for the Lioness."

A servant bowed. "This way."

Thom, the princess, and the prince watched, all looking grim. "Great," Thom said. "She has to go away again."

Kally sighed. "It's like Mama in raiding season," she told him. "We're lucky to have mothers who fight. Our fathers must stay home and protect their people."

"Da fights when they hit the village." Thom was a stickler for fact.

"Papa fights if he can." Roald tried to smile and failed.

Poor things, Daine thought. They miss their folks, coming and going all the time. At least while Ma and Grandda were alive, they were *there*.

"How about a run to the beach?" she asked. "The seals aren't that far out. If we ask nice, maybe they'll come in."

"Maybe I should wait," replied the red-headed boy.

"I'll have Gimpy keep watch," Daine wheedled. Usually the bloodhound's name made Thom smile, but not now. "He'll fetch us if they saddle Darkmoon."

"I'm not a *baby*. I won't *cry* or anything. It's just—I keep having bad dreams anymore." Thom looked down, biting his lip.

"Let's go look at the seals," Daine urged gently.

Gimpy was coming for them when the Lioness and Darkmoon passed him on the slope to the beach. The minute she stopped they knew it was serious: she wore full mail. A company of the Swoop's guards waited by the gate, wearing combat gear. One of them carried a banner, crimson silk with a gold lioness rampant—the personal flag of the King's Champion.

The knight slid from the saddle, hanging shield and sword from the pommel before kneeling to embrace her son. Thom fought tears.

"You know Fief Mandash?" She spoke to all three. Roald and Kally liked her and didn't look any happier than her son. "They've got ogres—three of them. They killed the lord and his son and have the rest of the family trapped in the keep. I have to go. We're the closest king's representatives."

Thom swallowed. "Ma, ogres are *buge*."

"Not *buge*, huge. The messenger says the male is eight feet or so. That's not bad, and he's the biggest." Alanna smiled, but her eyes spoke of worry and watchfulness. "I'm taking some men, all right?" That seemed to reassure the children. "Thom, mind your father and Maude, and don't get under people's feet. A hug and a kiss"—she took them—"and you be good." She tousled his hair and shook hands with Roald and Kally. "Tell your seal guests good night," she advised. "You need to clean up before supper."

All of them went to obey. The knight watched them pat the seals, pulling on an amethyst-stitched glove.

"Should I go with you, Lioness?" offered Daine. "If it's immortals?"

"No, with twenty men I should be fine. What gets me angry is I *told* Mandash to arm his people, if he was too cheap to hire soldiers. But *no*, we can't teach peasants to use weapons—what if they decide they don't like their overlords?" She sighed. "I shouldn't speak ill of the dead. I just don't like the timing, and I don't like it being immortals."

She took one of Daine's hands in both of hers. Her grip was powerful. "Will you and Numair look after my family? Don't let anything happen to them."

Chills crept up the girl's spine. "We won't, Lioness."

Alanna smiled. "Thank you." She drew a deep breath and went to bid good-bye to the children once more.

The Lioness had been gone for two days. Daine had collapsed early into her loft bed, worn out from her evening's lessons.

She dreamed: it was a pleasant night in her badger set. With her belly full, she listened to the kits play. She was about to go for a cool drink of water when her dreams changed. Trees and a moonlit sky tumbled around her. Boats filled with men came onto the beaches, and men crept among the trees. Speaking softly and fast, they lit fires, scorching the roosts and blinding her. Into flight she tumbled, over the roaring cold and salty place with panic in her throat. There was the light ahead, the one the forest bats had sung about, a beacon of safety. She was the greatest of the

People—she could protect them when strange men broke the night rituals!

Daine gasped and sat up. "Odd's bobs, what was *that* about?"

With her excellent night vision and the light of the full moon that came in the windows under the eaves, she saw that the rafters overhead were thick with bats. A good thirty of them, mixed breeds, watched her with nervous eyes. Three were hoary bats, named for the frost on their brown fur. By themselves they would not have been a surprise: they weren't sociable bats, not like the clusters of big and little brown bats that hung with them, or the handful of pipistrelles.

"Wing-friends, what's amiss?" she asked softly. "Come and tell me."

Within seconds she was a bat tree, with little bodies festooned on her curls and parts of her nightshirt. All of them trembled in terror.

"Hush," she told them. Closing her eyes, she thought of deep and even breaths, of safety in caves, of the drip and echo of water in high chambers. Slowly the bats took her calm into themselves. Small talons changed their grip, this time so flesh was not caught along with the cloth. The trembling eased and became a thin vibration. Some of the bolder ones returned to the rafters, to give her air. She sent the calm out with them, enticing more of those who clung to her to take the perches they were used to, hanging from wood. The ones left were the hoary bats and the leaders of each group.

Daine opened her eyes. "Now. Let's hear it—one at a time."

It was all she could do to stay calm when they described what they had seen. It was her dream: men, strangers, coming from the woods and from boats on the water, hiding under the trees. She had to clamp down on her witnesses a little to make sure of the numbers they were describing. Bats tended to count by the way they roosted: their idea of numbers was flexible, and depended on the breed of bat. Daine knew she couldn't tell the baron or the Riders her friends had seen six quarter-colonies or whatever the total was. Not only would that not be helpful, but they would think she was crazy.

To the hoary bats, who roosted alone, the men had arrived in flocks, like deer they saw grazing at night. Moreover, each bat had come from a different part of the wood that ran along the coast. After scribbling with a stick of charcoal on her drawing pad and squinting to read her own marks, she concluded that each hoary bat had seen nearly fifty men.

The big brown bats had seen at least two colonies—sixty men or so. Most of the pipistrelles were from one place and had seen less than half of one of their colonies—almost fifty. One lone pipistrelle from the wood north of the Swoop identified another half-colony. The little brown bats had come from the east and south. Each of their sightings came to two tenth-colonies; for them that meant two hundred men, all told.

All the bats assured her their counts had not overlapped, and that she took as truth. Their concepts of numbers might be odd, but a bat's knowledge of territory was precise to a pin.

Daine looked at the numbers, her skin tingling in shock. If the bats were right, they had seen more than five hundred strange men coming overland or by sea and landing near the cove. The bats were more familiar with the locals than those humans might have believed possible. The little animals insisted the strangers were not *their* humans. Moreover, the strangers all wore metal over some parts of their bodies, and all carried or wore wood tipped with metal, and bars of metal. Daine could see their faces in the bats' minds: they were the hard faces of warriors.

Carefully, without frightening the animals, she eased into her breeches and boots. In the process she talked two of the hoary bats into staying behind. The others, the head of each colony, the lone pipistrelle and one particularly scared hoary, clung to her nightshirt and hair. They would go with her, they said.

Sarge, who ran the trainees on night watch, and Kally sat in front of the stable, talking. From the look of things, the princess had been unable to sleep. "Daine?" Sarge asked when she emerged. The girl's blue eyes widened.

Abruptly Daine saw herself as they—as humans—must see her: small, wriggling animals swarming on her, clinging to hair and clothes. They tried their best to be clean, but a couple of them had lost control of their bowels.

I must look like a monster. Daine swallowed a lump in her throat. She hadn't realized how much Kally's opinion—or Sarge's—had come to mean to her.

"I have to talk to the baron," she whispered without looking at them.

Kally walked over hesitantly. She stopped, then reached out to touch a furry body. The little brown bat transferred his affections to her in a leap. She squeaked, then let him snuggle into her collar. "He smells you on me." Her tiny smile trembled and held.

Sarge got up, his brown eyes kind. "Come on, girls."

The master of the Swoop was in his study. The queen and Josua, the captain of the Swoop's guards, were there as well, seated in comfortable chairs, while Numair stared out one of the windows.

"What's all this?" George asked. His sharp eyes took in Daine's riders as well as Kally's small hanger-on. Thayet yelped when she saw Daine; Josua was on his feet, dagger half-drawn. Numair looked around, frowning.

"Please—don't startle them." The bats caught the surge of her own fears. She made herself take a deep breath and get under control. Don't open your eyes, she cautioned the bats. The room was cozily lit from a human standpoint, but not from theirs. "They won't hurt anyone."

"It's only bats, Mama." Sarge's mouth twitched: it was impossible to tell that Kally herself had been upset by them only a few minutes ago.

Thayet and Josua stared at Daine.

"It's important, sir," she told the baron. "I wouldn't have brought them if it wasn't."

"May I?" Numair asked, pointing to the hoary bat.

The animal's nose was already questing, having located interesting smells on the sorcerer's clothes. Gently Daine handed him over: in one of Numair's gigantic palms, the bat was dwarfed.

"What news have your friends brought for me?" George asked. Daine looked at his face, but saw no trace of mockery or disbelief.

Either he's the world's finest Player or he believes in me, she thought. "Have you a map?"

He gestured behind her. She turned and saw a table covered with sheets of parchment: on top was a map of Pirate's Swoop. Holding down a corner of it was a box of small, colored pebbles. Consulting with her friends, she put one at each location where strangers had been seen, explaining to the adults as she worked. "All this since twilight," she said when she finished. "We think it's more'n five hundred, all told." She looked at the picture she'd made, and blanched. The stones formed a half circle a mile away from the castle and village of Pirate's Swoop. They had been surrounded in the dark.

NINE

SIEGE

Things moved so fast Daine's head spun: Pirate's Swoop was more than prepared for night attacks. Within minutes Captain Josua, Thayet, and Sarge had left to quietly wake the village and bring the people back to the castle.

With them they took Daine's promise the livestock would move quietly. Once she had explained things to them, the village animals were eager to help. She felt ashamed of herself for showing them images of the raiders' imaginary stewpots in such gruesome detail, but told herself the cause was a good one. Even the geese and chickens had been willing to go along after that.

Next she asked the bats to return to their friends in her stable. You won't like the people I'm going to talk to now, she assured them, and they believed her. George had asked her for spies who would spook less easily than the bats, and that meant only one thing: owls. Daine had to admit owls were unnerving to deal with, and she *liked* them—the bats did not. While they weren't natural enemies, there was always a chance an owl could make a mistake, and apologies meant nothing to a dead bat.

With the bats gone, she went to the limits of her range, contacting owls and explaining her problem. She wasn't surprised to find that the silent predators were already angry about the invasion: the strangers had chased all the game worth hunting into burrows in earth and tree.

Waiting for the owls' report, she and Numair went to the observation deck. From there they watched as the Swoop's gates quietly opened and guards and Riders headed for the village, to help the people pack and move. Daine noted with approval that the hooves of all the horses and ponies were muffled. With the moon full and the night clear, they didn't need torches—a small blessing, since the invaders also had used moonlight to keep their arrival secret.

The owls reported, and Daine wrote their information on her paper. When they finished, she added the total with fingers that shook. She checked her numbers and came up with the same total. A third check bore the same result.

Her voice emerged as a squeak. "Lord Baron?" He had come while she was working. "I have the whole thing."

He raised his eyebrows. "So soon?"

"Owls are fast." She pointed out the total—a little more than six hundred men had infiltrated the woods. "The owls say they aren't moving. They're camped. No fires, but they've settled."

"Waitin' for dawn," the baron said. "Waitin' for *that*." He nodded at the sea. Two miles out a fog bank lay on the ocean, its top as high as the tower on which they stood. It took her a minute of looking before she saw what was wrong: the curved dome was clean, as if the thing were shaped by a sculptor. It was also dead on the water. Fog was neither tidy nor slow. It moved fast and overwhelmed everything in its way. This close, she should not have been able to see the sky, and she ought to have seen it move by now.

"Numair?" George asked. The sorcerer was leaning on the wall, his eyes closed. A transparent black cloud surrounded him; bits of light flickered in it like butterflies.

He shook his head. "It's opaque. I can't even feel the weather-working spells that are holding it in place, and there *have* to be spells. Fog is defined by natural law like any atmospheric creation. In the absence of those laws, we have to assume magic, which I *should* be able to detect. Since I *can't* detect it, that argues the presence of dampening spells in the fog."

"Dampenin' spells." George's face was tight. "We're boxed in, then—like rats in a trap. Whatever's in that fog will hit us in the mornin', sure as the Crooked God cheats. Why'd we have no idea this was comin'?"

The mage looked at his friend. "George, there are more illusion spells and diffusion spells than there are stars. Scrying is an inexact magic: I have to know what to look for.

All right, I'm good, but even I can be over-whelmed or outflanked. Alanna and Jon would tell you the same thing."

George put a hand on Numair's shoulder. "I'm sorry. I didn't mean you failed at your job. It's just been a long time since I've been sucker-punched. I don't like it." His face had taken on harsh new lines. "They'll crush us, between what's out there and those six hundred at our backs."

"And the army won't come before we're bruised at least," Numair said.

"Aye."

"How many warriors here?"

"Eighty—not countin' the Riders." George drew a deep breath and looked at Daine. "What can your friends do to help?"

She swallowed. "Don't ask me to make them fight," she pleaded. "They're not—this isn't *about* them. I can't ask them to fight and die for humans." Shivering, the girl remembered the marsh and the slaughtered birds. "Please say you understand."

George's silence drew out for a long moment and it was impossible to read what was in his face. At last he smiled and patted her arm. "I don't, entirely, but then I'm all too human. Will you ask them to watch, then? To let us know if more soldiers come, or if the ones out there start to move?"

She nodded, and whispered, "Thanks." Sending out her request, Daine settled to wait for her friends' reports from the woods. As she listened, guards and Riders began to return with the villagers. Never before had an evacuation gone so well. The livestock had been waiting for their owners to come out. There were no problems with catching animals, not even chickens. The trainees, at least, had a good idea of why this was so. The villagers did not, and fled to the castle as if their own animals had turned to ghosts.

Dawn. The first raiders came into sight, to find the village empty and the castle gates closed. The battlements were lined with warriors who did not look surprised in the least to see raiders outside their walls.

When the sun rose above the horizon, fog rolled over Pirate's Swoop.

A gentle hand was shaking her, and a wet tongue was bathing her face. Daine looked up and saw Onua, Kalasin, and Tahoi. "I'm sorry, I must've gone to sleep." She turned scarlet with embarrassment and tried to get up. Her knees buckled. "Goddess! How long have I been here?"

Onua caught her on one side, Kally on the other. "Since the middle of the night. The baron says we owe the warning to you and your friends."

"Thank my friends. I just passed the word on." She massaged the cramps from her legs. Kally gave her a roll stuffed with fruit and held a jug full of juice to go with it. Daine was still hungry when she finished. "What's going on now?" she asked, accepting a sausage roll from her young friend.

"We're in trouble. This"—Onua's wave took in the fog surrounding them—"isn't just fog. It carries dampening spells for the Gift—plenty of 'em. We're not sure how many sorcerers are out there holding it, but there have to be a lot of them. Whoever engineered this planned for everything."

Daine looked at the two humans. "That hurts you both, right? You're both Gifted."

Onua nodded. "Lucky for us, there's no

need for magic just yet. Numair got word out to the palace and to the king before the fog came in."

Daine looked at the woman, wondering if the mage had found anyone nearby who could help. Reading her, Onua shook her head.

"I'd best put on clean clothes, then, and get my bow." She caught an angry call from below. "And let Cloud know I'm alive. She's upset with me."

"Can I go with her?" asked Kally.

Onua smiled. "Of course. Just make sure you *stay* with Daine. If you run into your brother, have him report to me."

Daine glanced around to see who was there, and saw the queen, Numair, and the baron, with trainees and guardsmen armed and keeping watch. "Where should *I* report to?"

"Here. Take your time. Nothing can happen as long as this mess hangs over us."

She nodded. "Let's go, Kally. I need to clean up."

Roald and Thom were waiting for Daine in her loft. She shooed them downstairs while she changed, combed her hair, got her weapons, and comforted the frightened bats.

In the stable below she soothed the ponies, all of whom knew something bad was going on. She was uneasy, herself. She'd been fogged in before at the Swoop, but it wasn't the same. The mist felt dirty, and the hackles were up on the back of her neck. The two boys, both Gifted, were in worse condition than Onua and Kally, and clung to Daine's hands as she walked them back to the inner court.

On her trip down she hadn't looked at the new arrangements: now she did. Long tents were set up for healers. Water barrels were stacked everywhere. Temporary corrals held the village animals. Seeing them, Daine went to thank them, assure them they were safe, and reinforce the need for their good behavior. It was the first time anyone had explained that raider attacks were the reason why they were so often dragged up to the castle without warning. Understanding that, they were more than eager to help.

"Honestly, you'd think people would have *told* them before now and saved everyone trouble," Daine growled. "Speaking of people, where's their masters?"

"Some are on the wall," Thom said. Looking up, Daine saw villagers armed with bows, shields, and metal caps among the guards and Riders. "The rest are in the lower levels. We're dug into the rock. There's plenty of room down below."

She was startled. She'd never dreamed there might be more to the castle than what she saw. "How many more surprises does your da have up his sleeve?"

Thom grinned. "A *lot*."

Sarge waved to her from the wall. She waved back, hoping her face didn't reveal her thoughts. She had human friends here too—friends who might be hurt, or die. With Ma and Grandda gone, she'd thought she was free of that kind of pain, but she was less free than ever. She'd never love anyone as she had her family, but others had come to be important to her: Evin and Miri, who gave her acceptance; Onua, an elder sister; the Rider officers, respect for her judgment. Each of those people now was a potential wound.

Thinking grim thoughts, she climbed the outside stair to the deck, the children following her. I should've stayed wild, she told herself. I never should've got back up on my hind legs.

Never? another part of her asked. Never means not meeting sea lions and griffins. Never means not hearing whales sing. Never means not learning how to heal. She sighed.

On deck once more, she saw two guards and two trainees, Elnore and Padrach, on duty with bows strung and ready. The queen and Onua were armed as well. Buri, like Sarge, was elsewhere on the walls, keeping an eye on the other trainees. Baron George was talking quietly to one of the guards.

Thayet smiled at her and crooked a finger at her son and daughter. "Come talk to me," she ordered, and they obeyed. Thom went to stand with his father, and Daine sought out Numair.

"Are you all right?"

He looked tired and strained. His mouth was tight, as if he were afraid he might say too much if he opened it. He barely managed a smile for her. "I'm scared," he said quietly.

She looked up at him. I'm the only one who understands, she thought. If the Lioness were here, he'd've said it to her, but she's not and I am. There's magic in the air, lots of it, and everyone looks to him for a miracle. Right now he can't even tell if his magic is the right kind, and he's afraid.

She put her hand in his, and he squeezed it tight. "I hate to theorize without information, but I need a working plan," he told her softly. "As it is, I either hold the spells off the Swoop so the others can function, or I leave the dampeners on them and punch through myself, to fight with what *I* have. The problem is that as a warrior-mage my talents are limited, and I have no healing magic at all. If Alanna were here, we could work off each other, but—" His face tightened again.

"That's it, then," she said, trying to think aloud as he did. "They lured the Lioness off and put an army between her and us just for that."

He nodded.

"Which means they've been watchin' us all along." Daine and Numair both jumped when George spoke behind them. "They know we've the queen here, and the next two in line for the throne."

Daine and Numair looked at each other and chorused, "The Stormwings."

"*That's* why they were spying out the seacoast," Numair went on. "They were waiting for us to arrive and get settled. I'll bet they also made sure none of our army or navy was close enough to help." Something occurred to him, and his eyes lit. "Daine—your magic. How is it?"

She was surprised he even asked. "It's the same as ever. You told me, yourself, I couldn't turn it off."

"Wild magic," Numair breathed. "It's in everything. No matter how many dampeners they lay on us, *you'll* be able to function!"

Something tugged at the back of her eyes— something ugly and sour. "I can't send my friends to die," she warned, but already her attention had shifted. "Bows!" she yelled, getting hers off her back and putting an arrow to the string. "Bows! Stormwing in the air!"

George shoved Thom down between the wall and the floor of the deck, grabbed the prince and princess and did the same with them. Thayet and Onua had their weapons in hand. The trainees and guards were armed and ready. The baron had drawn his sword and dagger.

Numair swore so vividly that the children looked at him in awe and delight and added,

"The wind's shifting. They don't need the fog anymore."

"The dampeners?" George asked hopefully.

The mage shook his head. "Still there. The fog laid them down. Now the spells will stick to all that the fog touched."

Within minutes the fog was gone, and the world around them was lit by a midmorning sun. Daine gasped at the scene that lay before them. A fleet lay in the cove: five long boats, or galleys, rowed by chained men belowdecks, and seven smaller vessels, all bristling with warriors and their arms. Behind them lay four barges, huge, flat-bottomed boats with no apparent way to move. Large wooden structures sat in the middle of each, things that were wood, rawhide, and rope knit together. Each barge carried a stock of round stone balls, and a complement of barrels. Around their rims, and around the weird structures, were huge bags of sand.

"Such a big siege for such a little castle," Thayet murmured. "Where could they have sailed from?"

"Copper Isles," George replied quietly. "They're Carthak's allies now."

"What are the big, flat ones?" Daine asked, searching the air for the Stormwing she had felt.

The queen raised a spyglass to her eye. "War barges—the terror of the Carthaki navy." She offered the glass so Daine could see clearly. "The things in the middle are catapults. Each barge is counterbalanced with magic and ballast so the catapults can hurl stone balls or liquid fire. They can pound the walls of a place like this to rubble in the space of a day."

"So this emperor has declared war?" Daine asked. She had found the Stormwing, high above. He stooped, dropping onto the deck of the largest of the galleys, laughing as humans scrambled away from him.

"No Carthaki flags," Onua said. "This isn't official."

Daine stared at her. "Surely that makes no difference. A flag's only a bit of cloth, after all."

"A war's not a war until an official declaration is made and the armies march under flags." Onua pursed her mouth cynically. "None of those men or our friends in the woods are wearing uniforms, either."

"And he can *do* that?" Daine asked, outraged. "It's not a war till this emperor fellow *says* it is?"

"Or until His Majesty does," Numair remarked.

Onua said, "We can't expect *any* help from our navy?"

"A week ago Scanran wolf-boats hit all along the north coast," George told them. "Most of the navy is up there, or on our part of the Inland Sea."

"How nice," Prince Roald muttered.

"Heads up, darlin's," George said. "I think we're about to hear terms." The Stormwing was taking flight again, an elegant white flag in one claw and something much smaller in the other.

"This is not good." Numair too had a spyglass. "See the red robes at the bow of each ship? And there are at least four yellow robes per barge?" He lowered his glass. "A scarlet robe from the university in Carthak means you have your mastery—the same level as the Mithran black-and-gold robe. University yellow robes are adepts. They brought the barges here, and their spells keep them afloat and working."

"What robe are you?" Daine asked, watching the Stormwing's approach.

"None," he replied. "Ever put one of those things on? They're *hot*."

"He's a black robe," Onua said, hands tight on her bow as she watched the monster. "There are only seven of them in the world."

The Stormwing was a hundred feet away.

"Bows," Thayet said quietly. In the same movement she and all the archers on the deck raised their weapons, sighting on the messenger.

He hovered in the air before them, smirking. "Now, is that nice?"

Daine clenched her teeth. This was the one who'd come between her and her ma. This close, she could put an arrow clean through him.

The creature dropped a scroll onto the stone between Thayet and George. The queen didn't blink; it was the baron who picked it up and opened it. "'To Queen Thayet of Tortall and Baron George Cooper of Pirate's Swoop, from the Lord of the Free Corsairs, Mahil Eddace, greetings. By virtue of superior numbers and armament, I claim the castle, village, point, and waters of Pirate's Swoop for the

League of Free Corsairs. Should you prove obdurate—'"

"Obdurate?" Daine whispered without taking her eyes from her target.

"Stubborn," supplied Numair.

George continued to read, "'—I shall have no choice but to reduce the castle, enslave the survivors, kill all beasts, and sow its fields with salt. You have one chance only to avoid death, capture, or enslavement: surrender to me the person and effects of Thayet of Tortall and her children, Prince Roald and Princess Kalasin. You have what remains of this day and tonight to reflect. If the three persons named are not given over to us by such time as the dawn sun will clear the horizon, we will commence bombardment by catapult. If you wish to signify acceptance of these terms, you may do so by runnin' up three white pennants.'" Calmly he rolled the message up again, and as calmly ripped it to pieces and tossed them over the wall.

"Looks like Ozorne decided what advantage he needs against the king," muttered Onua.

"There was a time when your folk were no one's errand boys," the baron told the

Stormwing. His voice was even and almost friendly.

"We don't mind helping out," the Stormwing told him, baring his filthy teeth in a grin. "In a good cause, you understand." He looked at Daine. "Hello, pink pig. Zhaneh Bitterclaws will be here to see you soon." He nodded at Onua. "*Both* of you." Turning back to George and Thayet, he said, "Well? Your answer?"

The baron spat on the stone near his feet. "Get out, before I let them make you into a pin cushion."

The Stormwing's giggle was high and grating. "Oh, good. We *hoped* you'd say that." He pumped his wings, pulling away from them fast.

A hunter's screech split the air, and Daine's osprey friend shot past the humans. He tangled his feet in the monster's hair and hung on, pecking for the monster's eyes. The Stormwing shrieked in fury and tried to dislodge the bird from his head, but lacked the arms with which to do it.

"Daine, call him off," Numair said, his voice suddenly tight.

"I didn't call him on—"

"*Do* it!" her friend yelled. Before them gold fire was stretching above the galleys to form a great square, anchored by the red robes below.

"Come back," Daine yelled, putting her will behind it. "It's not worth it, come back!" Something was pounding through the air, making her ears hurt.

The osprey broke off the attack and returned. Onua grabbed the children and hustled them off the deck.

I almost had his eyes, the bird complained. Just one more wingbeat—

The gold fire in the square exploded, knocking everyone down. Like a nightmare, a horde of Stormwings blasted through, led by Zhaneh Bitterclaws. They filled the air with a degree of stench and evil that had not been felt in the world in four centuries. To that they added pure fear in a weight that crushed the humans before them. Something—something huge and red in color—almost seemed to shove the gigantic flock through the gate, but it vanished. It had only been an impression; Daine was too busy trying to breathe with a full pack of terror on her mind to think about it for more than a second.

She straightened: an act of will that took all the courage she had. At the palace she'd had a taste of what a flock of the monsters could be like, but it was nothing like this. She brought up her longbow. At the edge of her vision she saw Numair, then the baron, struggle to their feet. She smiled, blinked the sweat from her eyes, and loosed her arrow.

The messenger had chosen to attack with the flock. As she suspected, her arrow went clean through him. Before he had struck the rocks below she had another arrow on the string and loosed. It flew in a volley as the other humans released their arrows.

Battle raged. Archers, Daine included, fired bolt after bolt, making sure of the target before they loosed. Numair made a hard decision fast: sitting against the wall, where he'd trip no one up, he lifted the dampener spells. The people with lesser Gifts, including those who knew fire- and war-spells, got to work. Onua quickly drew a protective circle around the mage to hide him from the Stormwings.

Daine fought two wars. Her animal friends wanted to rescue her, but she refused to let them. She soon learned that keeping her will on so many species, in the woods, the castle, and the air, was impossible. Pain shot through her head: twice she lost control of the gulls and ospreys. With triumphant screams the birds leaped into the air to harry the Stormwings. With claws and beaks they attacked, trying to drive the monsters onto the rocks or into each other.

Tears rolled down Daine's cheeks. Mechanically she fired as birds fought and died, cut by steel wings or torn to pieces by steel claws and teeth. There was no chance that her power to heal would be pulled from her in this battle as it had been in the marsh: a wound here was death on the rocks below.

When the Stormwings attacked, so did the land raiders, reinforced by the fleet once the fog lifted. For the rest of the morning and into the long afternoon they tried to bring rams and ladders up to the castle walls, and were driven back.

Eventually the Stormwings lost interest in the battle and went to feast on the enemy dead outside the walls. They had what they wanted, no matter who won. They left the air over the deck first, not wanting to go on defending themselves against the archers and the birds.

When the deck had been quiet for a while, George ordered Daine to rest. She found some shade close to Numair and sat, leaning her throbbing head on her updrawn knees. No! she told the animals, who wanted to fight. No, no, *no*! With her last refusal she tightened her grip, until they gave in.

"Look at you." While she'd battled her friends, Miri had come to the deck with Kalasin and one of the maids. All three carried laden trays and wineskins. The fisher-girl came to Daine, frowning. "Your skin's a nice lobster red. You landlubbers don't think about reflected glare—" She rubbed a cool salve into Daine's hot face and arms. "Kally, where's the tonic?"

The princess filled a tankard from her wineskin and handed it over.

"Drink, or you'll be sick." Miri put the tankard to Daine's lips. She took a gulp and choked—it was tomato juice laden with salt and other things. "Drink it all."

"Goddess, that's nasty!" she croaked. She had the Smith-god's own headache. Her hands throbbed, and her fingers refused to close. The muscles of both arms were screaming. She had never shot so much in her life.

"Nasty it may be, but it'll keep you from collapsing on us. Have some more. Maude brewed it up special for you. Only think how her feelings would be hurt if you refused it."

She sat up, wincing as her head pounded. Maude?—the old woman in charge of the nursery. "That's right—she's a healer, isn't she?" From her cradle Daine had been taught to do as a healer said. She drew a deep breath and drank what was in the tankard as fast as possible. For a moment her stomach surged and her head screamed; then most of the pain and sickness were gone. "Goddess bless all healers," Daine whispered. Even her hands had improved a little.

She sat up, and the maid gave her a bowl of stew and a roll. Daine took them and began to eat as Miri and the servant looked at Numair. "Should you even be out here?" she asked Kally.

"Onua put a protective circle around this place," Miri said over her shoulder.

Daine smiled at Kally, then looked at Miri. "How's it going?"

"Not bad." That came from Numair. He sat with his head tilted back against the wall, his eyes closed, his face pouring sweat. Pillows had been put around his sides to make him comfortable. Someone—a redheaded six-year-old, Daine suspected—had tucked his prize stuffed bear under one of the mage's big hands. "They can't breach the walls—can't even get near them. They're having a *horrible* time with the archers. We're holding our own."

"Can you drink or eat?" Kally asked. "Maude says you should if it won't distract you from the spells."

He nodded. The girl fetched a cup of water from a nearby barrel and held it to his lips. He drank without opening his eyes. "How are you doing, Your Highness?"

"Please don't call me that." The girl's voice cracked. "It's 'cause of me being a princess that all this is happening. It's my fault and I hate it!"

Daine rolled to her knees and went to the child. "Here, now—stop that," she said, patting Kally's shoulder. The girl turned and buried her head in Daine's shirt. She was crying, and fighting hard to keep from making any sound. She's only eight, Daine thought sadly. "You got it all wrong, sweetling. Those men would do this no matter who they're after. They could have asked for Numair, here, who's in trouble in that Carthak place, or Sarge, that's a runaway slave. It isn't 'cause of you or Roald or anybody. You're just the excuse. If you must blame somebody, blame them Carthaks."

"Carthakis," Numair corrected. He was smiling a little. "Daine's right, Kalasin. The person who commits an action is the one responsible for it, not the people he commits the action upon."

"But they *said* it was 'cause of Mama and Roald and me." Kally blew her nose and wiped her face.

"So they would." Daine burned with fury. The Riders, the guards—even she had put herself in spots where a fight might sometimes be the only answer. They all knew the risks. But to twist a little girl's mind so she blamed herself for the fight—that was horrible. "Evil people say evil things to make good people cry and doubt. Don't let them get that hold on you. It's because they're too cheap to buy food. They druther steal it if they can. That's *really* what it's about."

"Kalasin?" Maude was at the stair, calling. "I need you below. There's healing to be done."

Kally sniffed and wiped her face again. "Coming."

Daine watched her go. "But she's only a child."

"That child is a strong, natural healer." Numair hadn't once opened his eyes. "She's partly untrained, still, but Maude can talk her through whatever has to be done. How are you managing?"

Daine looked at him warily. "What d'you mean?"

"I mean your friends out there must be dying to go after the raiders, and I definitely recall you saying you won't let them fight. The birds got away from you this morning, didn't they?"

Daine clenched her fists and immediately regretted it. "I'm all right."

"Liar." He said it almost with amusement. "Is it a strain?"

The air was singing to her. "What?" She got to her feet. Where was it coming from? "Numair, do you hear that?"

"Hear what?"

It was like the griffins, only different, a singing coming from the north, low and close. It filled her eyes and ears and beat against the sore palms of her hands.

Onua was with George and Captian Josua, trying to talk Thayet into going below, when she felt her circle of protection on the deck evaporate. "Down!" She pushed the queen to the floor. George and Josua had their swords out as the source of the music came thundering up from below to surge over their heads. Numair was on his feet instantly, his watch over the castle shattered.

The dragon shrieked its fury and broke away, to head out to sea; she turned and came back. Everyone was on the floor but Daine. She stood on the wall, scant inches between her toes and empty air, awed by the glory before her. Scarlet wings and scales glittered like rubies along that long and graceful form. The wings, fashioned like a bat's, were huge, delicate structures of deep red, lit from within by silver bones. As the dragon passed inches over her head, almost knocking her onto the deck, she could see orange and yellow scales

313

decorating the great creature's belly. Like the Stormwings, her claws and teeth were silver, but not the hard silver of metal.

Her song almost deafened the girl. She struggled to force the notes into a form she could understand, until she heard: —*Kidnappers! Filthy kidnappers! Rend them, take the raven-haired one to a cage on the ships!*—

Daine shook her aching head. What was she hearing?

The dragon came in low and almost seized Thayet before having to reverse her flight. —*Bring me here? You will send me home with your human tricks!*—

The girl closed her eyes. What tricks? she shouted with her magic, as loudly as she could. Tahoi yelped. Below the horses screamed, their delicate ears in pain.

The dragon came in again and yanked the sword from Josua's fist. The man was flung to the stone, where he lay stunned.

"Stop!" Daine yelled. "Stop! What kidnappers? What lies?"

The dragon was coming again. —*Send me home! I demand it!*—

Numair threw fire at her, fire that settled on

her like a cloak and blew away. The long head twisted around to focus on him. —*Human mage, you will pay for stealing me!*—

Daine threw herself at Numair and knocked him down. The long shadow fell over them, and stayed. The stone beneath them quivered. Somewhere distant a number of people screamed.

The deck was sixty feet across. The dragon had taken twenty of those feet for her person, forefeet to hind legs, and cluttered a good twenty feet more with her tail and wings. Everyone but Daine and Numair, between her forepaws, was pressed to the wall or had made it to the stairs.

Daine jumped to her feet and raised her hands. I *think* I have the knack of it now, she thought, or please Goddess I *hope* I do. . . . Putting her hands on that scarlet breast, she called, —*Listen, wing-sister!*—

Information flooded into her mind as the dragon let out an ear-rending screech. Daine's nose began to bleed; the intensity of her contact with the dragon's mind had overloaded her body's limits.

—*Who speaks?*—

Daine drew a breath, forcing her heart and lungs to slow down. —*Me.*—

—*Joking.*— Disbelief was loud in the dragon's mind and in hers.

—*No joke,*— Daine said. —*What did they tell you, the red robes on the ships?*—

Why did she feel as if she were healing something? A quick look inside showed her copper fire streaming through her hands, being pulled out of her and into the dragon. When she tugged, she realized she couldn't yank away. Her palms were locked against the dragon's scales.

The dragon was hesitant now. —*They say—they say, raven-haired one and her kits stole me from home, brought me here to destroy boats.*—

—*Can't you smell a lie?*— Daine asked. She was getting a sense of the mind behind the huge, catlike eyes. This dragon was not much older than a human of Miri's age, say, and very frightened: panic-stricken, in fact.

—*Only smell on red robes was Eaters.*— The Stormwings were vivid in the dragon's mind.

—*They brought you, the robes. They brought you with the Eaters.*—

—Do not understand . . . — The dragon was confused and scared. She was quivering under Daine's hands. *—Tired. Sick. Little one . . . —*

Daine felt the dragon's hide ripple. It was like a convulsion—or a contraction! Ma's daughter realized.

—You're having a baby!— she cried.

Suddenly the dragon's mind filled with a hot excitement that shattered Daine's magical hearing. Her hands dropped free of the dragon, and she clapped them to her ears.

The dragon screeched and launched herself into the air. Before Daine realized she was leaving, she had gone, flying north along the cliffs. Her image blurred, then vanished.

She can do magic, the girl realized with awe.

Numair got to his feet and jerked her into his arms. "You little idiot," he whispered, hugging her so tightly she squeaked.

"She was in labor and on her way home," Daine told him, feeling mashed. "They opened the gate nearby, and it pulled her in. I think it killed her baby. Maybe it would've killed her—but it was just what you said, the wild magic was just sucked right out of me, so I think she's healing. And she's been educated,

Numair, from books! Her mind—it's all organized, like you've been after *me* to do—"

Around them the others were coming forward. In Josua's and the guards' eyes she saw an emotion that looked like fear.

Someone ran up to the deck—Farant. "Master Numair? The healers are asking if something's wrong. If you don't shield them now, we'll lose Sarge."

"Oh no," Thayet whispered.

Numair released Daine and sat against the wall once more. His eyes closed, and the quality of air around him changed.

Daine decided she might like to sit down for a while herself. Her legs folded before she told them to, and she never remembered hitting the ground.

TEN

LISTENING FAR ENOUGH

Someone had carried her below and put her on a cot in what she realized was the baron's study. Tahoi lay nearby, worried; a couple of the bats clung discreetly to the hangings. The osprey—missing an eye, but miraculously alive—sat on the perch, letting Onua feed him raw fish. Daine sat up. Her head pounded worse than ever, and she felt her stomach heave. "I think I'm going to be sick," she whispered.

Onua got a basin to her just in time. "What's the matter?" she asked when Daine finished vomiting. "Was it the dragon?"

"No," she croaked. "How long've I been out?"

"Not too long. It's just after sunset."

Looking at her shirt, Daine saw it was a gory mess. "What happened?"

"You had a nosebleed. What's wrong with your head? Can you tell?" Onua smoothed her hair. "It's important. *You're* important."

They knew she was awake and their struggle to get free increased. She didn't even know she'd stopped answering the K'mir until coolness entered her veins, driving back the hot fire of the headache. She opened her eyes. Kally held one of her hands, Thom another. The coolness had been theirs.

"Hello," she said. Her voice sounded like a rusty gate. "Thank you."

"You're wearing yourself out." Maude stood behind the children, looking stern. "You have to let some spells go. I know your magic is different, but your body's just like anybody else's. You're doing too much. Release some of your spells, or we can't answer for the consequences."

Daine looked at Onua as the old woman steered Kally and Thom out. "Easy for her to say," she muttered when the door was safely closed.

Onua brought over a tray of food and put it on the table beside her cot. "Eat. What magic do you have going, anyway?"

Hotcakes, drenched in butter and syrup, fruit juice, hot cocoa. The sugar cleared her head as she ate. "I can't let them fight," she said, her mouth full.

"Let who fight?" Onua scratched Tahoi's ears, and patiently allowed the bats to settle on her shoulders as they listened to Daine.

There was cold water, to cut the sweetness. She drank half a tankard in a gulp. "Them." She waved her fork in the direction of the woods outside the castle. "The wild creatures—they won't let me be. They want to fight the raiders—they've been wanting to all day."

Onua moved her fingers to Tahoi's spine, and the great dog sighed. "I don't understand. Is it so bad if they fight? It's their home too."

Daine glared at her. "They'll get *killed*! They're animals. It's not for them to get tangled in human stupidness!"

"You won't like any of that," Onua told the bat that sniffed the tray. To the girl she said, "It seems to me we tangle them in our stupidity

321

all the time. At least if you tell them *how* to fight, they have a chance."

Daine got up and paced. "You don't understand! Once I meet them or talk to them, I *know* them. They're my friends; they're part of me. When they get hurt and die, it hurts *me*." She pounded her chest to make her point.

"You think it doesn't hurt me, when one of my horses dies?"

Daine blushed, embarrassed. "I forgot. I'm sorry."

The older woman sighed. "We share this world, Daine. We can't hold apart from each other—humans and animals are meant to be partners. Aren't we, Tahoi?" The dog wagged his tail. "He knows. He saved my life, when my husband left me to die. I've saved his life since. He can't cook or sing, and I can't chase rabbits, but we're partners all the same. The Riders' ponies are full partners with their master. They have to be, and that's what I train them to be, so everyone has a better chance of surviving.

"The Swoop's animals are in the same trap we are. Men broke into their homes, killed their families, threatened you—and you won't let them *do* anything for fear *you*'ll be hurt. That's selfish. How would you like it if I took your bow and said I cared too much about you to let you fight?"

Daine winced. "I see your point."

"You've made your friends helpless, just like bandits made you helpless when they killed your family. Of course the animals fight you." Onua sighed. "We have no choice in being hunted—not animals, not humans. That's how the world is. The choice we *do* have is to take it—or fight. Why don't you show them how not to get killed, and let *them* decide?" She studied her nails and added, "I'll be honest with you. We need all the help we can get."

Daine went to the window, fingering her badger's claw. I know what she means, she realized. They'll start with the catapults in the morning and smash our walls. Then they'll come take Thayet and the children if they're alive. And the rest—Thom, the twins, Gimpy and Cloud and Mangle . . .

There's got to be something my friends can do to help.

Suddenly she remembered a talk she'd

heard Buri give the trainees. "If your numbers are small—a Rider Group, say—it's idiotic to attack face-on when the enemy has superior numbers. *But,* enemies are only men, and men scare easy. Use booby traps: snares, pits covered with branches, pebbles strewn across the road to cripple them and their mounts. Foul their water sources. Sneak into camp and ruin their food, if you can. Keep up a racket all night so nobody gets any rest, and you've got the sentries shooting at ghosts. Do they buy or steal food from the locals? Make sure the food they get their mitts on is moldy, stale, or wet.

"An enemy that's tired, ill fed, and scared is an enemy who's half beat."

We could do that, Daine thought now. If the soldiers here on land are crippled, Thayet and everybody else might be able to fight their way through and escape before the ships get their warriors to the castle.

Closing her eyes, she opened her mind to the extent of her range. The countless animals in the woods around Pirate's Swoop began to clamor. They wanted her to release them. They wanted to tear, and gnaw, and leap—

Quiet! she yelled.

They obeyed.

She reached first for minks, weasels, and martens—clever, small animals with sharp claws and teeth. They were quick to grasp the images of leather wrappings, rope, and bowstrings. They must not be seen, she said over and over, with all her will behind it; they mustn't be caught. She pressed the images of bows, knives, and swords into their minds, until they knew to run or hide if they saw a human with a weapon in his hand.

Bears, wild boars, and woodchucks went after supplies, once she'd made them promise to run at any signs of human attack. She left them pulling apart sacks and boxes of grain, cheese, salted meat, and vegetables. Shrews and voles offered to take care of the tea and coffee supplies. If there was an edible or drinkable scrap in the camp by morning, she would be surprised.

Foxes she asked to free the picketed horses and mules. Once she had explained things, the strangers' mounts were happy to leave their masters and run for the woods. Some of the enemy's mules, once they were freed, came back to give water barrels a kick or a roll downhill. Owls and bats volunteered to keep the guards busy. Sentry after sentry had the unpleasant experience of an owl dropping on him silently from above, or of a bat flying directly into his face. Raccoons walked away with arrows and knives. Wolves howled on the fringes of the camp, to be answered by wildcats of all sizes.

Gods go with all of you, she thought sadly, and broke off the contact.

The room was empty. Surprisingly, it hadn't taken long to muster her army at all: the candle that marked the time had burned down one hour's mark and half of another. *I guess it's easier to get them to do what they want than it is keeping them from doing it,* she thought.

Please Goddess, don't let my friends be hurt.

She put on the clean clothes that lay on the cot, and let herself out.

Numair was right down the hall, in a room filled with books. The skin around his face was slack and gray; his nose thrust out like the prow of a sinking ship. His crisp mane was matted with sweat, his face drenched with it. Checking the water jug on the table beside him, she saw it was empty. She went back and brought her own water to him. This time, when she came in, his eyes were open. They were dull and tired.

"Thanks," he whispered as she poured water for him. His hands shook when she gave him the tankard.

"Wait." She supported his head and shoulders, steadying his grip on the tankard with her free hand. "You're still keeping those dampeners off?"

He nodded as he drank, and gasped when he was done.

It hurt to talk casually when he looked half-dead. You won't help him if you turn into a baby, she told herself sternly. "Can I get you some food?"

"I'll just throw up." He smiled. "How do you like your first siege?"

"That's very funny," she told him sourly. "I'm *so* glad you've hung on to your sense of humor. Only think how scared I'd be if you hadn't."

He closed his eyes and smiled. "That's my magelet."

"Can't you let up awhile?"

He shook his head. "The healers. They're still going. Daine—this afternoon. You said the dragon can *think*? It's educated?"

"She. *She's* educated. Even the griffins are like my animals, with all that's in their heads jumbled together higgledy-piggledy. Not her. She's read things in scrolls—I saw them in her mind."

"Amazing," he whispered. "I'd heard stories— just never believed them."

"What stories?"

"They're mages. Well, we saw that. She came right up on us. Even you didn't hear her until she was close. And she vanished. Do you hear her now?"

Daine listened, hard. "No, sir. But like you said—I didn't hear her until the last." She pulled off his boots and put a cushion under his feet. More cushions went behind his head. She noticed that he still clung to the toy Thom had put in his hand. "There's got to be something else I can try. I let the land animals go. They'll do some damage. There's not enough creatures on the ships to work with, though. It's mostly rats out there. I can't work with rats. I've tried, but they don't even want to listen to me."

"Whales? Ask them to swim up under the barges—capsize them. The catapults are the biggest danger. Then the red robes on the galleys."

She thought it over. "If whales're out there, I can't hear 'em. They're not in range." She chewed on a thumbnail until he knocked her hand away. "I'm fair tired too. The dragon sucked me almost dry." This time she didn't even get the thumbnail to her mouth before he grabbed her wrist. "Pity I can't reach the sea. If there's a cold spot in the cellars—"

"Find George. He'll figure out a way to get you to the water."

She saw another danger. "What if the mages on the ships catch me?"

"It's a risk, but you stand a better chance than anyone with the Gift. Only a very few can detect wild magic. It's a skill mages in Carthak are discouraged from acquiring. Remember, *they* think it's old wives' tales. If someone out there *could* sense it, he'd have a difficult time convincing the others. If you're detected, you can escape among the seals and sea lions." He sighed. "I know it's dangerous, and I hate to drive you this way, but—we need a miracle.

I'm hoping you can come up with one."

She got up. "Wish me luck." She hesitated, then kissed his cheek.

He gave her a feeble hug. "Luck, magelet."

Daine looked down the length of rock at the castle's rear. George and Evin stood by with ropes and a sling. "You sent folk down this way before?"

"It's a better ride than it looks," the baron assured her. "They won't see you from the water, because you're goin' down a rock chimney. When you return, just get in the sling and give the rope three big tugs"—he showed her what he meant—"and three little tugs. I'll have someone I trust on watch here for you. Got it?"

She nodded and fitted herself into the rope sling between the two men. "Good thing I grew up in the mountains and I'm not afraid of heights," she said with false cheerfulness, easing herself out over the edge of the wall. "I told you this was a long shot, didn't I?"

"Several times," the baron assured her. "Don't worry, I'm expert in long shots, youngling. Been takin' them all my life."

"What will you do for light?" asked Evin.

She looked at him in surprise. "I don't need any. There's the moon, after all. And I see well in the dark."

George nodded. "Try to be topside when the fun starts in the mornin'."

She smiled up at him. "Wouldn't miss it for the world."

The trip down the rock chimney seemed over almost before it started. At the bottom she found herself on the beach. Here she climbed out of the sling, pulled off her boots, and rolled up her breeches. At a brisk walk, she followed a strip of beach north, along the cliff face. She needed a place where she could anchor herself among the rocks. It wasn't her intention to be washed out to sea.

Finally she reached a spot that looked good. The cliffs were at her back. To the north lay more rock. The castle bluff shielded her from all sight of the enemy fleet, riding at anchor in the mouth of the Swoop's cove.

Gripping her badger's claw for luck, she wedged herself between two boulders and lowered herself into the ocean. She had to bite a lip to keep from shrieking at the cold wetness. Within seconds she was numb to the waist. For good measure she immersed her hands and sent her magic out.

The salt water made her feel as if the dragon had never drained her magic. Her mind raced past tumbles of rocks and kelp, past quite a few sunken ships. So *that's* why this is Pirate's Swoop, she thought. They swooped out from the cove.

She found the seals first and called a greeting. They wanted to play, but she explained she hadn't the time just now. On she went, beyond her normal range and into deep water.

Whale songs rose all around her to fill the sea with their magic. She had found a pod of nearly forty blue whales. Three quarters of them were adults, each at least eighty feet long and weighing over one hundred and forty tons. Daine faltered, awed by their magnificence, then called, —Hello!—

In a cave high over Daine's head, the dragon stopped nuzzling her little one. It was the mage-child, the one who had restored her baby to life when she had thought it dead in her body. The dragon couldn't mistake that atrocious accent.

Whales came into Daine's mind, huge shadows

staring at a girl-shadow. One—a hundred feet if he's an inch, Daine thought, a bit frightened—moved ahead of the others with grace and majesty. —*Who calls!*—

This was nothing like talking with land animals, seals, or fish. Whales seemed wise, in their own fashion, and words only partly conveyed the things they said. To their question she gave them what she was, or how she saw herself, an image embroidered with feeling and ideas.

They were amused. —*Why do you seek us out, tiny human calf?*—

With images and ideas she explained the siege, the Carthakis, the release of the Stormwings and the dragon. —*They want to take our freedom and they're hurting my friends. I came to ask your help. If four or five of you came up under the barges and overset them, and maybe one or two of the large boats, we'd have a chance. I know it's a big favor to ask. I can't say they won't hurt you—maybe they can. But you're my best hope, you see.*—

The chief whale heard her out politely. His answer, when it came, blasted into her mind and ears. —*No.*—

She barely remembered that she was out in the open in time to choke back a scream. She bit deep into her own wrist to smother it.

—*You don't understand!*— How could she explain so they would care? She gave them Onua's wry humor, Thayet's leadership, Miri's love of the sea, George's intelligence, Numair's curiosity. —*The enemy kills humans and animals who never hurt* anyone. *They brought monsters here.* (She gave them spidrens as well as Stormwings—it never occurred to her to add the griffins or the dragon.) *We have calves there—little ones who depend on us to keep them safe.* (Roald, Kally, and Thom were as fresh in her mind as if they stood with her. She offered them to these distant, cold judges.) *You wouldn't let your calves die. Grown humans may hunt you, but not these. Help me save them!*—

The dragon looked at her newborn. Knowing the kit was dead in her belly had sent her in a rage to attack the humans. She had blamed them for stealing her from home at the start of her labor, had blamed them for the magic voyage that had killed the life in her. Her kit, her first, had been dead—until this girl-child had put her hands on her breast. The pangs had begun again—her kit had been born. Dragons do not give birth lightly, do not face the loss of young lightly.

—*You do not understand, mortal calf,*— said the whale leader.

—*Explain it to me, please?*— She struggled to be polite. There had to be a way she could talk them around.

—*We will not fight or kill. Not for your cause—not for any cause. Violence against higher life-forms is disgusting. For centuries the People have vowed that the taking of a higher life is an abomination.*—

—*But Miri told me, you've attacked ships that kill your kind. . . .*—

—*No.*— Once again the force of the reply hurt. —*There have been accidents. There are times when one will go insane. Always, when the one who has fought understands what took place, that one starves himself, herself to death, to pay for the sin. We will not fight. We will not kill.*—

She had never heard such absolute refusal. It sounded in the marrow of her bones and through her nerve endings. Under its pressure her head began to pound again. —*We'll die, then. Their machines will break our walls— they'll have us out as an octopus has a hermit crab out of its shell. My friends, in the air, on the land—they'll have died for nothing.*—

—*You should not have asked them to fight.*—

—*I* didn't *ask them! They wanted to— because they're my friends!*—

—*There is no good reason to fight. There is no good reason to kill.*— The whales' voices were growing faint.

—*Where are you going?*— Tears rolled down her cheeks. They were her last chance, and they wouldn't even listen.

—*If ships are here, there is a chance of an accident. We cannot accept that risk. We go, far from this place where you make a killing-ground.*—

—*I* didn't *make it!*— she yelled, furious. —*They came to me!*—

The whales were gone. The only sound in her mind and ears was the lapping of waves. It would happen again, just like at home. The queen would die before she'd let Carthakis take her or her children. Numair would burn out. The raiders would win. If she'd learned her lessons better, if she'd explained things at the palace instead of waiting till the badger came to her at the beach . . . She put her face in her hands and sobbed.

If you listen *hard and long, you can hear any of us, call any of us, that you want*. It sounded now, so clearly that she looked up, trying to find the badger. He was nowhere to be seen.

If you listen *hard and long, you can hear any of us, call any of us, that you want*. That's what he had told her. Maybe she could catch up to the whales, convince them. Maybe she could bring them under her will. Surely that was like calling anyone she wanted to, wasn't it?

It's wrong to force the whales to fight, a small voice in her mind argued. Not when they hate it so.

I won't let my people die, she told the voice. I *can't*.

She took a deep breath, and another. She let go of herself, opening her mind entirely to wild magic. Grabbing her up, the copper fire took her west.

She rolled along the ocean's bottom like a wave, hearing each click and gurgle the sea creatures made. Her awareness spread in a half circle, hearing the fleet, finding the departing whales. She would have talked to them, but the copper fire wrapped tighter around her mind and kept moving. Deeper and deeper the ocean floor sank. With dreamy surprise she slid around a patch of islands—where had they come from?

She dropped into ice water that was black as ink in her mind. In the west, past the islands, he lay—ship killer, man-eater, old as time. The mages had missed him when they sealed the Divine Realms, centuries ago. He had lain on the bottom, the ultimate predator, dining on whales and human ships. His immense tentacles, each a mile long, stirred with interest.

The kraken had never seen a little fish like her.

Daine stared at him, aghast. His was the body of an octopus with far too many arms, his mantle a mile and a half across.

—*I will kill any fleet you like, little fish.*— His voice was filled with soft, deadly good humor. —*You were talking to the whales. Pacifists, all of them—enough to make me vomit. Just show me where those nasty raiders are. I can guarantee they won't trouble you for long.—*

—You'd never make it on time,— she said, to cover her real thought: I could never get rid of him!

—Leave that to me. Come, my dear—this is no time to be squeamish.—

Deals with demons, she thought nervously. It's a deal with a demon . . . Wait—what about Numair? Once he returns to full strength, he'll be a match for this monster. I hope he will, anyway, because this kraken is the only hope I have left.

Please Goddess and Horse Lords, let this be a good choice!

Daine thrust what she knew of the fleet at the giant thing, and fled as his laugh echoed all around her. She flashed through the water faster than she would have believed possible. It was hard to say what she was doing: running from the kraken or racing to get to the Swoop before sunrise.

It was too late. When she opened her eyes, the incoming tide was up to her chin, and the sky overhead was pink.

She struggled, fighting to get her tightly

wedged body out from between the rocks. Everything was numb; her hands couldn't get a purchase anywhere. How can I reach the castle, let alone the deck? she wondered, panting as she tried to free herself. And what can I tell them, anyway? If those islands are what I *think* they are, they're the Copper Isles, four days' sail out. *If* I didn't dream that whatsits, that kraken, there won't be anything here in four days for him to eat—

Curved silver bars closed around her middle, gently. She looked up into the dragon's catlike eyes.

—*I will take you to your friends, little mage.*—

The dragon wrapped her other forepaw around the one that gripped Daine. The girl held on to those silver claws, running her hands over them in awe. There was a tremendous jolt, and they were airborne. She screamed in delight to see the earth fall away below them, forgetting briefly all she had been through, and all that was coming, in the joy of flight. Behind her she could feel the surge of the dragon's wings as they soared higher and higher. To their left she saw the enemy, and the Stormwing that dropped to Mahil Eddace's ship. The red robes in the galleys and transports sat or lay at the prows of their ships, many clutching their heads in their hands. Slaves, bare but for a loincloth and a collar, ministered to the red robes.

Her appearance—the dragon's appearance—had dramatic results. Men pointed and screamed; archers scrambled for their weapons. One red robe got up and did something that involved waving hands. It resulted in a yellowish cloud that boiled their way.

—*Amateurs,*— the dragon said coldly. When the cloud reached them, she blew on it, and it vanished. She banked gracefully, heading for the Swoop. Tiny figures on the deck pointed at them, while any of the archers who might be in range had their bows up. Someone on the deck recognized Daine and called an order. Slowly the weapons came down.

She peered at one of the dragon's toes, examining the bone structure and the violet scales. (She picked up several tiny cuts on the scale edges, which were razor sharp.) "Excuse me—weren't you red yesterday?"

—*I was angry. We may change color, to suit*

our wills—or to reflect strong emotion.— The great creature hesitated, then went on, *—I heard you speak to the whales.—*

She swiveled to face her bearer. "You did? But these days nobody else hears when I'm talking to just one species."

—That may be so, among mortal *creatures.—* (It occurred to Daine her rescuer was a snob.) *—We are mages of the air.—* Sounding anxious, she added, *—Could you send me home? I do not understand how I came to be here, and I wish to be with my family.—*

"We don't know how," Daine replied sadly as they descended. "We're trying to learn, though. If you stay with us, we'll find a way to send you home—if we survive, that is."

The dragon touched down, more gracefully than she had the day before, and released Daine. Onua, Roald, Kally, and Thom ran to hold her up as the great creature rose into the air and flew back along the cliff. Once more she vanished in midair.

"Any luck?" the baron asked as he and Thayet came over, their faces worn and exhausted. Daine looked around and saw Numair, seated on the wall. He waved a shaky hand.

"No," she told her audience quietly. "The whales said no." She couldn't even bring herself to look at Numair again. "There—there might be something, but—I don't know. I don't think it can be here in time. I'm sorry."

The queen patted her arm. "You tried. You've done so much already. I don't think the men from the camp outside the walls are fit to go into battle today, thanks to your friends."

"The dragon?" George asked Daine.

"I don't know. She's not very strong. I could try and call her back—"

"Well, well. All the little pigs tidy in one pen." Zhaneh Bitterclaws hovered overhead, just out of bow-shot for the deck's guards. The Stormwing queen's looks had not improved: her eye socket continued to ooze. *Whatever other magic they've got,* Daine thought to herself, *healing isn't part of it.*

Daine glanced around for her own bow and quiver: they were in Numair's lap. Thom sidled away from their group, backing up toward the mage with his hands open behind him. "What's the answer, mortals? Will you surrender the three we want?"

"We surrender nothing to you and your

handlers," Thayet spat. "Tell them they've just bought my husband's eternal enmity— and *mine.*"

"You won't live long enough to care about enmity!" Bitterclaws snarled.

Something hard and something leathery pressed against Daine's cold fingers. Thom had brought her bow, already strung, and her quiver. The girl's numb muscles couldn't respond fast enough. The Stormwing laughed and climbed away when she tried to get her bow into firing position. Daine swore, flexing her hands to get them limber again.

"Children, get below!" Thayet snapped. They wavered, and the queen roared, *"Now!"* They obeyed at a run.

The girl looked seaward to find what had made the woman raise her voice so uncharacteristically. In the night, the four barges had been moved to the front, ahead of the ships, and each catapult was assembled and loaded with a stone ball. Two of them fired; the balls struck the cliff face below the tower with an earsplitting boom. The stone beneath their feet shook.

The two remaining barges shifted. Must be

the sorcerers that move them, Daine thought, since there were no oars and no sails. Their catapults let fly. The first stone ball smashed into one of the other towers; the second hit the curtain wall. Already men were reloading the first two catapults.

The dragon, her scales flaming gold, dropped on them from what had looked like empty sky. She immediately put flight to the stories that her kind spat flame from their mouths. The fire came from her forepaws, and devoured the sails on Eddace's flagship. Banking hard, she cut directly across the face of one of the catapults to seize the stone ball loaded in it. Her flight sagged from the weight of the stone, but only momentarily. She dropped it on the next barge. The flat boat immediately listed to the side.

Numair propped himself on Daine's shoulder. "Wasn't she red yesterday?"

"They change color. Numair, she's not big enough."

"Maybe she's big enough to stop them. And it's justice, my magelet. They're the ones who brought her here in the first place."

Archers shot at the dragon uselessly. The

red robes tried their magic, but like Numair's, it washed off her. She hurled fire at a transport, burning it entirely, before heading back to the catapults.

Stormwings broke out of the woods on land and streaked to defend the ships. Daine watched, sobbing, as their claws cut deep into the dragon's sides. "Can't you help?" she demanded, forgetting the state he was in.

"I wish I could. Call her back this way, if you can. Our archers can swat the Stormwings away from her."

Daine called, hard. The dragon ignored her to fall on the red robe at the prow of Eddace's vessel. With him in her grip, she rose into the air and dropped him among a knot of Stormwings.

They exploded. Scared for the lovely creature though she was, Daine cheered as the other red robes fled to more protected parts of their ships.

Another catapult fired. Moving fast, the dragon was on the missile and had it in her talons. This time, when she dropped it onto a barge, she waited until she was much higher over it. When the stone hit, it went straight through the wooden bottom. With the other stone balls off-balance and rolling everywhere, the barge began to sink.

"Oh, gods," Numair whispered. "Call her in, Daine. Quick!"

"She won't listen! What's wrong?"

"They're loading the slings with liquid fire. Call her in *fast*!"

Daine *screamed* with all the wild magic she could find.

The dragon's only reply was a vision of a cave, high above the sea, with light coming out of its mouth.

"She won't come," Daine whispered, and tried again.

The Stormwings gathered before the dragon, forcing her back. She fought to rise above them or fall below, but they blocked her. At the right moment, the two remaining catapults fired—not stones this time, but balls of a clear, jellylike substance. They splattered over the dragon, and burst into flames.

She uttered an earsplitting shriek that none who saw the battle would ever forget, and dropped. Her flaming body crashed into a barge, and sank it.

Daine wailed her grief. "I'll kill them!" she

screamed, putting an arrow to her bow with fingers that shook. "Let 'em get near enough and I'll kill them!"

The catapult that remained in action fired. Its stone thudded into the wall at the base of the tower. "Fall back!" George ordered their guards, who obeyed. "Onua, Daine, Numair— let's go!"

Numair looked out to sea and froze, his hand locked tight on Daine's shoulder. His eyes opened so wide they started to bulge. "What dice did the Graveyard Hag roll?"

Someone on the wall below screamed as a huge black tentacle darted out of the water to grip the catapult that had just fired. Clutching it as a baby might hold a rattle, the tentacle yanked the catapult and the barge it was fastened to onto its side.

Another tentacle shot out of the water beside Eddace's flagship. Up and up it soared, until it reached the crow's nest. Delicately, with precision, it gripped the nest—and the man inside—and snapped it off the mast.

"Friend of yours?" Numair asked. His voice was very quiet, but she could hear him perfectly. No one at the castle was making a sound.

"Not exactly," she whispered. "I guess he moves faster than I thought."

A third tentacle crawled over the rim of the last barge, the one the dragon had knocked off-balance. It snaked all the way across the bed, gripped the opposite rim, and flipped the entire thing over.

Daine gulped. "Oh, dear—I think he's going to be nasty."

"How big did you say it was?" George had come to stand with them, his face white under its tan.

"I didn't," she replied.

Tentacles sprang up around the fleet like a forest of snakes, hemming it in. More tentacles groped into the boats, to begin a systematic destruction.

Numair straightened, blinking. "The dampening spells are breaking up."

Thayet had run to the opposite side of the deck, the part that looked out over the rest of the castle. "Listen!" she yelled.

Horn calls split the air. From the woods to the east came a company of the King's Own and the rest of the Swoop's guards, the Lioness at their head. From the northern woods came another company of the King's Own. They fell on the raiders outside the wall, as the Stormwings converged on that battle.

Onua, Thayet, and George raced down the stairs to reach the curtain wall, where they'd have a better view. Numair sagged to the floor of the deck. "I'm all used up," he told Daine, smiling at her. His eyes fluttered shut.

"Rest quick," she told him. "You and Lady Alanna are going to have to get rid of Himself, out there."

He fluttered his hand at her—of course, of course—and let it fall. Within seconds he was out cold.

To her surprise, she heard the sound of hooves on stone. Cloud emerged from the stair, her withers streaked with sweat. *I have been looking all over for you,* the pony told her crossly, coming to sniff Daine from top to toe. *First they tell me you got sick, then they tell me you went down to the ocean, then—uh-oh.*

Daine looked up. Zhaneh Bitterclaws had returned.

"I suppose you think very well of yourself, girlie. I suppose you think you did something wonderful, calling up that greedy-guts." She jerked her head in the direction of the kraken, who continued his breakfast of ships.

The girl shook with fury. She hadn't taken her arrow off the string, but it would do no good. Even supposing she could aim her bow, she had lost the strength to draw it. Numair wasn't the only one to be all used up.

The Stormwing queen knew it too. She fluttered closer. "You're mine," she said with a grin. "I'll be on you before you make the stair. And maybe I'll cut up your long friend here too, before I go. You think about that for a moment—it'll be your fault that he dies."

"Liar," Daine spat. "Folk like you always lay the blame on somebody else. If I'd listened to talk like that, I'd've let myself get killed by my own people months ago."

"They *should* have killed you, girlie." The Stormwing drew in closer yet. "You call me a monster—what are you? My gods made me. You're just a freak. All you do is get your friends killed, like that poor dragon. They'd be better off if you just threw yourself off the cliff right now."

Cloud leaned against Daine's thigh. Suddenly the girl was filled with energy; she was as fresh and strong as if she'd had a full night's sleep. Lightning fast, she swung her bow up and loosed.

The arrow went clean through Zhaneh Bitterclaws' neck as the creature gave voice to a choked scream. She dropped, trying to claw the arrow out of her flesh, until her body smashed to the rocks below. As she tumbled end over end to the sea, her own wing feathers cut her to pieces.

Daine and Cloud stuck their heads over the low wall, watching the Stormwing die in silence. Finally the girl straightened. Her newfound strength was gone. "Is she right?" Daine asked her pony.

She isn't, Cloud said firmly. Your friends all make their own choices to live or die for you. I've yet to see you force death on a friend.

Carefully, muscles aching, Daine unstrung her bow and coiled the string, tucking it into her pocket. "Did *I* know you could do that?" she asked. "Give me strength like you did?"

Of course not, was the pony's smug reply. We People don't have to give you all our secrets.

"*Now* she tells me." Daine sat with Numair and curled up against him. "Wake me in time for supper," she told Cloud tiredly.

Of course, the mare said, knowing her human was already asleep. There was a blanket where Numair had been sitting when the dragon returned Daine to the castle. Cloud dragged it over, covering the man and the girl. She assumed a guard stance near the two of them and waited for the rest of the fighting to end.

EPILOGUE

Her dreams were filled with the vision, the one the dragon had given her of a hole in the cliff. At first, the silvery light from the cave had been strong, almost enough to read by. As she dreamed the same thing, over and over, the light dimmed. Just before she awoke, it was almost gone.

"How long?" Her voice emerged in a whispering croak. Her throat was so dry she began to cough.

Numair hauled her into a sitting position and put a canteen to her lips. "Drink!"

Daine gasped, swallowed a mouthful of liquid, gasped again, and drank some more.

Finally she drained the canteen. "How long?" she asked again.

"The rest of the day the kraken arrived, then yesterday and today." He gave her a cake, sweet with honey and filled with raisins and nuts.

Daine ate it and took another. "I have to go out."

"Don't be silly," he told her. "You're weak. You're staying here."

"That's where you're wrong," she replied. She swung her feet off the bed and stood. For a moment the room spun, then settled into place.

She was in the stable. They had placed her cot in an empty stall, where the ponies could watch her. Her bat friends hung in the rafters overhead, where the loft ended, leaving plenty of room for the one-eyed osprey to perch. None of the animals were pleased when Daine started to pull on her clothes. Cloud in particular glared at her over the partition.

Remembering something, she froze. "My friends—the woods creatures—"

"Some were killed," Numair said gently. "Once the enemy was driven off, we found the injured ones. They've been cared for. There weren't as many casualties as you'd think. You gave them the right advice."

"Good," she said, a weight off her mind. She went on dressing.

"You *need* to rest and eat. I'm still weak on my pins myself."

"There's something I have to take care of," Daine said. *"Now."* She stuffed her feet into her boots.

Her friend sighed. "Then wait a moment. We need an armed escort. There may still be enemies out there. And let's get horses. Where are we going?"

She closed her eyes and recalled the vision. "Northwest," she said finally. "Along the cliff. We have to hurry."

He smiled at her. "Then we'll hurry."

She couldn't even manage Cloud's tack. Soon after the mage had left, Miri raced in. "Master Numair says you need someone to help you saddle up." She gave Cloud a wary look. "You behave," she told the mare, "or Wave-walker help me, I'll singe your tail."

Cloud stood meekly and did as she was told.

Daine was glad to sit on her cot and watch. "What time is it?"

"Afternoon," the older girl said. "You beat

Master Numair by half a day. He got up this morning."

"He looks a lot better." She gasped. "I forgot—the kraken!"

Miri grinned. "Don't worry about *that* one," she said, tightening cinches. "Once Master Numair was up, him and Lady Alanna had a talk with that old ship killer. You should have *seen* him scuttle out of the cove! He sucked the water after him and left the bottom dry. The Lioness had to pull it back in!" She patted Cloud's withers. "There you are—all set."

Daine rose and took the reins. "You've come a long way since we met."

Miri grinned shyly. "Thanks. It means a lot to hear you say so."

They waited in the courtyard as castle hostlers brought out Darkmoon, Spots, and horses belonging to the King's Own. Here, shading her eyes from the sun, the girl saw the repercussions of what she had done. The stable hands had liked to talk to her, before the enemy invasion. Now they avoided her glance and kept well away from her.

A small explosion struck her back and almost knocked her off her feet. It was followed by a second, and a third. Whatever the hostlers might think, Roald, Kally, and Thom were glad to see her up. Her eyes stinging, Daine knelt to return the hug. "There, there," she whispered, more to herself than the children. "It's all right. It's over."

"Can we go too, Ma?" Thom asked the Lioness as she approached.

"No, my dears. Some other time. We're not sure the enemy is completely gone." The knight grinned at Daine. "You've been a busy girl."

Daine grinned back. "So have you." Looking at the men of the King's Own who followed Alanna, she recognized Hakim and his companions. "It's good to see you," she told them.

"The honor is ours," Hakim replied gravely.

"You said it was urgent?" Numair reminded her.

The group left the castle at a trot, following Daine. The vision's lure was powerful in her mind. Following it, she guided Cloud onto a road that ran along the cliff face, high above the sea. Gulls followed them, filling the air with their cries.

Alanna drew level with the girl. "I've yet to thank you," she said quietly. "I never thought you'd have to keep your promise in such a way."

She smiled at the knight. "What happened? They lured you off, didn't they?"

Alanna nodded. "The ogres were real enough. They kept us busy for more than a day. By the time we felt we could return, there was a small army between us and home. Lucky for me Hakim rode in with two companies of the Own. They were still in Corus when Numair sent word you were up to your eyeballs in trouble."

Daine held up a hand: they were close. Listening, she dismounted. "Stay put," she ordered Cloud.

Numair came after her on foot. "What are we looking for, exactly?"

She was about to say she wasn't sure when the ground dropped under her. For a second time she had the doubtful pleasure of being picked up to hang in midair—this time, at least, she wasn't half-drowned. Looking down, she saw she had almost gone through the roof of a cave that opened in the cliff face.

"Can you set me down in there?" She wasn't sure who had her, Alanna or Numair. "I found it."

The Lioness chuckled. "You have a unique way of finding things." Gently Daine was lowered through the hole she had made, until she was on the stone floor of the cave below.

There was a rustle nearby, and a chirp. A silver shape, no bigger than a large cat, came over on legs that hadn't yet mastered the skill of walking.

She knelt. The little creature stared at her with slit-pupiled blue eyes. Tiny, scaled forepaws gripped her breeches: the baby dragon pulled herself up onto her hind legs.

Daine's eyes brimmed with tears. "I'm sorry," she told the dragonet. "I guess I'm your ma now." She scooped up the armful of kit and looked up at the hole she'd made in the roof. Alanna, Numair, and Hakim stared down at her. "The dragon had a little one," she explained. "She's hungry."

Carefully the Lioness raised her and the dragonet up through the hole, to stand them on solid ground.

Daine managed to construct a bottle that would hold up under the kit's small, but sharp, teeth. After consulting with the healer Maude, she warmed goat's milk and loaded it with butter, to make it even richer. The dragonet gulped a pint of the mess, burped, and fell asleep in Daine's lap.

The entire operation was watched, in awe and fascination, by the queen, Alanna, George, Numair, Buri, Onua, Maude, and the children.

Gently Kally ran a finger along the sleeping animal's flank. "She's so *soft*," the girl whispered. "What's her name?"

"Skysong," Daine said. She frowned—where had that knowledge come from? "I guess her ma passed that on to me too, before she—died." Coming to a decision, she looked at Onua. "I don't think I can stay with the Riders past the summer. My duty's to this little one, now."

"You can still make your home with us," Thayet told her. "That is, if you wish. I know my lord and I would prefer to have you in the palace."

Daine stared at her. *"Me?"*

"You." Thayet took her hand. "Veralidaine Sarrasri, you saved my life and the lives of my children. A home is the *very* least we can offer you."

Daine lowered her head, to hide her beet red face.

"But we want her to live here," objected George. "Surely we're more suited as a home, bein' on the sea and near Master Numair and all." He grinned. "And bein's how our girl's made so many friends in our woods."

"I don't see why she can't live in my tower," Numair protested. "She *is* my apprentice, after all."

"A girl's got to have females to talk to," Alanna informed him. "You haven't even gotten a new housekeeper since the last one interrupted one of your experiments."

"Come live in the palace," Kally and Roald begged, tugging her arm. "We'll be good forever and ever if you will."

Skysong sneezed and shifted in Daine's lap.

"Shh," Maude ordered. "You'll wake the baby." The children hushed, guilty faced.

"You don't have to decide now," Onua pointed out. "I don't see why rearing Skysong should interfere with helping me this summer."

Daine looked at these unusual people who had become friends, and laughed. "It's fair funny," she explained. "I've gone from having no home to having too many!"

The Lioness smiled and put a hand on her shoulder. "Welcome to Tortall," she said.

Turn the page for a preview
from the second book in

THE IMMORTALS SERIES:

WOLF-SPEAKER

The wolves of the Long Lake Pack, gorged on a careless mountain sheep, slept as they digested their meal. Only Brokefang, their chieftain, was awake to see the moon rise. He sat on a stone outcrop, thinking—an odd pastime for a wolf. In the last full moon of summer, on the advice of Old White, the wolf god, he had sent his best travelers, Fleetfoot and Russet, in search of a two-legger who once belonged to his pack. Their orders were to bring her to him, to speak to the local humans on his behalf. The sight of that night's full autumn moon reminded him that winter was coming. What if his messengers couldn't find

Daine? What if something had happened to them?

He did not like "what if" thoughts. Until he'd met Daine two winters before, he had worried about nothing but eating, mating, ruling his pack, and scratching fleas. Now he had complex thoughts all the time, whether he wanted them or not.

Soft chatter overhead made him look up. Two bats had met a stranger. Clinging to a branch over his head, the three traded gossip in the manner of their kind. The newcomer brought word of a two-legger on the other side of the mountains, one who was human outside and Beast-People inside. She carried news from bats in the southwest, and if a Long Lake bat was hurt, she could heal him with her magic. She traveled in odd company: two horses, a pony, an extremely tall human male, a big lizard, and two wolves.

The local bats exclaimed over the news. Their colony should hear this, they decided. Would the visitor come and tell them in their cave-home? Along with their guest, the bats took to the air.

Brokefang stretched. One new thought had

been that he could learn much if he listened to the talk of nonwolves. Now he could see it was a good thought, so perhaps the others were good, too. He was interested to hear that Daine also had learned new things since leaving the pack. Before, she could not talk directly with bats. Her healing was done with stinging liquids, needles, thread, and splints, not magic.

He stopped in midstretch as he remembered something. When Fleetfoot and Russet had gone, the pack was laired near the valley's southern entrance, where a river flowed from the lake. While they eventually could find the new den in the valley's western mountains, it might take them days to locate the pack.

He would take his wolves south and guide his visitors home.

Two days later, the girl called Daine watched rain fall outside the cave where she and her friends had taken refuge. For someone Brokefang regarded as Pack, she looked quite human. She was five foot five, slim for her fourteen and a half years, with blue-gray eyes the color of the clouds overhead. Her curly brown hair was tightly pinned up, her clothes as practical as her hairstyle: a blue cotton shirt, tan breeches, and soft-soled boots. Around her neck a heavy silver claw hung on a leather thong.

She played with the claw, thinking. She had been born in mountains like these, in a town called Snowsdale over the border in Galla. The first twelve years of her life were spent there, before she lost her family. When she left Galla to serve the king and queen of Tortall, she had hoped that she might never see the mountains again. And here she was, in a place that could be Snowsdale's twin.

Soon she would be with the wolves that had hunted in her old home. They had left soon after she did: Fleetfoot and Russet, her guides, had told of fleeing human hunters to find their new home by the Long Lake. What would it be like to see them again? To be with them again?

"What are you thinking of?" a light male voice asked from deeper inside the cave. "You look grim."

Daine turned around. Seated cross-legged by the fire, a traveling desk on his knees, was her teacher, the wizard Numair Salmalín. He wore his springy mass of black hair tied into a horsetail, away from his dark face and out of his brown eyes. His ink brush was dwarfed by the hand that held it, an exceptionally large hand that was graceful in spite of its size.

"I'm just wondering if Onua is managing the Rider horses all right without me. I know the king told her he needed us to come here, but I still feel as if I should be helping her."

The man raised his eyebrows. "You know very well Onua managed the Rider horses for years before you came to work there. What's *really* bothering you?"

She made a face. She never could distract him when he wanted to know something. "I'm scared."

He put down his brush and gave her his full attention. "What of?"

She looked at her hands. They were chapped from cold, and this was only the third week of September. "Remember what I told you? That I went crazy and hunted with wolves after bandits killed Ma and Grandda and our animals?"

He nodded. "They helped you to avenge the deaths."

"What if it happens again? When I see them, what if I forget I'm human and start thinking I'm a wolf again? I'm s'posed to have control of my wild magic now, but what if it isn't enough?" She rubbed her arms, shivering.

"May I remind you that the spell that keeps your human self apart from your magic self is one I created?" he teased, white teeth flashing in a grin. "How can you imply a working performed by your obedient servant"—he bowed, an odd contortion in a sitting man—"might be anything but perfect?" More seriously he added, "Daine, the spell covers all your contacts. You won't lose control."

"What if it wasn't the magic? What if I simply went mad?"

Strong teeth gripped her elbow hard. Daine looked around into the bright eyes of her pony, Cloud. *If I have to bite you to stop you feeling sorry for yourself, I will,* the mare informed her. *You are being silly.*

Numair, used to these silent exchanges, asked, "What does she say?"

"She says I'm feeling sorry for myself. I don't think she understands."

I understand that you fidget over stupid

things. Cloud released Daine's elbow. *The stork-man will tell you.*

"Don't fret," said the mage. "Remember, you allowed me into your mind when you first came to Tortall. If there was a seed of genuine madness there, I would have found it."

Daine smiled. "There's folk who would say you're the *last* man to know who's crazy and who's not. I know a cook who won't let you in his kitchen, a palace quartermaster who says he'll lock you up if you raid his supplies again—"

"Enough!" Numair held up his hands in surrender.

"Just so you know." Feeling better, she asked, "What are you writing?"

He picked up his ink brush once more. "A report to King Jonathan."

"Another one?" she asked, startled. "But we sent one off a week ago."

"He said *regular* reports, magelet. That means weekly. It's a small price to pay for being allowed to come to the rescue of your wolf friends. I just wish I had better news to send."

"I don't think we'll find those missing people." In March a group of the Queen's

Riders—seven young men and women—had disappeared in this general area. In July twenty soldiers from the Tortallan army had also vanished. "They could've been anywhere inside a hundred or two hundred miles of us."

"All we can do is look," Numair said as he wrote. "As wanderers we have seen far more than soldiers will. Even so, it's a shame the whole northeastern border is opaque to magical vision. I hadn't realized that a search by foot would be so chancy."

"Why can't you wizards see this place with your magic?" Daine wanted to know. "When I asked the king, he said something about the City of the Gods, and an aura, but then we got interrupted and he never did explain."

"It has to do with the City of the Gods being the oldest center for the teaching of magic. Over the centuries magic seeped into the very rock of the city itself, and then spread. The result is a magical aura that blanks out the city and the lands around it for something like a five-hundred-mile radius."

Daine whistled appreciation of the distance involved. "So the only way to look at all this mountain rock is by eye. That's going to be a job and a half."

"Precisely. Tell me, how far do you think we are from our destination?"

Fleetfoot and Russet had measured distance in the miles a wolf travels in a day. Daine had to divide that in half to figure how far humans might go on horseback. "Half a day's ride to the south entrance to the valley, where the Dunlath River flows out of the Long Lake. From—" She stopped as something whispered in her mind. Animals were coming, looking for her. She ran to the mouth of the cave as their horses bolted past.

Here they came up the trail, wolves, three in the lead and four behind. Two of the leaders were her guides to the Long Lake: the small, reddish white male known as Russet and the brown-and-gray female called Fleetfoot. Between them trotted a huge, black-and-gray timber wolf, plumed tail boldly erect.

🍁 🍁 🍁

From *New York Times* bestselling author

LISA McMANN

lisamcmann.com